W9-BAF-839

"OH, MY GOD," GRIMALDI WHISPERED

A pall of smoke rose above the fireburst, curling and swelling into a mushroom shape. The dust and debris sucked up into the superheated air began to fall back to earth. A dark cloud formed over the scene of destruction.

"Carl, what happened?" Brognola demanded.

"Listen hard, Hal," Lyons said from the chopper. "There's been a massive explosion near Bucklow. I mean massive. Call in all emergency services in the vicinity. Now."

"What does it look like?"

"Like Hell landed on the county with a vengeance."

"Carl, Gadgets is down there."

DON PENDLETON'S

STONY

AMERICA'S ULTRA-COVERT INTELLIGENCE AGENCY

MAN®

GATHERING STORM

FREEDOM FIRE BOOK I

A GOLD EAGLE BOOK FROM

W RLDWIDE®

TORONTO • NEW YORK • LONDON
AMSTERDAM • PARIS • SYDNEY • HAMBURG
STOCKHOLM • ATHENS • TOKYO • MILAN
MADRID • WARSAW • BUDAPEST • AUCKLAND

If you purchased this book without a cover you should be aware
that this book is stolen property. It was reported as "unsold and
destroyed" to the publisher, and neither the author nor the
publisher has received any payment for this "stripped book."

First edition April 2005

ISBN 0-373-61960-X

GATHERING STORM

Special thanks and acknowledgment to
Mike Linaker for his contribution to this work.

Copyright © 2005 by Worldwide Library.

All rights reserved. Except for use in any review, the
reproduction or utilization of this work in whole or in part
in any form by any electronic, mechanical or other means,
now known or hereafter invented, including xerography,
photocopying and recording, or in any information storage
or retrieval system, is forbidden without the written permission
of the publisher, Worldwide Library, 225 Duncan Mill Road,
Don Mills, Ontario, Canada M3B 3K9.

All characters in this book have no existence outside the
imagination of the author and have no relation whatsoever to
anyone bearing the same name or names. They are not even
distantly inspired by any individual known or unknown to the
author, and all incidents are pure invention.

® and TM are trademarks of Harlequin Enterprises Limited.
Trademarks indicated with ® are registered in the United States
Patent and Trademark Office, the Canadian Trade Marks Office
and in other countries.

Printed in U.S.A.

GATHERING
STORM

Freedom comes at a high price and requires constant guardianship. Taken for granted, it can slip away all too easily. When the hand weakens and the eye turns aside, the time may come when the resolve needs to be strengthened. And in those times there may be a need for armed conflict to restore the balance. As always it is the men and women of the Armed Services who must carry that burden. They bear the brunt of the inevitable clash of arms, and they do so in the spirit of the pledge they made to ever defend and protect our peace. Their fight goes on. They continue to suffer and often to make the ultimate sacrifice. They deserve both our respect and our enduring gratitude.

PROLOGUE

San Remo, Italian Riviera

Abe Keen had a lead. The freelance investigative re-porter was involved in a project chasing down former members of Saddam Hussein's administration, and he'd been working on his story for the past three months. Keen had succeeded in identifying and photographing four of the former dictator's cabinet members who had managed to escape from Iraq as the coalition forces moved in. Working from tip-offs from his not-inconsid-erable sources, Keen had journeyed to a villa on the Ital-ian Riviera, where he was expecting to find a group of the hard-line inner circle. If the information *was* true and he managed to get the final batch of photographs, the journalist would have everything he needed to com-plete his series of articles.

Keen was perched on an outcrop overlooking the villa. From his vantage point, armed with his camera and telephoto lens, he was able to look down on the pool and the patio surrounding it. Three hours had passed, but as yet he'd seen nothing of significance.

He was used to long periods of inactivity. It came with the job. The great pictures seldom came easy. Not in Keen's line of business. He wasn't looking for that defining moment when the lens caught a fragment of life at its most fragile. Keen was a hunter. His life paralleled the man in the bush, stalking his prey and waiting for the right time to squeeze the trigger. It was often a long time coming, and one of the first things the hunter had to learn was patience. The ability to sit for long periods, doing nothing. Just waiting. Waiting for that split second when his quarry presented itself in the crosshairs. Keen had honed his craft over the years. Now it was part of him. Just as breathing was a natural function, so was Keen's ability to let the moment come to him—and when it did he grasped it and froze it on film.

Below him there was movement on the poolside. First, the armed bodyguards. Even though the villa was behind high walls, with electronic warning systems, the bodyguards always came out and scanned the immediate area. They moved with the precise actions of men who breathed security. Once they had the poolside secure, they stood back while the principals came out and took their places around the table, talking among themselves.

Keen put his eye to the viewfinder of his 35mm camera, using the motor-driven, powerful telephoto lens to check out each of the four men around the table. As each one came into sharp focus, Keen pressed the release button and photographed him.

He knew them all well. They were all fedayeen, ex-members of Saddam Hussein's regime, faithful carriers of the flame still dedicated to Iraq's old guard. These men lived and breathed for the day they could return to Iraq and take up their former positions and rule the country once more. They were dreamers who closed their eyes to reality, fervently clinging to the tattered remains of a defeated and crushed dictatorship. Regardless of the inevitably of the outcome, they steadfastly refused to accept it.

Keen's diligence had paid off. Here, now, he had his final proof. The four fedayeen were gathered in one place, most likely discussing their plans for a victorious return to Baghdad. Watching them, Keen decided it might even be sad if it wasn't scary. These men were no amateurs. Far from being idealistic dreamers, they were hard, ruthless men, who had killed in the name of the old regime and who would kill again if the need arose. He had no doubts on that score. Whether or not they succeeded in their planned return to power, the quartet below would create a lot of death and suffering if they were allowed to carry on with their plans.

Sudden movement by the open sliding doors that led poolside caught Keen's attention. He swung the camera lens in that direction and saw a tall, broad figure step out of the villa. The man was dressed in light clothing, his dark hair cut short against his skull. He paused as the bright sun caught him and raised a large hand to shield his face. He turned and crossed to the table where the four men had pushed to their feet. Keen watched as each man stepped forward to embrace the newcomer.

For a few moments the group stood talking, and then, as if by some invisible signal, the four returned to their seats and waited for the newcomer to join them. There was a spare seat at one end of the table. The man moved to it and sat. He stared around the table, at each man in turn, speaking to them individually. He finally sat back, placing his large hands flat on the table in front of him and for the first time raised his head, giving Keen the opportunity to focus on his face. As the lens brought the face into sharp relief Keen's finger hovered over the release button, ready to take the photograph.

He froze, staring at the image the camera gave him. his finger hovered over the button as his disbelieving mind held him in immobility. He might have stayed that way if his professionalism hadn't clicked in. His finger came down on the button and the camera took a succession of shots. It was only as the sound of the shuttering mechanism intruded that Keen snapped back to reality. He took his finger off the button and sat back, still taking in what he had seen.

To be precise, *who* he had seen—a man who had been pronounced and identified as dead during the war. The man had been killed during a running battle with an American Special Forces team in the northern Iraqi town of Tikrit. He had been found in the ruins of an official party headquarters, his body having taken the full force of a grenade. In a local hospital, a doctor had examined the body and carried out an autopsy. When his report had been delivered, it had identified the dead man.

Razan Khariza.

A colonel in Hussein's military, Khariza had been hated and despised for his treatment of Iraqi citizens. He had a penchant for torture. For devising and utilizing terrible means for extracting information, or for simply inflicting pain on those who stood up against the former regime. Khariza was a man who had little respect for his own people. He had willingly participated in purges within the administration, turning against people he had previously called friends. In his other capacity he had undertaken the purchase and importation of weapons and technology aimed at improving Iraq's offensive ordnance. Khariza had traveled extensively on behalf of the regime, making and fostering contacts in a number of countries and with individuals able to arrange the purchase of weapons and equipment.

He had supposedly been killed during the hostilities.

But here he was, alive and well, heading a meeting with the very men he had commanded during the time he had served the former dictator of Iraq.

Now, with the image still large in his viewfinder, Keen realized he had stumbled on to something big. He had no doubt he *was* looking at Khariza. He knew the man's face well. This was no lookalike. Razan Khariza had never used a double. There had been no need. He'd never had high a profile. His work was done in the shadows, out of the light of day. And if he *was* dead, what would be the purpose of someone impersonating him?

There would be no logic to that. A double might have the appearance but wouldn't carry what was in Khariza's head. Keen was convinced he was looking at the genuine article, and the more he studied the man, the more he started to understand the recent activity among the group Khariza was talking with right now.

There had been a great deal of coming and going from the villa over the past few days. Keen had been curious as to why. Now he understood. The group had been preparing for Razan Khariza's appearance. Now he was here, in the flesh, and Abe Keen knew something was being organized.

He used up the rest of his roll taking as many shots as he could, then put his camera away. He slung his bag over his shoulder and backed away from his vantage point. He moved carefully, staying in cover until he was well clear, then gained his feet and negotiated the slope that would take him back to where he had parked his rental on the road that wound up into the hills from the main highway. It provided access to the villas scattered around the hills and cars were always driving back and forth through the area.

He unlocked the Peugeot's door and slipped in behind the wheel. He started the car and turned it around, driving back to the main road and heading for San Remo. His mind was full of questions he didn't have answers to. Keen was trying to work out what Khariza was up to. He hadn't shown himself simply to have a get-together party with his old friends from the regime. The five men seated at that table were hard-line loyalists of the former regime. Keen had no illusions. The five were planning something.

He just wished he knew what.

KEEN'S CAR HAD GONE, leaving only a faint mist of dust in the warm air. A man eased out of the undergrowth, pausing to brush a hand over his clothing. He carried an expensive digital camera in his free hand. He made sure it was secure before he slipped it into a pocket inside his suede jacket. The action pushed aside the jacket to briefly expose the Glock autopistol carried in a shoulder holster.

He made his way down the side road, having to step to the side as cars appeared and drove by. He returned to where his partner was waiting in a car some distance along the road that wound its way in the direction of the villa. He took out a transceiver. He activated it and raised it to his lips, speaking to the person who responded to his call.

"Yes. There was someone watching. We think he was taking photographs of the villa. It was too risky to do anything here. Too many cars up and down the road. But I know what car he is driving. We can trace him through that. And I took photographs of *him*. We can run it through our database. Once we identify him, something can be done. Don't concern yourself over that. It will be taken care of."

KEEN DROVE DIRECTLY to his hotel, parked the car and went to his room. The first thing he did was to rewind the film in his camera and remove it. He took out a new roll of film and put it in his camera, pressing the release button to expose about half the film. He placed the camera in its case, then he sat on the edge of the bed, studying the roll of film in his hand, debating his next move.

Ten minutes later Keen left the hotel and drove across town to a photo store. He knew the man who ran it. After a few moments discussing the price, Keen was installed in the darkroom at the rear of the store. An hour later he was done. He had processed and printed the images captured on the film. With the results in a manila envelope, he returned to where he had parked his car and drove back to the hotel.

He spread the photos out across the bed and studied them. He had printed off two sets. He slipped the negatives and one set of prints into a padded envelope and wrote his own London address on the front. Calling the desk, he asked for a seat to be booked on the next available flight to London. The desk returned his call ten minutes later and confirmed they had him booked on a flight that left at eight-thirty that evening.

Keen took a laptop from its case, placed it on the writing desk and connected it to one of the room's power points. From his equipment case he took a slim scanner and plugged it into the laptop. He disconnected the room phone from the socket and plugged in a modem cable from the laptop. He spent the next ten minutes scanning a number of the photographs, assigning them to document files before accessing his e-mail address book. He scanned the list of names until he found the one he wanted and opened a new e-mail. He typed in a brief message, attached the document files and sent the message. The files took time being transmitted, but Keen was eventually rewarded with the acknowledgment that his e-mail and attachments had been successfully delivered.

Working steadily, he disconnected his equipment and stored it all away in the carry bag, including the set of prints he had scanned. He reconnected the room phone, then glanced at his watch. Still plenty of time before his flight. Keen checked the room, making sure he had packed everything. Then he called the desk again and asked for his room bill. He picked up his luggage and left the room, making his way down to the lobby. At the desk he settled his bill, paying for his flight at the same time. His ticket would be waiting for him at the check-in at the airport.

His luggage was placed in the trunk of the Peugeot. Keen climbed in and drove away. He had things to do before he headed for the airport.

His first stop was at the main post office where he had the padded envelope weighed and stamped. He paid for airmail delivery, then returned to the parked Peugeot and picked up the route that would take him to the airport.

He had been driving for no more than five minutes when he spotted the tail car.

Abe Keen had been tailed before. The nature of his profession meant he often intruded on delicate situations and elicited a variety of responses. Investigative journalism of the kind Keen was involved in was far removed from celebrity probing. Keen's subjects had a more direct line of response than threatening an invasion-of-privacy suit. Over the years he had been physically assaulted, once run down by a car and had been shot at three times. On the second shooting he had taken a bullet through his left arm, but had kept his finger on the camera release button, actually capturing on film the moment he had been fired upon.

The sight of the black Mercedes some forty feet behind him made Keen aware of his vulnerability. He didn't carry any kind of weapon himself. He used a camera, not a gun, realizing and accepting the danger he placed himself in. He glanced at his watch. Still time before his flight. And it would take him another ten minutes before he reached the airport. He took another look in the rearview mirror. The tail car had dropped back behind a silver Toyota. Keen knew that if he could see the Mercedes, they could see him.

He stepped on the gas pedal, moving away from the Toyota. The car had closed in on his rear. As soon as Keen accelerated, so did the Toyota.

Keen realized he had a pair of cars following him. For what ever reason, the Toyota was upping the pace. Keen had the feeling the Toyota was ready to tailgate him if the opportunity arose, deliberately hit his back end and force him off the road. Anyone driving by would see it as a road accident, with one impatient driver clashing with another. No one would want to get involved. They would drive on by and allow the two parties to sort out the mess themselves.

The light was starting to fade now. If the tail car was going to do something, this would be the time, as the day gave way to dusk. Drivers would be even less ready to stop to see what had happened now. They would prefer to stay inside their own vehicles. Safe from what was going on outside.

Keen rammed his foot down hard, feeling the powerful car surge forward. The hell with them, he decided. If they wanted him they were going to have to work at it. He forgot about speed restrictions as the Peugeot hurtled along the road, speeding by the other traffic. He could see the Toyota falling behind a little. If they were going to make their play, it would have to be soon. Once it got full dark it would be easier for him to lose his pursuers. His other ace was the possible presence of the local cops. If he passed any patrol car at the speed he was going, he would attract their attention. It would be worth being pulled over just to make the tail cars back off.

As it was, there were no patrol cars in sight. No flashing lights or wailing sirens. Keen's high-speed drive brought him to the airport at Genoa far faster than he had anticipated. He was forced to reduce his speed as he neared the access road to the airport. He followed the road around to the parking area and eased the Peugeot into a slot. He opened the trunk and took out his luggage. Normally he would have taken time to return to the rental office and settle his account. This time around he was going to leave the car where it was. It would be located and the rental company informed. They would check out who had rented the car and follow through. By that time Keen would be back in London if everything went as planned and he would deal with the rental company then.

He entered the terminal building and made his way to the airline counter for his ticket. He had to go through the identification process, showing his passport and credit card before his ticket was handed over. Keen took it and made his way to the flight check-in desk where his luggage was weighed and tagged, vanishing from sight along the conveyor.

He was told the flight was on time and would be taking off within the next half hour. He walked through the busy terminal, searching for the departure lounge, then had to go through the usual delay at the customs desk. With that over, he passed through the barrier that fed him into the departure area. At least his pursuers couldn't get to him now. No one was allowed through to this section if they didn't possess tickets and passports. There were armed security guards and probably police patrolling the terminal building. Any sign of a disturbance and they would be on hand very quickly.

Keen located a bar and ordered a drink. He took it and sat at a table where he had his back against the wall and could see the entrance to the area. It never did any harm to be cautious.

So far, so good.

Abe Keen didn't let himself become complacent. He was thinking ahead. If his pursuers missed him here, they would pick up the pursuit once he arrived in London. It wouldn't take them long to work out who he was and where he lived in the U.K.'s capital city. Keen didn't need telling that Razan Khariza's people would quickly gain intel on him.

By the time they had finished, they would know everything there was written down about him. Regardless of the possible threat to him, Keen had no intention of going into hiding. It wasn't his way. Since he had taken up his profession he had accepted that situations might occur that might put him in danger. He wasn't going to change his way of life now. Not even for someone like Razan Khariza.

London, England

KEEN'S FLIGHT TOUCHED DOWN ten minutes late due to a sudden change in the weather. Rain hit just as the airliner had swung in over mainland U.K. and followed it all the way to Heathrow. He took the rail link into London, then picked up a cab to his flat in Camden Town. He glanced at his watch as he climbed the stairs to his floor. It was just after 3:00 a.m. Keen realized just how tired he was. It had been a long day.

His bags slung from his left shoulder, he put his key in the lock and pushed the door open. As was his usual practice, he reached out with his right hand to flick on the light switch. It clicked, but the hallway remained dark.

Keen was about to let go with a choice word or two but stopped in his tracks as he picked up the strong odor of a fruity aftershave.

He realized immediately it wasn't one of his.

And knew in that same moment that he wasn't alone.

He made to back off, out of the door, but a powerful hand caught hold of his arm and he was pulled inside with enough force to throw him to the floor. He hit hard, cracking his head against the tiles. The impact left him stunned, disorientated. Even so, he heard the door click shut behind him, and picked up the sound of movement in the seconds before he was lifted bodily and half dragged along the hall and through the door that led into his kitchen.

Discounting what he had thought before about not letting himself become threatened by Khariza's people—because he knew damn well that was who was behind this—he had to give them credit for locating his home so quickly. After the thought, he decided it was a strange thing to consider in his present situation.

He struggled to free himself from the two men who were holding him. All that achieved was a sharp rap across the mouth that split the skin and pushed his inner lip back against his teeth. He tasted blood in his mouth and could also feel it trickling down his chin.

It was still dark in the kitchen. Keen heard a third man moving around. He heard the sound of the Venetian blinds being closed. There was a soft click, and the light under the cabinet unit to his left came on.

The man facing him was leanly fit. He had strong shoulders under the long leather coat he wore. It was buttoned right up under his chin. His face was shadowed in the dim light, the curve of his shaved skull gleaming softly. His eyes shone like bright pinpoints as he leaned forward to stare at Keen.

"No time-wasting, Mr. Keen. We both know why we are here and what we want. Let us take it and this can be over quickly."

His voice was soft, with a Middle East accent.

"And then you'll let me go so I can report it to the police? You must imagine I'm stupid."

"Taking those photographs was not exactly the act of a smart man. Did you not think we would have taken precautions against such things?"

"We all make mistakes."

The man nodded.

"Certainly so in your case. Now, the photographs?"

"In my bag," Keen said. "The middle-size one."

His luggage was dragged off his shoulder. Keen, still in the grip of one of the other men, watched as the bag was opened and the contents spilled out across the wide work surface.

"Are these the only copies?"

"I only need one set to prove my case."

"Have you shown the photographs to anyone?"

"In the time I had in San Remo? Go figure."

The man in the leather coat pawed through the rest of the bag's contents. He held up a packet.

"These are the negatives?"

"Fuck you, find out for yourself. I don't figure I'm coming out of this alive, so why the hell should I make it easy?"

Leather Coat sighed as if he was disappointed. He said something to his two men that Keen barely heard.

The man gripping his arms swung Keen around suddenly. He placed one hand at the back of Keen's head and smashed the journalist facedown against the work surface. Keen's world exploded in stunning pain as his nose was crushed flat under the impact, blood squirting across the pale wood surface. His left cheekbone cracked and his lips split open. He groaned, trying to pull free from the grip of the man who had pushed his face into the work surface. Pain rose, engulfing his battered face.

He was in no condition to see Leather Coat reach out and pick a heavy cast-iron fry pan from the hook on the wall. Leather Coat stepped up behind Keen and slammed the pan down against the back of Keen's skull. Keen grunted in shock, arms flailing helplessly. Leather Coat repeated the blow over and over, the thick cast iron descending with terrible effect against Keen's skull. Flesh lacerated, bone crumbled and Keen's skull became a bloody, misshapen mess. The journalist's shuddering, twitching form became still. It was only the grip of Leather Coat's partners that kept Keen from falling to the floor. Leather Coat, breathing strongly, threw aside the iron pan. It was slick with blood and had fragments of bone and flesh adhering to the underside. The work surface itself was streaked with more blood and broken skull pieces.

On Leather Coat's orders Keen's body was allowed to slip to the kitchen floor. The killer gathered up the photographs and the negatives. He placed them inside his coat. He gestured to his pair of helpers and they followed him out of the kitchen, along the hall and out through the front door.

CHAPTER ONE

Memo: Barbara Price/Aaron Kurtzman to Hal Brognola
Recommendation for action based on collated data.

Major Kamal Rasheed. Member of the Ba'ath Party. Loyalist fedayeen. Hard-line Hussein man. He got out of Iraq once the writing was on the wall. He dropped out of sight for a while, but rumors started to circulate he'd been seen in Iran, then Afghanistan. As with other members of the inner council, this man won't let go. We've picked up Internet chatter he's working with other members of the old regime to make some kind of comeback. There's all kinds of speculation flying around, but there has to be some truth in among all the rumors. There are too many messages flying around the Middle East, calls for Islamic loyalists to come together to oust the Americans and their stooges from Iraq.

When we picked up details of increased movement down in Santa Lorca, Central America, concerning the increase in illegal arms, it didn't come as a surprise when information was received about a Middle Eastern buyer looking for small arms. The other matter tagged on to this was the hint that these weapons might be destined for the U.S. This could tie in with the information we've picked up from our main security agencies about upcoming strikes within the U.S. and their connection with the resurgence of ex-Hussein loyalists. One of our contacts came through with a photograph. Not the best, but when it was put through the computer program the closest match it gave was Kamal Rasheed.

We need to confirm just who it is buying weapons down there, because if it does turn out to be Rasheed, it more or less confirms that the data we were receiving about the old regime getting its act together is genuine.

I suggest we set up an operation. Get a team into Santa Lorca, offering a good deal on the kinds of weapons being sought, and identify the main buyer. If it does put Rasheed in the frame, our suspicions will be confirmed. An added bonus would be to get our hands on Rasheed and bring him back. Let our security services put him through a debriefing session. See what they can get out of him.

Santa Lorca, Central America

The man's name was Regan. His gaunt, lined face was tanned and unshaven. He was wearing a crumpled white suit. On the beer-stained table in front of him was a sweat-stained Panama hat, the brim curled and frayed. He watched the man across the table from him through watery blue eyes, constantly blinking as he toyed with the squat bottle of local beer.

"You better be straight with me, Bubba," he rasped. His voice was coarse, low, as if he was unable to raise it above a whisper. "This ain't fuckin' Paducah. Mess with the locals here and they'll cut off your balls and barbecue them in front of you. Understand me?"

The tall, rangy man facing Regan made no comment. He was calm, his hands mobile and sure as he rolled a cigarette using paper and tobacco. He stuck the finished cigarette between his lips and lit it with a battered black lighter. He took a long draw, visibly enjoying the taste of the smoke.

"You been listening to me, Bubba? I don't make speeches just to hear myself talk."

"You had me fooled," the other man said. His accent was British, hard-edged, and Regan became aware that he wasn't dealing with a novice. "Let's stop buggering about, Regan. Neither of us is here for the beer—and I can see why after tasting it. We arranged a deal. Why don't we cut to the chase so I can move on and you can count your money. Two weeks in this bloody place is playing hell with my social life."

"You can provide me with the ordnance I need? Anything from handguns to rocket launchers?"

"And everything in between."

Regan rubbed his stubbled chin. He glanced over the Briton's shoulder, just to make sure his two bodyguards were still in place. The pair sat at a table near the door, doing nothing except making their beer last as long as possible.

"Understand what I'm going to say next, Bubba. It isn't that I don't trust you, but the people I'm brokering this deal for are fussy. You know what I'm sayin'?"

"They want to see I'm not peddling you a load of scrap iron?"

Regan spread his hands. "You show up hawking a cargo of weapons. So you say. How do I know you ain't screwin' me around?"

The Briton nodded.

"I guess with the kind of money they're offering they have a right to see the merchandise."

"So it's no problem?"

"No."

"How soon can you show me samples?"

"Boat is standing by. I can pick up what we need and have it here later tonight. Your warehouse?"

Regan nodded, smiled and picked up his beer.

"Four a.m. I'll bring along my client. Let him check the stuff out. If everything is okay, we can complete by tomorrow evening. Just remember he'll want the full shipment up front before he hands over any cash."

The Briton stood. "I'll go and get my people working on it." He dropped a folded paper onto the table. "My hotel and room number. Give me a call if anything crops up."

As soon as the Briton had left the bar, Regan beckoned to his men. They came to his table.

"Follow him. Let's see if he's who he says. I don't want this deal screwing up."

"Don't you trust him?"

Regan smiled, scrubbing at his unshaven jaw. "I don't trust anyone."

One of the bodyguards grinned. "You trust us."

"Do I? Who the fuck ever said that, Bubba?"

THE BRITON LEFT the bar and made his way along the street. It was already dark. The night warm and sticky. He took his time, knowing full well that Regan would have him followed. It was what he would have done in Regan's place. He returned to his hotel, collected his key and went directly to his room. Inside he crossed to the window overlooking the street and saw one of Regan's bodyguards lounging against a storefront on the far side, half hidden in shadow. The man was lighting a cigarette and trying to look as though he belonged. He failed badly. No matter how casual his attitude, he still identified himself as an overmuscled hardman, even down to the bulge where his too-tight jacket fitted over the shoulder-holstered gun he was carrying. The other man had obviously gone into the hotel and was, even now, probably paying the desk clerk to take a look at the Briton's details in the guest register.

George Reese, British National. Home address, London.

That was what it said in the register. If a deeper probe into Reese's background was carried out, his background in dubious operations would show. Suspected of involvement in arms smuggling, some drug dealing. His sphere of operations would catalog deals in the Middle East, Asia, South and Central America. George Reese, though traceable if anyone wanted to follow through, was in fact a totally fictitious character who only existed in the computer files at Stony Man Farm, Virginia, U.S.A. Any requests for information on the character would be routed through to Stony Man, where his fictitious profile would be accessible to any tracer. George Reese was nothing more than a cover for one of the Phoenix Force operatives on this particular mission.

David McCarter.

TURNING BACK from the window, McCarter took off his jacket and tossed it onto the bed, went to the dresser and picked up a pack of Player's cigarettes. He needed one to take away the taste of the tobacco he had purchased from the hotel bar. It was rough, running a close second to the home-brewed beer they sold in the area. He lit the cigarette and took a long draw, sighing with relief.

He took a cell phone from his pocket and hit a speed-dial number. When his call was answered, McCarter asked, "Did you pick me up?"

Calvin James affirmed his query.

"We trailed you back to the hotel. Watched one guy go in while the other stood across the street. Hey, your first guy just came back out. He's crossing to meet the other one."

"Let's hope they bought my biography."

"Hell, these guys don't exactly look like they work for the *Oxford English Dictionary*."

"You and T.J. follow them. See where they go. Who they meet. Call me if anything happens we need to know about."

McCarter broke the connection, waited a couple of minutes, then made another call. This time it was to Gary Manning and Rafael Encizo. They were on board the sixty-foot motor vessel anchored off Santa Lorca, along with the cargo Phoenix Force was offering for sale to Regan.

"I did my deal with Regan," McCarter told Manning when the Canadian answered his call.

"And?"

"I show him samples. Early morning call. Four a.m."

"Okay. Let's hope he brings his buyer along. If he doesn't, we've come a long way and set this deal up for nothing."

"Took our pessimistic pill this morning, did we?"

"You have to admit this has been a hell of a long shot from the word go."

"So? We've worked thinner operations before."

"Yeah? This one is so thin Stevie Wonder could see through it."

"Bugger me, is that Canadian humor I hear?"

Manning chuckled softly. "I'll see you later."

McCarter glanced at his watch. A long time to go before he made his rendezvous with Regan. He figured to allow himself a couple of hours to get to the boat, pick up the samples and get them to the dock area where Regan's warehouse stood. Until then he had little to do, so he decided to relax. If anything cropped up, the others would let him know. James and Hawkins were keeping in the background, acting as shadows to cover McCarter, without showing themselves to Regan or his men.

McCarter sauntered down to the hotel bar and asked the man behind the counter if he had any chilled Coke. To his surprise the barman produced cold bottles from a cooler. The Briton took half a dozen and climbed the stairs back to his room a relatively happy man. He closed the door and settled down on the bed, switching on the TV set. It was lucky he had the Coke. It helped to ease the pain of watching old U.S. series dubbed in Spanish. He did some channel hopping and came across three Western series, yet another rerun of *Star Trek,* and ended up watching *Mannix,* with every character mouthing out-of-sync Spanish.

McCarter watched the episode, through. He smoked three more cigarettes and downed two bottles of Coke. He was feeling better. He switched off the TV, eased his long frame off the bed and crossed to the window. It was quiet down below. The Briton spent a few minutes at the window, letting the faint breeze cool him. He was about to turn away when he picked up a sound from the other side of his room door. McCarter stepped away from the window and crossed the room to stand against the wall to one side of the door. He turned his head slightly and picked up a scrap of sound. It was the sound of a floorboard creaking under weight. The weight was quickly removed but only made the board creak again. A man's hushed voice expressed impatience and elicited a sharp response.

At least two.

But what were they doing outside his room?

The Briton decided he wouldn't have to wait long to find out. As he eased his Browning Hi-Power from the shoulder holster he was wearing, the door handle moved slightly as pressure was put on it from the other side. He flicked off the main room light, leaving on just a small lamp on a table beside the bed.

The door swung open and two men stepped inside, scanning the room as they did. Both were armed with pistols. Seeing the room apparently empty seemed to confuse the pair for a few seconds and McCarter used the time to his advantage. He booted the door shut and as the gunners swung around he launched himself into action.

The barrel of the Browning cracked down across the wrist of the closer man, the hard blow numbing his grip on the pistol he carried. As the man grunted in pain, McCarter rapped the Browning against the side of his skull, hard, stunning the guy. As the first man slumped to his knees, McCarter turned his upper body and drove his bunched left fist into the second man's face. The blow was delivered with full force, cracking against the target's jaw. His head snapped around, blood spraying from a split lip. The guy fell back against the wall. The Phoenix Force leader was already closing on him, his right knee coming up in a blur to drive into the guy's exposed stomach. The breath gusted from his slack mouth and the man clutched himself. He offered no resistance as McCarter snatched his pistol from his hand. Stepping back, the Briton kicked the first guy's gun across the room, then backed up himself to cover the two men.

"I don't suppose you bums are room service? No? Didn't think so. So who are you?"

"Someone you don't want to mess around with."

McCarter glanced at the speaker. The accent wasn't local. There was something familiar about it. European? Slavic maybe? Difficult to tell. The man had been mixing with other cultures and had lost a degree of his native cadence.

"Might be a good idea if you stopped watching cheap movies," McCarter said. "Coming up with a line like that. Bloody terrible. Now why don't we stop being silly. Just tell me who you are and what you want."

"We want you out of Santa Lorca. We do business here. This is our territory."

McCarter grinned. "Losing out, are you? Tough. You blokes never heard of competition? Now I suggest you get the hell out of my room and stay away from me."

"You don't understand."

"Oh, I understand. But take it from me, chum. If you keep this up I'll kill you. No second chances.

Keep that thought when you leave. Now get the fuck out of my room."

The two men glanced at each other. They were in a bind. No weapons, and it was plain to see that the man they had come to hassle was in no way disturbed by their presence. They gathered themselves and moved to the door. McCarter followed them into the passage and stayed until they had disappeared down the stairs. He went back into his room, closing and locking the door. He picked up the discarded weapons and placed them in his leather holdall. Then he got back on his cell phone and spoke to James again. He explained what had happened.

"You think this could cause us problems?"

"If we've stepped on the toes of the local union of gunrunners it could get busy. The sooner we have our meet with Regan's buyer, the better. All we need is to identify the buyer, grab him if he fits the bill, then get the hell out of this sweatbox and go home."

"Our boys here only went back to the bar and spoke to Regan. Looks like he was just checking up on you. We'll keep an eye on them."

"Okay."

McCarter put in a call to Manning and gave him an update.

"Let's hope they don't decide to do something drastic like hit the ship," McCarter said. "Losing a piece of action is making these guys a little tetchy."

"Let's hope your meet goes smoothly," Manning said.

MCCARTER PULLED UP outside Regan's warehouse, cutting the engine of the battered Jeep 4x4 he'd rented from a local contact. He checked out the dock area. It appeared deserted, but the Briton never took anything on face value. There were a hundred places where a man with a weapon could hide. Taking that thought to its logical conclusion, McCarter realized there could be a hundred armed men in hiding. It was a sobering thought. Enough to make him pull a pack of Player's cigarettes from his pocket and fire one up. The smoke he took in eased his tension a little. McCarter exhaled and glanced quickly at his watch. Almost time.

At the far end of the dock a car appeared, easing around the edge of the most distant warehouse. It moved forward slowly, headlights picking out McCarter's parked Jeep. The Phoenix Force leader reached across to make sure his Browning was still beside him on the passenger seat.

The advancing car came to a stop twenty feet away. Both front doors opened and Regan's hardmen stepped out. They moved to the rear doors and opened them. McCarter saw Regan step out of one door. The man who emerged from the other side of the car was unknown to the Phoenix Force commander. Dressed in a dark suit and shirt, even down to a black tie, he stayed a few steps behind Regan, who led the way along the dock until he was no more than a couple of feet from the Jeep.

"At least you're on time, Bubba," he said as McCarter stepped from his vehicle.

"And I've brought your samples."

McCarter turned to the rear of the Jeep and lifted out a rolled tarp. He carried it to the front of the vehicle and laid the tarp on the hood. McCarter unrolled the bundle to expose two M-16 A-2 rifles, one fitted with an M-203 grenade launcher. There was also a Beretta 92-F and a LAW rocket launcher.

Regan stepped forward to look over the weapons.

"Go ahead," McCarter said. "They won't fall apart."

Regan picked up one of the M-16s and examined it thoroughly. He knew his weapons, expertly stripping the rifle and reassembling it with practiced ease. He did the same with the Beretta.

"Good condition," he said. "If I asked where you got them?"

"You'd get the same answer I would if I asked who you banked with."

Regan chuckled. He turned to his rear seat passenger. "You want to check these out?"

The man moved forward into a patch of light. He was lean, his complexion dark, a trimmed beard and mustache covering the lower half of his face. He wore steel-rimmed glasses. He barely glanced at McCarter as he reached out to pick up one of the Berettas, turning it over, working the slide. Once he had the weapon in his hands his attitude visibly changed. His stance relaxed, his gaze fixed on the pistol. The weapon worked like a drug, soothing him. He nodded slowly, his lips moving as he carried on some inner conversation with himself, slender fingers caressing the smooth, cool metal.

McCarter felt the hairs on the back of his neck rise slightly. The man was a little creepy, he decided. The Briton glanced across at Regan, who returned his gaze and offered a brief shrug.

The prospective buyer placed the Beretta back on the tarp. He gathered his thoughts and cleared his throat.

"Excellent. I believe we can make our trade. You know what we require, Regan. The price as agreed. I will bring cash. U.S. dollars. Make your arrangements." He offered McCarter the briefest of glances. "I will take delivery myself."

He turned then and made his way back to the car, leaving McCarter and Regan alone on the dock.

"I thought he was going to make a bloody date with that Beretta," McCarter said.

"As long as his money is genuine, I don't care if he takes the fuckin' thing to bed with him, Bubba."

"Regan, you're all heart."

"Ain't I just. You got enough stock on that boat to fill this order?"

"No problem. Just tell me where and when."

"Right here. How about this evening? Around eight?"

McCarter wrapped his weapons back in the tarp. He placed them in the rear of the Jeep.

"I'll have the boat in the harbor, waiting for my call," he said to Regan.

Regan nodded and turned back toward his car.

McCarter waited until he was alone before he took out his cell phone and called Manning.

"ID confirmed. The buyer *is* Kamal Rasheed."

"Have you arranged the deal?"

"Eight o'clock tonight. Regan's warehouse."

"I'd better let Jack know. We want him standing by at the airstrip. This is where it could get hairy."

"It's been quiet up to now," McCarter said. "I don't feel comfortable with the setup."

"You worry too much."

"Somebody has to."

MANNING CONTACTED Jack Grimaldi. The Stony Man pilot was waiting at a small airstrip a few miles along the coast from Cristobal. He had an old but fully maintained Douglas DC-3 on standby, ready to airlift Phoenix Force out of the country. He had flown in two days earlier after receiving a signal from Manning. In Santa Lorca, anything more sophisticated landing at the airstrip would have aroused deep suspicion and questions.

"I'll be ready and waiting," Grimaldi had said after Manning had advised the deal was to go through the following evening. "This going to be a quiet farewell party? Or do I break out the flak jackets?"

"Anybody's guess, Jack. You know how these things can change. David did have some unwelcome visitors at his hotel. Santa Lorca Mafia tried to scare him off."

"Wish I'd been there to see that."

"Just keep your eyes open in case. I have a feeling when we come to hitch our ride we'll be in a hurry."

"No problem. Let me know when you're getting close."

Manning cut the call and turned to Rafael Encizo. "Let's go check the charges."

Encizo nodded and the Phoenix Force pair went belowdecks to check out the thermal charges Manning had installed in the motor vessel's hold. They were more for protection than anything else, a noisy distraction in case the team needed to make a rapid withdrawal.

JACK GRIMALDI HAD the DC-3 ready and waiting by late afternoon. He had topped up the fuel supply, paying the owner of the strip in cash. The man had retreated to his control hut, putting up the shutters for the rest of the day.

With the instincts of a born pilot, Grimaldi had spent the previous few hours running checks on the aircraft. It wasn't in his nature to leave anything to chance. Faults that occurred at fifteen thousand feet took on a significance that might not have seemed so bad on the ground. Grimaldi had too much respect for his, and the team's, lives to allow something like that to happen.

With the DC-3 locked down, Grimaldi retreated to the cockpit. He had the plane positioned so he could see the approach road from Cristobal. He settled into the pilot's seat and leaned over to check the 9 mm Uzi and Beretta 92-F stored at his side.

Satisfied, he relaxed and wound down to wait. As a backup pilot for the Sensitive Operations Group, much of Grimaldi's time was spent waiting. He usually didn't resent it. His was one of those functions that required him to be there when he was wanted, and when that time came he had to be on the spot, with all engines running. He got involved in the action from time to time, and always acquitted himself well. Jack Grimaldi was no slouch when it came to battle. Conversely he had learned the combat soldier's creed of always resting when the situation allowed. The same applied to food and drink. Any break in hostilities meant weapons checks, food and rest. Once the heat was turned up again there was no way of telling when there would be another lull. So refueling, mentally and physically, were the priorities. Grimaldi's mentor, Mack Bolan, had opened the ace pilot's eyes to these unwritten rules. He had taken them to heart and lived by those rules every time he went on a mission.

Port Cristobal Dock

CALVIN JAMES AND T.J. Hawkins were in position on the roof of the next warehouse along from Regan's. They had been there since late afternoon, clad in blacksuits and armed with their personal weapons and M-16 A-2 rifles. For communications they wore lightweight Tac-Com headsets.

Down on the dockside McCarter wore similar gear, as did Manning and Encizo on the boat.

They were on the far side of the harbor, in among a scattering of moored vessels, waiting for McCarter's signal to bring the boat in.

The Briton glanced at his watch. It was seconds before eight. Shadows were starting to crawl out of the corners, pushing over the dock. A soft red glow spread across the Pacific. It would be full dark in an hour.

The Phoenix Force leader turned as sound caught his attention.

The roller door to Regan's warehouse began to open, rattling against steel guides. As it reached head height, figures appeared in the opening. Regan, flanked by his two hardmen.

Just behind, still in his dark clothing, was Kamal Rasheed. He was carrying a black leather attaché case in his right hand. Three men stood close by him, almost blocking him from McCarter's view.

"Seven, I can see," McCarter said softly into his microphone.

"Affirmative. Seven," Calvin James answered.

"Just remember trust is for children and cute puppy dogs," McCarter added. "And incidentally, it's my arse on the line down here."

"Sorry, boss, didn't get that last line," Hawkins said.

Regan walked across the dock and stared out over the harbor. He glanced at McCarter.

"Cute outfit."

"My tennis whites stand out too much."

"When you're ready, Bubba," Regan said, reaching across and tapping McCarter's microphone.

"Okay, boys, bring her in," the Briton said.

The boat eased into view, moving out from the cluster of other vessels and heading toward dockside. Manning was at the wheel, with Encizo standing at the bow. As the craft reached the dock, Manning brought it around, easing the vessel up to the mooring point. Encizo threw a rope to McCarter, who looped it around a mooring ring. The Briton secured the line. Manning cut the engine.

Regan turned to signal his men.

McCarter heard a soft voice in his earpiece.

"Four coming in from north end of dock," James said. "On foot. All armed."

"I can't see them," McCarter growled. "Where?"

"Behind the yellow dock crane. They're moving out now."

The sudden flurry of movement caught McCarter's attention. He spotted the armed newcomers as they broke into a run, rapidly closing on the warehouse frontage. He reached inside his jacket and hauled out the Browning.

"Friends of yours, *Bubba*?" he asked Regan.

"Fucking hell, no," the man yelled, pulling his own handgun.

There was one of those extended moments of immobility as everyone assessed the situation.

And then the dock was racked by the sound of autofire.

The first volley of autofire reached out in the direction of Regan's hardmen, punching into flesh and taking out one man, dropping the second to his knees. Even as the man tried to pull his weapon, a second burst from one of the attackers tore through his throat and dropped him on his back, blood bubbling from his torn flesh.

Rasheed took a step back, his trio of bodyguards forming a human shield around him. One gave a startled cry as he took a couple of slugs in his right shoulder. The impact pushed him off balance and he fell against Rasheed, knocking the man to his knees. The wounded bodyguard pulled a stubby SMG from under his coat and turned to return fire as the other bodyguards bent to help Rasheed.

From his position on the warehouse roof, Hawkins settled his sights on the lead attacker and put two 5.56 mm slugs in the guy's chest. Dead on his feet, the target fell, legs giving way under him. He flopped onto his back, the rest of his team pushing forward, still firing.

McCarter, down on one knee, brought his Browning up double-handed and fired. His two shots hit one of the attackers in the shoulder, tearing through the padding of flesh and shattering the man's collarbone. The guy went down, on his knees, all thought of aggression wiped from his mind as the initial numbness gave way to pain. He put a hand to his shoulder and fingered ragged shards of bone protruding from the wound.

"Gary, Rafe, take Rasheed."

"You got it."

Encizo, wielding a 9 mm Uzi, scrambled onto the dock. Manning was behind him, pausing only long enough to activate the timer that would transmit the detonation of the incendiary package he had laid in the hold. On the dock, he followed Encizo.

Hawkins took out another of the attack group, his 3-round burst slamming the guy to the dock in a twisting tumble. The man tried to get to his feet in a show of sheer resistance. Hawkins fired once more, laying the 5.56 mm slug through the top of the target's skull.

Kamal Rasheed was yelling wildly to his remaining bodyguards. They formed a line in front of him, pushing him back toward the warehouse door in an attempt to get him under cover. At the same time they lifted their pistols at the advancing Manning and Encizo.

Regan turned his attention on the remaining attacker. The man had a transceiver in his hand and was yelling into it.

"Son of a bitch," Regan screamed, losing control. He raised his pistol and began to fire, pulling the trigger in a frenzy of rage. "Try to queer my deal, you assholes!"

The majority of his shots missed, but enough found their mark, driving the target backward, bloody eruptions bursting from his chest.

McCarter swung around and moved to assist his partners. As he did, Encizo, ignoring the shots peppering the dock around him, took out one of Rasheed's remaining bodyguards, placing a single shot in the guy's head. As the man fell, Calvin James triggered a close shot that removed the surviving bodyguard.

"Let's move," McCarter yelled.

He took off across the dock, reaching Kamal Rasheed as the Iraqi ducked under the warehouse door. McCarter caught hold of the man's coat collar and hauled him back. He snatched the attaché case from Rasheed's grip.

"You cannot…" Rahseed protested.

"I'll tell you just once. Shut it, keep it shut, or I will bury you here and now."

Rasheed stared into the Briton's eyes and saw a gleam of wildness there that convinced him he would be wise to do as he was told.

"Fire in the hole," Manning warned as he glanced at his watch, seeing the second hand sweeping toward the end of the time set on the explosive pack.

The Canadian's estimate was out by around three seconds. There was a muted thump as the detonators went off, followed by a harsh crackle and blinding light that burst out of the open hatch covers. The intense power of the incendiary charges spread and began to burn the motor vessel.

"Reassemble," McCarter said into his microphone, calling James and Hawkins down off the roof.

He caught Encizo's attention. "Go and bring the wagon. We need to be out of here fast."

"What the fuck is going on here?" Regan yelled.

McCarter rounded on him. He barged straight in, stiff-arming Regan in the chest and bouncing him off the warehouse wall. Regan made a token gesture with the gun he still held in his hand. McCarter ignored it, pushing the muzzle of his Browning into the soft flesh under Regan's chin. The gunrunner made a soft sound. He let his own weapon fall from his fingers.

"Think before you answer, *Bubba*, because if it isn't the one I need..."

"What?"

"Where did chummy over there want those guns delivered?"

Regan was many things. He wasn't a fool. He'd seen the way these men operated. His death wouldn't mean a thing to them, so he raised both hands in surrender.

"Same place as the other shipments. Mexico. Nuevo Laredo. Local guy named Luiz Santos. Then over the border into the U.S. But I don't know where. You can blow my balls off and I still wouldn't be able to tell you."

McCarter kept up the pressure, pushing until the steel muzzle really hurt.

"Let me make one thing clear. If we go to Mexico and find Santos has got the word, you *will* expect us back here. And balls could well be at the top of our list. Understand, *Bubba?*"

Regan nodded.

"No second chance, Regan. We get burned, we always come back."

"Christ, looks like I got enough problems with those local suppliers we just tangled with. Last thing I need is you on my fuckin' back. I don't know who you are, and I don't need to."

"We're just a collection service," McCarter said. "We've got what we came for."

Regan eyed Rasheed. "Him? He's worth all this trouble?"

"He's worth it," the Phoenix Force leader said.

Behind them the boat's fuel tank ruptured and sent a fiery cascade across the water. Some of the burning fuel spilled across the edge of the dock.

"Tell me something," Regan said. "The guns on that boat. They real, or was that part of the scam?"

McCarter smiled.

"Real. But they were all spiked. Except the ones I showed you. Hell, Regan, don't you know it's against the law to sell stolen weapons?"

"Son of a bitch."

"Aren't I just."

The Jeep 4x4, Encizo at the wheel, swung into view from behind one of the warehouses. The moment he braked, Manning opened one of the rear doors and pushed a resisting Kamal Rasheed into the vehicle. James and Hawkins appeared. James climbed into the

Jeep, so that Rasheed was between him and Manning. Hawkins took the center position in the front, leaving the final space for McCarter. He climbed in and slammed the door, feeling the Jeep surge as Encizo pushed the gas pedal to the floor.

Leaving Port Cristobal, Encizo picked up the road that would connect them with the airstrip. Once they left the town behind, the tarmac surface petered out so that they were driving on a dusty, uneven strip that had more ruts than they had ever seen in one stretch of road.

"Any chance you can get more speed out of this thing?" McCarter asked.

"Right now we're close to takeoff speed," Encizo told him. "If we come off this road we'll probably launch into orbit."

McCarter laughed. "I wish."

"Hey," Manning said, "I think someone has called in backup."

McCarter looked in the rearview mirror, recalling one of the attackers on the dock sending a message via his transceiver. A dark SUV was trailing in their dusty wake, clinging to the rough road as if it were on rails. The big and powerful vehicle was brand-new. It looked as if it had the power to overtake and run the ancient Jeep off the road.

"Look at him move," Hawkins said.

"Confirms one thing," James said. "There are two maniac drivers in Santa Lorca and I'm a passenger with one of them."

"You want to live forever?" Encizo asked.

"Maybe not, but the next ten minutes would be nice." James grinned.

Following on his remark came the crackle of auto-fire. Winks of light showed from the pursuing vehicle. A couple of slugs clanged against the Jeep's bodywork. The rear window cracking as a stray slug bounced off the toughened glass.

"Those bastards are bound to get lucky before we hit the airstrip," Hawkins said.

The Jeep began to climb a long incline. Manning checked the position of the SUV, then leaned forward to watch the crest of the slope coming up.

"Foot down, Rafe," he said. "If there's a downslope on the other side, keep the speed up until I tell you, then hit the brake."

Encizo nodded. He trod on the gas pedal and put the Jeep along the road at dizzying speed. He saw the crest coming fast, then the Jeep cleared the hump and left the road for long seconds. It came down with a thump that jolted the passengers violently. The Jeep bottomed out, scraping up earth and creating a thick swirl of dust that misted the air behind them. Encizo felt the wheel wrench in his hands and had to use all of his strength to keep the vehicle on the road.

"Hey, Rafe," Hawkins said, turning to check behind them again. "You know how they do that in movies and the cars come out in one piece?"

"So?"

"I think *we* left some bodywork behind us."

Manning's guess had been correct. There was a slope

on the far side of the hump. The Jeep bowled along it, bouncing once again as it hit the level road.

"Now," Manning demanded.

Encizo hit the brake and hung on to the wheel as the Jeep slowed, sliding to one side.

The moment the speed had dropped to a safe level, Gary Manning eased open his door and cleared the vehicle. He turned immediately and faced the slope they had just come down, bringing his M-16 to his shoulder.

As Manning raised the rifle, the roar of the pursuing SUV's powerful engine increased as it burst into view over the hump in the road and sped in their direction.

Manning watched the SUV as it sped toward him. Once it was in range, he stepped forward and tracked in the M-16. He knew the American rifle well. He was also the team's lead sniper, deadly accurate with a rifle. He was entirely comfortable with the M-16 and now he sighted in on the oncoming SUV. The driver had to have seen the Phoenix Force commando's armed figure. He jammed on the brakes, putting the big vehicle into a dust-kicking skid.

Manning wasn't about to allow the opposition time to take cover. He opened fire, placing his shots in the visible front tire, the 5.56 mm slugs tearing and shredding the rubber. The tire flattened and the SUV's steering went leaden in the driver's hands. The vehicle lurched and rocked, threatening to overturn, but remained upright as it came to a juddering halt.

One of the rear doors swung open and an armed man sprang out, swinging his own weapon into play. Manning hit him in the chest with a pair of rounds. The man bounced off the side of the SUV, pitching facedown in the dust. Manning immediately switched his aim and began to jack off shot after shot into the windshield and the side windows. Glass imploded and they could see shapes inside the SUV struggling to get clear. The driver's door opened and an already bloody figure tumbled out, hauling his SMG into play. He fired a burst in Manning's general direction. Manning hit him with a single shot that entered just above his right eye and cored through and out the back of his head, blowing brain scraps onto the SUV's door.

The big Canadian took another couple of steps forward, the M-16 already following its next target as another gunrunner emerged from the far side of the SUV. He had stayed low until the moment he raised his head above the hood of the vehicle, searching for the shooter who was eliminating his partners. He never even had time to see his killer. Manning's M-16 cracked once and the bullet blew off the back of his skull. The man did a complete turnaround before he slammed facedown on the ground.

It became very still after that.

Manning remained on full alert, watching the enemy vehicle. He couldn't see any movement inside the vehicle and decided that his shots through the windows of the SUV had taken out any others still inside. He took a couple of steps back, freeing the magazine from the M-16 and feeding a fresh one into the receiver.

McCarter stepped up beside him. "Persistent buggers, aren't they," he commented.

"Were," Manning corrected.

The Briton touched him on the shoulder. "Let's get the hell out of here before the Santa Lorca militia decide to chip in."

"This burg got a militia?"

McCarter shrugged.

They returned to the Jeep and Encizo moved off. He pushed the vehicle as fast as was safe on the dirt road. A couple of miles out from the strip, James put in a call to Jack Grimaldi.

"Crank up that crate, Flyboy. We'll be checking in anytime now."

"Ready when you are, ladies. Make sure you wipe your boots before you come aboard. I run a clean ship."

ENCIZO TOOK the Jeep across the airfield and parked just behind the DC-3. The engines were already running, turning over smoothly. Grimaldi leaned out of the cockpit, waving at his passengers as they made for the open hatch. As the last man in pulled the hatch shut, the Stony Man pilot released the brakes, boosted the power and the aircraft began to move. Grimaldi coasted to the end of the runaway and waited until he had the engines balanced and trimmed. Then he upped the throttles and the DC-3 began to roll along the strip.

They lifted off into a sky that was darkening around them. Grimaldi banked the aircraft onto its correct heading once they were out over the Pacific. He settled back in his seat, enjoying the experience of piloting an aircraft like the DC-3. It was real flying as far as he was concerned. No digital readouts or satellite-controlled flight settings. Just his hands on the controls, a far cry from supersonic jets and even his beloved *Dragon Slayer.* For Jack Grimaldi this was a flight of pure indulgence and he was enjoying every minute of it.

KAMAL RASHEED HAD BEEN handcuffed to his seat with metal handcuffs. He resented Phoenix Force, making his feelings known whenever anyone came close to him.

"Do all the ranting you want, mate," McCarter told the Iraqi. "When we reach the U.S. you'll be handed over to the people who are going to be looking after you from now on, and I can tell you they aren't as nice as we are."

Rasheed glared at the Briton. "You should reconsider what you are doing. Do you realize who I am?"

"Don't remind me. Kamal Rasheed. One of Saddam Hussein's little helpers. We have a nice long file on you. And what a bloody charmer."

"You dare to judge me?"

"Damn right I do."

"Because I am Muslim you have decided I am your enemy."

"Change the record, Rasheed. You people keep bleating on about your religion like it's the reason for everything. I don't care who you worship. This isn't about religion. It's about a bunch of bullies who held their own country to ransom, put everyone who wasn't in their club in fear. You terrorized them, tortured them, kept them in ignorance and stole every bloody thing you

could get your thieving fingers on. Kids died from mal-
nutrition while you miserable bastards had gold taps fitted to your bathrooms, ran around in luxury cars and
salted away billions of dollars in your personal accounts. That had nothing to do with religion of any
kind, so don't throw that one at me."

"Because you have me, do you think it will stop what
we are going to do? We have God on our side, and we
will win."

"See? You can't open your mouth without using your
religion as an excuse. Just for once talk to me man-to-
man. Stop bloody hiding behind God."

The expression in Rasheed's eyes hardened. "You are
not fit to speak of him. This is why we will destroy you.
Maybe not this year. Or the next. But we will in the end,
because we are chosen."

McCarter backed off, shaking his head. "What the
hell am I wasting my breath for? This bloke is on automatic pilot. Open him up, I'll bet you find a recorder inside with a tape-loop quoting the phrase of the day."

"Hard to communicate with someone tuned out of
real conversation," Hawkins said. "Hey, boss, what do
we do with this?"

He held up the attaché case. McCarter reached out
and took it.

"We sneak a look."

He sat on one of the side benches bolted to the
DC-3 deck. McCarter laid the case across his thighs and
examined the locks. He tried one and the clasp sprang
open. McCarter repeated the operation with the other

lock. He raised the lid. Stacked inside the case was a thick layer of one hundred dollar bills. The layer was four deep.

"What have we got here?" Hawkins asked.

"My next month's salary," McCarter said. "Short a couple of bucks."

He took out one of the banded stacks of bills and flicked the end with his finger.

"Man, you could buy all the cigarettes you'll ever need with that," Hawkins breathed, visibly impressed by the amount in the one stack of bills.

"And have change for a few cases of Coke."

Hawkins raised his eyes to look across at Rasheed. The fedayeen had his gaze fixed on the case.

"I think we pissed him off lookin' at his stash," Hawkins said.

McCarter replaced the money as something else caught his eye. Resting in the leather pocket on the inside of the case lid was a grained-leather personal organizer. The Briton reached for it, pulling it from the pocket and turning it over in his hands.

Unable to conceal his panic, Rasheed lunged forward in his seat, coming to an abrupt stop as he reached the limit of the handcuff chain. The metal of the bracelet dug into his flesh, drawing blood. The Iraqi ignored the pain as he watched McCarter examining the organizer.

McCarter heard the sound as Rasheed fought his handcuffs. He realized it was the discovery of the organizer that had agitated the Iraqi, not the money.

"T.J., I believe we have Mr. Rahseed's attention."

CHAPTER TWO

War Room, Stony Man Farm, Virginia

Hal Brognola was a worried man. He had reason to be. Things were happening that had given him sleepless nights for the past few days, and his recent visit to meet the President had only added to his concern. The incidents, occurrences, breaches in security and rising tensions—however they were wrapped up in diplomatic words—had spoken volumes to Hal Brognola. They had told him in no uncertain terms that the current status quo was about to be rocked once more.

And when those things happened, or threatened to happen, Brognola took on the full weight as head honcho of the missions that were carried out by Stony Man operatives.

Stony Man Farm was the President's covert intelligence agency, a dedicated off-the-books operation used by the Man when other considerations had been rejected. Then SOG's talents were brought on line and the combat teams given their orders.

There were times when objectives needed to be reached, situations brought under control and individuals prevented from executing their personal plans. In areas where the normal protocols had no valid acceptance, the Sensitive Operations Group's commando teams were given their own mandate and sent out on covert missions. Brognola was waiting for his teams to join him in the War Room.

Separated from the relatively new Annex with its state-of-the-art Computer Room and Communications Center, the War Room sat beneath the original farmhouse that was the public face of the Stony Man complex. The house, the wood-chipping mill and sundry outbuildings were all that was visible to the casual eye. The vital sections of the SOG operation lay underground, concealed from prying eyes. Protected by thick concrete walls and surrounded by electronic sensors, the unseen heart of the complex was manned day and night, all year round. Terrorism and its associated threats didn't operate on a nine-to-five basis, and neither did Stony Man. Everything about the Farm was covert, from buildings, equipment and personnel. It wasn't supposed to even exist. Stony Man was the President's secret weapon. A totally dedicated force ready to respond to any global threat aimed at America, her allies or simply a threat to stability. One of the problems with incidents in Stony Man's remit was the probability of escalation drawing in other nations and the U.S. being caught in the ripples.

Stony Man had learned, through experience, that reaching out to stomp on a possible threat at its inception often prevented it developing into an out-of-control epidemic of death and destruction. The Stony Man combat teams were used to being handed missions that came out of scant information that grew and intertwined with alarming speed.

Able Team had arrived from different locations earlier that morning. The other group, Phoenix Force, was due to arrive within the next half hour. It had recently returned from a mission in Central America, where its members had infiltrated a gunrunning operation to identify the buyer. What the team didn't know, but would soon become acquainted with, were the details included in one of the folders Brognola had on the War Room table. The players in the weapons-buying deal were one of the reasons the big Fed had called his people together.

What he was about to brief them on had the potential to be both wide-ranging in its implications as well as threatening to the security of the U.S. mainland. The situation was building to become disturbingly serious unless Stony Man did something about it quickly.

One of the telephones rang. Brognola picked it up and heard the gruff tones of Aaron Kurtzman, Stony Man's cyberchief. He was a big man, with a commanding presence that swamped the fact that he was confined to a wheelchair. He was capable of being hard on his cyberteam when the need arose, but they would work for him until they dropped, such was the depth of their respect for the man. Right now The Bear, as Kurtzman was known, and his team, were immersed in collating and analyzing information coming into their domain from varied sources. It all had to do with the matter at hand and the moment he recognized Kurtzman's voice, Brognola knew things had gone up a notch.

"You want the bad news first, or the bad news?"

"That's what I like about you, Aaron. You always wrap things up nicely."

"Didn't you once tell me I was hired because of my winning ways?"

"I don't think so, pal."

"Okay. We are picking up reports of activity along the Turkish-Iraqi border. It appears the Kurds have made a couple of incursions in Turkish no-go areas and attacked a military post. One Turkish soldier killed and a couple more wounded. The Turkish authorities have started to move military units into the area and there have been warnings about reprisals if this sort of thing happens again."

"This information reliable?"

"Oh, yes. No doubts on that."

"Why now?"

"I'm heading down to see you. There are other things I need to discuss. All related." Kurtzman paused. "You got any of that War Room coffee on the go?"

"Yeah."

"Thought so. I'll bring my own."

Brognola grinned as he put the receiver down. Kurtzman bringing his own coffee was as much of a threat as anything that might come in via the communications setup.

He picked up his copy of the files he was about to

present to Able Team and Phoenix Force. For the next few minutes, Brognola went over the data. Not for the first time. He had been reading during his helicopter flight to Washington and his briefing with the President. He had gone over it all with the Man, and he had skimmed through it on the return flight to Stony Man. It made compulsive reading, despite the content, which was far from uplifting.

In essence, there was a growing threat from a number of sources. In isolation each item was disturbing. Linked together they formed an alarming scenario that implied a concerted effort to destabilize the Middle East region and also pointed at some large-scale security threat to the U.S. itself.

The current incident concerning the Kurdish attack on a Turkish outpost was one of a number of similar incidents. The way they were happening suggested, at least to Brognola, a pattern. Pieces of a puzzle that needed fitting together. The President had made it clear he wanted the SOG to take on the task of dealing with the affair.

The White House, earlier same day

"YOU'VE SEEN the photographs Leo Turrin sent in?"

"Yes, Mr. President."

"How in hell did this happen, Hal? Khariza was supposed to be dead. Out of our hair. Now he's shown up on the Italian Riviera alive and well and having a poolside chat with his old regime cronies. Did somebody slip up, or have we been had?"

"Right now, Sir, I don't have answers."

"Get them. Put your people on this full-time. Last thing we need right now is the Middle East blowing up in our faces on top of this mainland threat. It's just what the extremists want to happen. Stir up feelings until the whole thing goes out of control. Security assessment teams are indicating some kind of terrorist strike here on U.S. soil. The way this is going, now would be an opportune time for such an attack. We have commitments in the Middle East. A large percentage of our efforts are channeled in that direction. We don't know that these Mideast incidents are a distraction or part of an overall plan. We need to know, Hal. People are dying out there. And there are Americans on the list. Something has to be done. Damned if I'm going to sit back and just let things slide."

"I understand, Sir. Phoenix Force has already had contact with one of Khariza's group. Kamal Rasheed. They picked him up in Santa Lorca, trying to buy weapons. We handed him over to the CIA."

"There's something in the wind, Hal. Too many things happening out there that tell me we could be in for a bumpy ride. All these incidents. Rumors flying around. Familiar names keep cropping up. Linked to Khariza's inner circle. And now he rises from the dead. It all sounds a little too neat to me. Get your people on the job, Hal. If there's a tangible threat to mainland security, I want it handled soon as. I want Stony Man to take it on board. I don't have the time or inclination to go sparring with Agency protocols. They'll want to discuss it in committee, weigh the various arguments and options, advise me it isn't the right time. I want something done now. There's too much bullshit coming at me from the other agencies. Hal, I want direct action on this. Last thing this country needs is another World Trade Center disaster. The American nation has suffered enough. Find the bastards behind this mess and come down hard on them."

"I already have my people pulling in all the data they can. Soon as we get it all together, maybe we can pin something down."

"Hal, this is priority. Find out what's going on and shut it down. Any problems over anything you need, call me. I'll leave contact details so you can access me at anytime."

Brognola recalled some of the hot spots the information had indicated. They were widespread across the Middle East and Europe.

"Glad you mentioned that, Sir."

Stony Man Farm, Virginia

BROGNOLA HEARD the War Room door open. He glanced around to see the men of Able Team entering and making their way across to the conference table.

Carl Lyons, the team commander, Rosario Blancanales and Hermann Schwarz, were skilled, seasoned individuals. Each man had his own unique personality. For the most part, Able Team handled missions within the borders of the U.S. With the spread of terrorism, the associated threats and the expansion of the playing fields, Able Team was sometimes to be found taking trips well beyond the territorial boundaries of the U.S. mainland. In the end they went where the mission dictated.

Blancanales took himself to the coffee station that held the simmering pot of coffee and poured himself a mug.

"Hey, anyone want coffee?"

"I'll have one," Brognola said, recalling Kurtzman's promise to bring his own. "Black. No sugar."

"That it?" Blancanales asked. No one else spoke.

Lyons dropped into a seat close by Brognola, studying the big Fed closely.

"You okay?"

"I could do with a couple of days somewhere quiet and deserted. Apart from that, I'm doing fine, but thanks for asking."

Schwarz, sitting a little distance away, leaned forward. "Why don't you go with him, Carl? A break would be helpful right now."

"I don't need a break."

"I was thinking about me and Pol," Schwarz said, his face blank.

"One day, when I'm really gone, you'll remember all the things you said."

Blancanales placed Brognola's coffee on the table, then took a seat. He glanced across at Lyons.

"No, we won't. We'll be too busy having f-u-n."

The War Room's door opened and Aaron Kurtzman rolled his wheelchair across the floor. He was carrying the familiar coffeepot he kept brewing 24/7 in the Computer Room. Behind the broad-shouldered cyberexpert was Barbara Price. Tall, blond and utterly capable, Price was Brognola's mission controller. She thrived on a crisis alert, remaining calm and in control, whatever the situation. She moved ahead of Kurtzman, reaching the conference table and depositing a stack of files in front of her seat.

"Phoenix has arrived," she informed them as she took her place. "Be down any minute."

Kurtzman had moved across to the coffee station. He placed his pot down and plugged it into one of the power sockets.

"Never leave home without it," he said as he took his place at the conference table, in front of the panel of controls he used to illustrate his findings on the large TV wall screens. He tapped the keyboard and the screens snapped to life. Images and data were displayed in sharp profile.

"Any new material?" Brognola asked.

"Try this."

Kurtzman brought up a report from the Arabic TV network Al-Jazeera. The station, broadcasting all across the Middle East, had become known for its strong, uncensored images during the Iraq war. It had come under some criticism for the way it showed the news, but countered that it was primarily there to broadcast to the Arab nations and to depict the incidents as they happened, not in the sanitized versions shown to Western audiences.

"Say what you like about these guys," Kurtzman remarked, "but what you get is what you see."

The item showed a bullet-riddled car skewed across a street. Doors were open and bodies were seen in the vehicle or hanging half out of it. There were also three bodies on the road. The whole scene was familiar to the Stony Man crew. An ambush, the car riddled with autofire and the passengers killed before they could react.

"Do we know who the victims are?" Price asked.

"UN personnel based in Baghdad. The three on the ground outside the car were Iraqi police. They were in the car just showing on the right side of the picture."

"Did this actually happen in Baghdad?" Schwarz asked.

Kurtzman nodded. "Our mystery players are starting to get confident. No more hiding in dark alleys. They're showing they can do this with impunity. In broad daylight."

Phoenix Force came into the War Room at that point, taking their places at the table.

"We miss anything?" David McCarter asked.

Brognola indicated the screen image. "Aaron was just showing us the latest incident in Baghdad. UN team ambushed and shot. Three Iraqi police officers, as well. That's on top of the Kurdish attack on a Turkish military post."

"From intel reports we've been monitoring there seems to be a lot of activity in the Middle East region," Price said. "Now, I understand there's always something going on, but in the last week or so, this activity has gone up a notch. There's a concentration around Iraq. Attacks on U.S. and U.K. personnel. The UN. Covert intelligence suggests there's a deal of background rumblings in the major Iraqi cities. And we've all heard about the renewed incidents in Israel and Palestine. We have information on recruitment in the Mideast and Europe of hard-line Ba'athist supporters. Loyalists of Saddam's regime. All low-key at the moment. We were hard put to get a trace on the who and the why, but these photos have kind of got us on track."

Price spread out copies of Abe Keen's prints.

"Khariza?" Manning said. "He's supposed to be dead."

"Looks anything but deceased to me," Calvin James remarked.

"The journalist—who took these—Abe Keen, was found murdered in his apartment in London the same night he got back from Italy where he had taken the photos," Brognola said.

"Aren't those others from his old group?" Blancanales asked, glancing up from examining the prints.

Brognola nodded. "They're all there except one. And we know where he was."

"Kamal Rasheed. Brokering a deal for arms in Santa Lorca," McCarter said by way of explanation.

"Phoenix broke up the connection in Santa Lorca and got a name. Luiz Santos. Aaron ran a make and it seems he's been in the business some while. The information we got was that the weapons Rasheed has previously bought went via Santos into the U.S. What we need now is where they went after that and what they are going to be used for. The organizer Phoenix found in Rasheed's attaché case may give us some answers about Rasheed's dealings."

"Anything from it yet?" James asked.

"Most of the entries were in Arabic script. They're being translated now. If and when we get anything useful, it will be sent to the appropriate team," Kurtzman said.

"Are we looking at anything significant time-wise?" Gary Manning asked. "What I mean is, are we looking at a special date? A reason to launch any possible attacks on a particular day?"

Price shook her head. "There is a significant Iraqi election of provincial leaders coming up. It's taking time to build the permanent inner council to run the country. You all know the timetable. A couple of less-than-successful attempts. Clashes between political and religious thinking. Intertribal rivalry. Only this time 'round, everyone is hoping the various parties can reach an amicable working agreement. If these incidents keep occurring they could throw the various groups into doubt. And that would go down a treat with Khariza's group."

"So an incident on the day of the election would give cause for concern," Manning said.

"It's a point worth noting," Brognola said.

Calvin James stood to fetch a cup of coffee.

"They'll be voting Saddam back into power next."

"May not be as wild as you think, Cal," Price said. "Not Saddam Hussein, but members of his old regime may be trying to get sympathizers into the ruling party, even if it has to be by the back door. That came from our Israeli sources. They have confirmation on ex-fedayeen behind troubles on the Gaza Strip. Stirring things up among the Palestinians."

"I wondered when that bunch would stick its head over the parapet again," McCarter said.

"We knew the fedayeen wouldn't just fade out of existence," Brognola said. "They cut and run, but they're still out there. They won't quit. Not as long as there's even the remotest chance they might be able to get back into power again."

"Bit like the Nazis."

"David has a point," Brognola said. "Look how long they carried on after WWII. Even though they were scattered all over the globe, they plotted and planned their comeback. Okay, it didn't amount to much in terms of retaking power, but they still recruited believers and kept the old guard protected while they were able."

"The Nazis had a lot going for them," Encizo pointed out. "Look at the money they had salted away. That gave their organization a lot of clout. Enough money can buy you a lot of power."

"We've already seen an example of Khariza's fedayeen shopping for weapons," Brognola said. "This was small-scale dealing. I figure they're using money they managed to haul out of Iraq once the war started to go against them."

"Small change," Kurtzman said. "Cash they kept around for emergencies."

"The money recovered in Iraq is nothing to what the regime hid over the years," Brognola said. "Now that we have intel that Razan Khariza is on the scene, it suggests he and his crew are making moves. The big accounts have enough cash in them to buy a couple of small countries. If the fedayeen get their hands on those they'll have finance to run a war. But until they get their hands on the real money, they are going to use every means available to them. Beg, steal or borrow, Razan Khariza isn't going to sit back and wait. Hence the weapons deal Phoenix interrupted."

"What kind of money are we talking about?" Manning asked. "How big does it go?"

"I doubt if anyone knows exactly just how much money the regime salted away over the years," Brognola said. "It's common knowledge that the money came from a variety of sources. In the region of $2 billion was literally stolen from the shah of Iran some years back. Then there was oil revenue. Kickbacks on deals. Money siphoned off aid programs. Back-door deals. The regime had backing from investors who helped them negotiate special terms. Even banks chipped in. We've had figures of $30 billion in total, but the stuff is so spread about we may never know the actual figure."

Kurtzman opened one of his files.

"Money was handled by agents, brokers, companies created so that cash could be made to vanish. The regime made extensive use of electronic cash transactions. They were able to move it back and forth across the globe. In effect, the cash was being laundered."

He brought up an image on one of the large wall screens.

"From Iraq to London. Across to South Africa. Hong Kong and Japan. Even Russia. Down to the Balkans."

"Looks like it's done some traveling," James said. "Aaron, isn't it possible to follow the electronic trail?"

Kurtzman sighed. "Not as easy as it sounds. The way the money has been pushed around lessens the chances of tagging it. Each transaction weakens the electronic trail. One big chunk would be broken up and distributed among a number of recipients. They would push it further along the path. Some would be put into legitimate businesses. It's like shuffling a pack of cards before you deal. There's no way of knowing where a particular card will show up. By the time the cash comes together again, no one knows where it originated."

"The whole system was designed to conceal what was being done," Brognola added. "And to make it difficult for what is being attempted now. M-I6, Mossad, CIA, they all have teams out looking for the regime's missing billions. One thing we did come up with. Aaron put names and faces through the system—Saddam's agents, his brokers, whatever you want to call them. Key individuals have disappeared. Others we know have died in suspicious circumstances. The conclusion is they were killed by regime hit men as a way of guaranteeing their silence, preventing them giving any information as to where the money might be."

"If Khariza was such a big noise," Manning asked, "how come he doesn't have access to at least some of the cash?"

"Small amounts, no problem," Brognola said. "But he'll need the big money to broker his main deals, the kind of money he can't get without access to the right accounts."

"Our friend from Mossad, Ben Sharon, has a contact

who might be able to give us some guidance," Price said. "His name was mentioned in Rasheed's organizer."

Brognola nodded. "Aaron."

The screen image changed to show a head-and-shoulders shot of a man in his forties—black hair, clean-shaven, a lean face, bright eyes staring directly at the camera.

"Ibn el Sharii. According to background checks, he was part of Khariza's staff," Kurtzman said. "Big Saddam loyalist until the regime had his brother executed as a traitor just before the war. Something about him having been caught in meetings with pro-Western groups. Rumor has it Khariza carried out the execution personally. Insider information tells us that Sharii took the news badly. He realized his own time was running out, so he got out of Iraq before he went the same way as his brother. Before he left he set up a virus in the computer program where the access numbers and codes were stored. The moment anyone tried to access the system to get the account codes, the virus would just corrupt the whole thing and wipe it completely. Sounds like he wanted to leave the regime something to remember him by."

"Giving the finger to the fedayeen isn't a good way to stay healthy," James said.

"Maybe Sharii decided he didn't have anything more to lose. He stayed low, out of sight in Europe, finally reached London. It was a Mossad agent who spotted him there. Sharon connected the information Abe Keen sent to us with Sharii's knowledge. Mossad agreed to let Sharon follow through with us because we've worked with him before. Mutual needs, really," Price said. "One more thing. Khariza still has plenty of sympathizers out there. People who agree with his aims. Groups who want us to suffer. They'll give him help with what money and equipment they can, and they'll point him in the direction of anyone who he wants to get his hands on."

"Thing is, you're right," Blancanales agreed. "There's a whole world of help out there for someone like Khariza."

"They'll be crawling out of the bloody woodwork," McCarter said. "Sad thing is, we'll have people from our own countries ready to help, too."

"They have their beliefs as much as we do, David."

McCarter glanced at Brognola. "Don't I know it. All I'm saying is it makes it harder for us to get to the right people."

"Aaron has got some more intel for you," Brognola said. "It should give you background on the missions you'll be assigned once he's through. Barbara has logistic details and backgrounds for cover identities. This is up and running, people. The way things are accelerating, we have to start in top gear. It's obvious the opposition is operating in a number of different areas, so we have to cover what we can. We're going into this with minimal information. You know my feelings on that, but the President has the bit in his teeth and I can understand his motives. Situations can change fast, and if we don't stay on top we could be too late if the main event comes out of left field. I know this is throwing you in without much background. It means you're going to have some location changes. Can't be helped. Let's find out what Khariza is up to. Go for anything that might give us answers. The President has given this to us because he knows we'll locate and terminate without interagency rivalry or internal agendas getting in the way."

"Any contact with other agencies as a matter of interest?" Calvin James asked. "We've had problems before from them because they don't know us and we don't know them."

"If anything gets in the way, you pass it to me. I'll field it and get the President to step in."

"Hal, with due respect, that's a crock," Lyons said tersely. "We end up in a face-off with some agency rule-book geek, there isn't much chance for time-out so we can call home and get clearance."

Brognola held up his hands in surrender. "You got me there, Carl. In the field you have to call whatever you feel is the right choice. If there's no time and it's a case of being compromised, then do what you have to. It comes down to the choice about which is the priority decision. Let's call this what it is, guys. We are in a war situation. The ex-regime groups are out to do two things. Inflict as much pain and suffering as they can on specified Western targets and stir up trouble in the Middle East. At the back of all this are the attempts to get hold of power in Iraq. Do I have to spell out the end results if we don't go out and stop it?"

Kurtzman picked up a printed sheet. "This is an extract from one of the Intelligence Analysis think tanks. Something to bear in mind. 'Ex Ba'ath Party members will seek out their stolen money so they can rearm themselves. Part of their strategy will be to move into organized crime in order to reestablish themselves. It has to be remembered that these people were used to the best of everything and will want to retain their status. But they will also do what they can to infiltrate the Iraqi ruling party to destabilize it and get some control over the government. They will attempt to stir up trouble between all the various classes within Iraq society. Their ultimate aim will be to create unrest. Mistrust. A sense of loss of national identity.'"

Lyons leaned back in his seat. His question had been answered. It was the same for all of them. In an ongoing tactical situation, where balances had to be weighed, there were times when choices to be made might not look so clean-cut in the light of day. There was no easy way around that kind of dilemma. A man had to deal his hand and live with the consequences.

"Initial missions," Price said to break the contemplative silence. "Able, you need to follow up these mainland threats. Pick up where Phoenix left off. Nuevo Laredo. Your contact in there is Tomas Barranca. If there's any talk about these arms deals Phoenix hit on, Barranca is your man." She handed over files for the team to study.

"Aaron," she said.

Kurtzman brought images and data on-screen. "Tomas Barranca. This is the house he rents on the

Nuevo Laredo outskirts. His car. This is the cantina he frequents. He's pretty friendly with the guy who owns the place. That's him."

"Who does this guy work for?" Blancanales asked.

"You could call him a freelance," Price said. "In the past he's had associations with the CIA. Did some good work for the DEA in tandem with the Mexican drug squads. Lately he's been doing fieldwork for Justice. His name came up when Leo handed over those photos of Khariza."

"Sounds a risky way to earn a living," Schwarz said. "How does he do it?"

"Simple," Price said. "He's careful."

While Able Team worked on the research Kurtzman had collated, Phoenix Force took their missions on board.

"I don't like splitting you guys," Price admitted, "but we've got too much ground to cover. Gary, Rafe, Cal— Italian Riviera. San Remo to be exact. See if you can get a line on Khariza and his people. Check on the villa where Abe Keen spotted them. We have to start somewhere. That's as good a place as any. See if they're still in the area. Everything current we have on Khariza and his buddies from the old regime is here in these files.

"David, you and T.J. are booked for London. You'll meet with Ben Sharon and he'll brief you about Sharii. Right now that's all I can give you. Sharon says the guy is terrified of Khariza's people finding him."

"Not the wisest choice of places to hide out then," McCarter observed. "There are a bloody lot of Iraqi expats living in London, as well as the illegal visitors. Sooner we get there, the better."

"Get your stuff together," Price said. "You'll be going home courtesy of the U.S. government's own airline."

McCarter groaned. "U.S. Airlift Command again? Christ, have you ever eaten the bloody stuff they serve on those flights?"

Hawkins grinned at the Briton's grumbling. "Cheer up, old fruit," he said in mock English. "Let's get you to Blighty and you can 'ave a plate of fish and chips down the Old Kent Road."

McCarter glared at the younger Phoenix Force commando. "T.J., don't you ever do that again. If I even thought I sounded like that I'd go and join Bin Laden in a bloody Afghan cave and never show my face again."

In the background Lyons's dry tones were heard. "Does he mean it?"

"We live in hope," Blancanales replied.

"Okay, people, listen up," Kurtzman said. "No moving out until we go through the rest of my background data. I managed to locate another batch of photographs showing more of Khariza's Iraqi buddies. They'll come in handy if you come up against them. Always helps to know the players."

There were groans all around.

"Somebody give me a tranquilizer," Blancanales said.

Kurtzman beamed at them. "That's what I like to hear. Enthusiasm. Now somebody bring me some of my coffee. I wouldn't want to dry up halfway through."

CHAPTER THREE

Aboard the Petra

"So, my friend, are matters progressing as you wish?"

Razan Khariza raised his head from its contemplative position on his chest and studied the speaker. His host. His lifelong ally.

Radic Zehlivic, an Albanian Muslim, stood in the middle of the luxurious saloon of the oceangoing motor vessel *Petra*. Zehlivic was a multimillionaire. He had made his fortune over the years from astute playing on the world stock markets. He was a man who took great chances, investing in risky markets that had paid him back handsomely. Any money made was plowed back into further dealings and Zehlivic's fortune had grown and expanded. He had investments in property, land, in oil and ship building. He played the Western world at its own game, using wealth and an inborn intuition to manipulate the financial game for his own gain. He had percentage holdings in innumerable companies across the globe and was respected within the financial and business communities. Yet his name seldom made the headlines. He was as reclusive as he was smart. He stayed true to his faith, doing little to advertise his wealth beyond his close circle of friends, using his money to fund those who were working against the West. There were few people he trusted. Oddly, despite the man's reputation both inside and out of Iraq, one of his trusted circle was Razan Khariza.

Zehlivic's mother had died giving birth to him, and his late father had been a clever and industrious man who had made his money from property dealings in his own country. His talent for turning quick, profitable deals had also made him enemies. In the end he had transferred his money to London, moving himself and his son there, where he had restarted his business operations. The British had been easy to manipulate and no one ever knew the duplicitous methods Zehlivic Senior used to work his deals.

Father and son lived in a country house in Buckinghamshire, just outside a small village. Zehlivic Junior still owned the house and used it often on his visits to the U.K.

He had met Razan Khariza at the private school they had attended in England. In fact they had spent much of their youth in the country, and though their paths went in different directions in their early twenties, each had kept in touch with the other, Radic's admiration and devotion to his Iraqi friend becoming ever stronger.

In the tumult of the military action that had deposed Saddam Hussein and had seen the total dispersion of his regime's high-echelon members, Khariza might have died or been captured if it hadn't been for the assistance he'd received from his friend. A telephone call from Zehlivic had offered help during Khariza's darkest hour.

Through Zehlivic's chain of contacts, his knowledge of the country and a considerable outlay of money, Khariza had been spirited out of Iraq just ahead of the attack that hit Tikrit. A body had been substituted for Khariza, dressed in his uniform and carrying identity papers and personal belongings. When the local party headquarters was hit during a running battle, the body was deliberately mutilated with a grenade and then taken to a local hospital where the medical examiner, bought and paid for by Zehlivic, carried out an autopsy, making sure that all files and details matched the dead man identified as Razan Khariza. Members of the fedayeen were never fingerprinted or had medical details revealed during the regime, so there was nothing for the Coalition forces to match to. All they received was the formal declaration and postmortem photographs of Khariza's badly mutilated body.

Though Khariza had been an important functionary within the regime, his death was accepted as a minor victory within a larger canvas. He was listed as dead and as he had no family to claim him, the body was handed over to the hospital for interment. It was, in fact, quickly cremated and the ashes scattered.

The doctor who had performed the autopsy had pre-

pared to leave Tikrit himself once the formalities were
over. With his few belongings packed along with the extremely large amount of cash he had been paid, the doctor had been picked up by some of Zehlivic's people and
driven away late at night. He was never seen again. As
soon as the car he was in reached a safe distance from
Tikrit, it stopped and the doctor was taken out. He was
shot twice in the back of the head and his body buried.
The car drove on, taking away the doctor's luggage,
along with the money. The body was never found.

Razan Khariza, out of Iraq, went into hiding, courtesy of his friend Zehlivic. He remained in obscurity for
as long as it took for the hostilities to cease and Iraqi
reconstruction to start. When other members of the late
regime began to surface, and Khariza heard of their survival, he began to contact them. They, glad to find out
he was alive, rallied to his call. They needed someone
with his leadership qualities to ferment their plans for
a return to Iraq.

In their eyes, America and its allies might have won
the initial engagement. What they didn't realize was
the true fact that the war was far from over. In truth, for
the fedayeen, it had only just begun.

They wanted their country back as it had been before,
with control in the hands of the Ba'ath Party.

So they began to organize resistance, to create diver-
sions that would confuse the enemy and allow the fedayeen time to get their own people into place. They
would locate the immense hoards of cash that had been
sent out of the country and placed in secret accounts.

As soon as that money was in their hands, they could buy any weapons they needed to mount major offences.

That, however, seemed to be a stumbling block at the present time.

Which was why Radic Zehlivic's question jarred Khariza's mood.

Khariza pushed to his feet and crossed to gaze out the window, watching the gentle swell of the blue Mediterranean. The sky was cloudless and hazy blue. Peaceful. Calm. Khariza felt a pang of guilt. Here he was, safe and far away from the struggles in Iraq. He countered that thought with the realization there was little he could do in any physical sense at this point in time. Until he had the various strands under his full control, all he could do was wait. Khariza disliked the feeling of helplessness. He was a man of action, of control, and he was feeling impotent right now. There was so much to do. To arrange. Matters were progressing, but at an alarmingly slow pace.

Until the huge money caches were back in his hands, all he and his people could do was initiate the low-key portions of the operation—the individual removal of interfering officials, the strikes against various factions that would lay the blame on others. Important as these incidents were, they paled into insignificance when compared to the main events. And those couldn't be brought online until Khariza had the money to pay for the ordnance purchases. They wouldn't come into his hands until money had been exchanged. It was simply a matter of business. The amounts of cash being talked of were extreme and Khariza's suppliers weren't going to deliver purchases until they were paid. It was as simple as that. If Khariza took the items, then failed in his intentions, the sellers would find themselves losing both goods and payment, and that wasn't how they operated. Khariza's policies didn't interest them any further than the cash in hand. His goals were his business, not theirs, and they had no intention of coming out the losers. So the Iraqi had to curb his impatience and wait.

There had been an unexpected complication in the form of the journalist, Abe Keen. Despite Khariza's security, the man had discovered the meeting at the villa. He had taken photographs and had slipped away before any of Khariza's people could stop him. By the time he had been located, Keen had left his hotel in San Remo and was on his way to the airport. Although Khariza's men had followed him, the journalist had reached the airport and had even gone through Customs to wait for his flight in the departure lounge. Unable to prevent him leaving the country, Khariza had contacted his team in London, where Keen lived, and had given them the instructions that would lead to the eventual death of the man.

Now Keen was dead and the photographs he had taken were in Khariza's hands. Why then, he kept asking himself, did he still feel uneasy?

Perhaps because he wasn't totally convinced that Keen hadn't sent copies of the photographs to other interested parties. With that thought uppermost in his mind, Khariza had quit the villa and brought his team on board Zehlivic's boat. It would serve as a floating base of operations until Khariza could arrange other accommodations.

"So, my friend, are matters progressing as you wish?"

"Not as well as I had hoped by this time. We have to find Ibn el Sharii. And quickly. Until I can get those damn code numbers, I cannot release that money."

"Razan, you know I'd help if I could. But the amounts you need to satisfy those…"

Khariza turned from the window and smiled at Zehlivic.

"You've done enough already. Helping me out of Iraq, providing the villa, funding much of the U.S. project. All this. What have I done to deserve such a friend?"

"You have helped me in the past. So I return the favor. What kind of a friend would I be if I turned my back on you?"

"Thank you, brother. I will speak of you in my prayers as always. Your loyalty will not go unnoticed."

Zehlivic bowed his head. "Nothing is more important to me than your friendship. You honor me, Razan Khariza."

"We honor God. In his name we pledge ourselves to this cause. And because we are walking in the light of truth we cannot do anything but succeed."

Zehlivic crossed the saloon to the drinks bar and helped himself to a large glass of chilled fruit juice from the cooler.

In his early forties, he was a large man, carrying too much weight for his frame. He had tried all kinds of diets to reduce his bulk. Nothing worked for him. His physician had examined him, run tests and had only one thing to tell him. That his condition was hereditary and there was little that could be done. He would always be overweight. Zehlivic had really known this already. His father had been a big man who enjoyed his food, too much wine and too many large cigars. But once he had accepted the inevitable, Zehlivic decided he might as well enjoy life's pleasures while he could.

He stood beside the cooler, drinking the large glass of juice, a little out of breath from simply walking to the bar.

"How is that young wife of yours, Radic?" Khariza asked. "Still in Paris spending your money?"

"At the moment," Zehlivic said.

"And does she still make you happy?"

Zehlivic smiled. "What can I say? She keeps me young. She may well be the death of me, but I'm not complaining."

Khariza joined him at the bar and helped himself to a glass of Zehlivic's finest whiskey.

"Don't look at me like that, Radic. I am only testing the corruption of the West so I can better understand how to fight it."

Zehlivic couldn't help laughing. He knew Khariza had a liking for whiskey, and who was he to deny his friend such small pleasures.

A telephone rang. It was at the far end of the bar. Zehlivic answered it, then held the receiver out to Khariza.

"For you."

Khariza took the phone. "Yes?"

"We have located him. He *is* in London."

"Are you there yourself?"

"Yes. I am on my way to London now."

"Have you informed your people?"

"Yes. They are seeking him out as we speak. We do have a problem, though."

"What?"

"The Israelis have also located him. It seems he was seen by a Mossad agent in London going into a local mosque. Since then they may have spoken to him. Perhaps made him an offer of protection."

There was silence as Khariza absorbed the information.

"Find Sharii first. Do what you have to. Use whoever you need. I don't care how many Zionists you need to kill to get to him. Especially if they are with Mossad. We have many scores to settle with them. Just keep me informed. And remember the importance of finding this man. He must be taken *alive*. Understand? He's no use to us dead."

"Of course."

"I hold you fully responsible. There cannot be any mistakes."

"Depend on me."

Khariza replaced the receiver.

"Now we wait," Zehlivic said.

"And while we do, we must plan ahead."

Khariza drained his glass. "I need to talk with the others. Please ask them to join me, Radic."

TEN MINUTES LATER they were all assembled. The same four men Khariza had met at the villa in San Remo. In the time since that day and the discovery they had been seen and photographed, each man had moved on to progress his own particular section of the long-term plans they had formulated. This meeting on Zehlivic's boat was the first time they had come together again.

They had gathered in the luxurious comfort of the main salon. They sat in deep leather armchairs, with rich, thick carpet beneath their feet. The low ceiling reflected the gleam of polished wood paneling the walls. The armchairs were set in a loose circle around a wide, oval coffee table made from polished teak. On the table, a large silver tray held a steaming coffeepot and small cups. One of the men handed Khariza a cup of the hot coffee. He took it, inclining his head in thanks, then sank back in the armchair.

Khariza tasted the spiced coffee, taking the opportunity to gaze around the assembled group. *His* group. Faithful to the party. True men of the fedayeen. In Khariza's eyes they were the saviors of the Ba'ath Party, dedicated followers of Saddam Hussein. But in truth they were all Razan Khariza's men.

While following the party line he had groomed them over the years to follow his way, which would insure continuity in the event of any breakdown of the regime. Khariza, if nothing else, was a man who lived in reality. In as much as he had been true to Hussein, the dictator of Iraq had been less than cautious in his ways. There had been times when Khariza, watching and listening, had been disappointed by his leader's attitude. There had been too much dependence on the tried and trusted ways of the regime, an entrenched stubbornness to even contemplate anything might change, never any moves that might have strengthened the grip the party had on the country. And the increasing voraciousness of the central ruling group had done little to bolster confidence. Too little attention had been paid to the overall readiness of the military. The belief had been that despite the threats of the West, no one would actually take that final step and invade Iraq.

When it had come, the shock had left the whole of the regime in near panic. There had been varying degrees of reaction. Some had grabbed what they could and had left the country. Others had immediately surrendered. The order from the top had been that every element of the Iraqi defense machine stand and fight to the death. There was to be no capitulation. Doubters were openly executed in front of their brothers-in-arms. Television and radio fell silent. No one was allowed to see any news reportage in case it showed the true state of affairs. And as the days wore on and the Iraqi strongholds fell one after another, the propaganda machine worked in overdrive to put out ludicrous claims of how the brave and victorious Iraqi military was defeating the American-led incursion at every turn.

It had been a short-lived war. Resistance crumbled quickly and, apart from the odd, stubborn holdouts, the main campaign reached its conclusion very speedily. The regime tried every desperate measure it could to remain in power, but the Americans had overcome them all. Death and destruction overwhelmed Iraq. The clique of hard-line rulers, from the top down, saw the end coming and had made their escapes. There were still many loyal to the regime, and there was no difficulty making their bids for freedom. Many already had places arranged where they could go to hide. The money they had hidden away during the years of rich pickings went to insure they wouldn't lose the luxurious lifestyles they had become used to. Secret accounts in global banks made sure of that. Others simply went to their secret hoards and packed bags full of banknotes, taking them with them when they fled.

In the first months of enforced exile, the flickerings of anger at the brutal removal from their exalted positions began to stir thoughts of a return. Khariza and his group, men of former high rank, saw the possibility of working their way back into Iraqi life. Khariza's own exile had proved a frustrating time. Matters moved slowly as he'd gathered his people and made his initial moves to pull back from the brink and look to the future. There was a great deal to accomplish—retribution as well as a return to his homeland.

The Americans, the catalysts of the whole affair, wouldn't go unpunished. They still imagined they were masters of the world, and their arrogance was sometimes astonishing. Khariza wanted to challenge that assumption. He had studied the Americans and their ways, and he knew well enough that they had their weaknesses. He would exploit those weaknesses and deliver a strike that would make them think again.

Khariza had loyal followers already living in America. They were established in jobs and, after the Coalition strikes against Iraq, they were more than ready to make America pay. They would be given their orders at the right time and Khariza knew they would carry out those orders to the letter.

The buildup, by necessity, would be gradual. There was much to do to prepare. Khariza wanted to achieve two main goals. One was a powerful strike that would deliver suffering and pain to the Americans. He also wanted to initiate long-term aggression in the form of guerrilla strikes within the U.S. Simpler, but still effective, would be small, well-armed bands of his followers moving around the American mainland, striking here, vanishing, then striking again at some distant point. America was a vast continent, too large to police as thoroughly as the administration would like. Isolated communities, great distances. He knew, from reports, that in the great heartland of America, people knew little about the world at large. Often they had scant information about places within America itself. They lived in their own communities, safe and content to go about their daily business, believing that what went on across the other side of the world would never touch them. Sudden, shocking events occurring in their rural, self-sufficient communities would bring home the events taking place in the real world. Khariza saw this as an ongoing campaign. Something that would upset the tranquility of their self-indulgent lives.

To that end Khariza had sent one of his followers, Kamal Rasheed, to purchase weapons and explosives and arrange to have them shipped to locations inside the U.S. Rasheed, a born deal-maker, had ventured abroad during the regime's tenure. He had contacts. And more than that, he was a man who had a fascination with weapons. Guns were his preoccupation when he was free from his official duties. His personal collection of firearms was legendary, and he had even managed to take most of them along with him when he'd left Iraq.

Rasheed had been making headway, already having completed a number of deals. Shipments of weapons had been transported over the Mexican border into the American southwest, where they were picked up and relocated in the place chosen as a main base for the armaments.

Disaster had struck when an American undercover team set up a fake deal in the Central American state of Santa Lorca. The heaviest loss, as far as Khariza had been concerned, was the capture of Kamal Rasheed. The Americans had taken him out of Santa Lorca, and Khariza assumed that Rasheed was now being detained somewhere in the U.S. In the hands of the Americans, Rasheed would be tortured for information and probably executed out of sight. His death would be a blow to Khariza's plans, but he would at least receive his just reward in the afterlife. One thing was certain. No matter what the Americans did to him, Rasheed would never divulge the information he carried inside his head.

The money Rasheed had been carrying had also been lost. That meant little to Khariza. There was ample money available in the short term to purchase what they needed for the American campaign.

Thoughts about money brought Khariza to the problem he still had to resolve. If anything contributed to his concerns, it was money. To be exact, the huge deposits of cash locked away in a number of bank accounts. Accounts that were denied to Khariza until he got his hands on the access codes that had been stolen by an ex-member of Khariza's group.

Khariza had to get his hands on those deposits. There were literally billions of dollars salted away in those restricted accounts. Offshore accounts. Swiss banks. Khariza tried not to let the frustration get to him. If he did, he might easily lose his composure. Ranting and raving wouldn't solve the problem. But he had to get to that money. Without it his ambitions to forment unrest in the Middle East region might not come to fruition. There was so much depending on that money.

Not just a strike at the very seat of power within Iraq itself, but far-reaching plans to initiate full-blown destabilization across the region. One of the focal points would be the Israeli-Palestinian situation. Peace plans were ongoing. There was always mistrust, suspicion, hard-liners on both sides just waiting for a chance to point the finger given the excuse. It wouldn't take a great deal to unleash the pent-up hatred and turn the area into a war zone. Already, Khariza's people were making inroads. Small incidents, created to resemble attacks by each side on the other. The next step would be to launch a strong attack on one side, then create a retaliatory strike from the other. Well orchestrated, it would have the Israelis and Palestinians at each other's throats. There would be similar incidents within the region, planting suspicion within rival groups, destroying trust and opening age-old rivalries. With the Middle East in turmoil, the attention would be drawn away from Iraq, albeit for a short time. The Americans would be in a quandary, unsure what to do and realizing that even with its vast military machine it couldn't police every incident. And while the world stood back in dismay, Khariza would make his own move.

His master plan depended on his being able to purchase the ordnance required. The financial outlay was immense. It needed the clout of the billions held in the locked accounts. Being denied that money was forcing Khariza to place his operation on hold.

He brought his attention back to the moment and specifically to Ibn el Sharii. One man was preventing Iraq's destiny being altered. Khariza tried to understand how he had missed the change in the man's feelings. He had, he now accepted, made a grave error when he had executed the man's brother. At the time it had seemed a wise move. When it happened, Sharii had been under the illusion his brother was still being held in prison, as Khariza had told him. There had been no doubt as to Sharii's brother being involved with an outlawed pro-Western organization. Proof had been obtained. Photographs and audio recordings had been stolen and shown to Sharii as proof. Sharii had exhibited anger and then embarrassment. His own position within the regime had been placed at risk. Then Khariza still believed in Sharii. His trust was lost to Sharii, unbeknown to him at the time, when the pro-Western group managed to get their hands on evidence of what had been done to Sharii's brother while he was in prison. Graphic evidence showing the extreme torture that had been inflicted on the man, leaving him a pitiful, ruined victim. The final, damning evidence, had been the moment when Khariza himself had executed the man.

IBN EL SHARII HAD concealed his feelings following the revelations. He had realized there was nothing he could do in the short term. The Americans were commencing their military action and the country was starting to fall apart. He was aware of Khariza's intention to flee the country, along with the close group he had within his sphere of influence. Sharii had become aware, too, that his safety lay in his own hands. And at that time he realized there was something he could do to harm Khariza's plans.

The answer was almost too simplistic.

Sharii had unrestricted access to the regime's bank accounts. He had, in fact, been deeply involved in setting up the computer program that controlled the accounts. Within the data banks were all the codes and passwords to those accounts. It was a simple matter for Sharii to go into the data banks, extract the information and record it on a disk. As a precaution, he made two copies. The next step was to create and plant a virus program within the main data bank. His skill as a computer programmer gave him the opportunity to devise a virus that would lie dormant until someone accessed the account data. The moment the program was opened, the virus would be initiated and it would spread rapidly through the entire database, wiping it completely with no way of rescuing any of the information. Sharii refrained from deleting the program immediately because if it was discovered before he managed to leave Iraq himself, his life would be in danger before he reached the city limits. It was simply a delaying tactic he hoped might give him precious time to escape.

His involvement might have gone unnoticed if the regime's paranoia hadn't already reached its highest escalation. There were hidden TV cameras in every sensitive area of the establishment, placed there so that even the most trusted of the trusted were under observation. Sharii's attention was fixed on what he was doing and it never crossed his mind that he was being watched. There was too much going on within his head that he let his concentration lapse in that area. Luck was on his side initially. Because of the situation with the advancing Americans, there had become a need for all available people within the administration to help with vital tasks. The man assigned to observe activities on the TV monitors was assigned to something else. To cover the period he was away from his post, the man flicked on the banks of video recorders linked to the cameras. All activities seen by the cameras was caught on tape for later viewing.

By the time the tape from the TV camera in Sharii's office was seen, he was long gone. Once he had the virus installed and his copied disks in his pocket, Sharii had

walked out of the office. He had made his way out of
the building, nodding and speaking to people as he did
so. He even saw Khariza himself at a distance. Outside
the building he had paused to watch the smoke rising
from targeted buildings American bombs had hit the
previous night. Sharii had turned in the opposite direction from where his car was parked and had made his
way along the wide avenue until he'd spotted a cruising taxi. He had hailed it and asked to be taken to his
apartment. The driver had been calm, discussing the
current situation as though he was talking about an everyday event. It had surprised Sharii just how normal everything seemed within Baghdad in the daytime. The
night before, there had been explosions, flashes of light
and the wail of sirens. With daylight the city returned
to normal.

At his apartment Sharii packed a few belongings,
his passport and a hoard of cash he always kept for
emergencies. When he left the apartment, he made his
way to a public telephone. A quick call put him in contact with the pro-Western group. He told them he
wanted to leave. They agreed to help him out of respect
for his brother. A car picked him up within thirty minutes. The next few days passed in a daze. Sharii was
moved and passed from group to group as they transported him across the country. He finally found himself
on board a freighter leaving for Europe. When the
freighter reached Holland, Sharii was smuggled into
the country and hidden out by the group for two months
until he decided to move on, aware he was taking up

their time and resources. He had family in the U.K. and made the move to enter the country, asking for one last favor from the pro-Western group. They had done what he asked. Two days later Sharii was in the U.K., in a cramped flat in London's Bayswater.

He was on his own now. The flat overlooked a busy thoroughfare, with people and traffic moving back and forth all day and most of the night. Sharii sat in that small flat, staring out of the window and trying to make some sense out of his current position. The ceaseless flow of humanity below, going about their business, oblivious of the conflicts raging inside his head, was a blur to him. He had broken all ties with his home country, placing himself in danger because of what he had done.

During his stay in Europe, news had filtered through that Khariza himself was dead. Killed by the Americans during fighting in Tikrit. Sharii heard the reports and for a short time he felt relief. That relief was short-lived. The more he thought about it, the stronger became his belief that Khariza was still alive. It was nothing more than a feeling, which became stronger as time went by. He couldn't explain it. He didn't express his feelings to anyone else. But he became convinced that he was not mistaken. Khariza's death was nothing more than a distraction. Something to throw the Americans off the trail.

As his time in London began to put a strain on him, and his enforced stay in the flat brought on a mild depression, Sharii knew he had to do something to prevent himself from falling apart.

He had, during his infrequent forays out of the flat—

to buy food and other necessities—discovered a mosque at the far end of the main thoroughfare, set back off the road. One evening, when his solitary existence became too strong to fight any longer, he went out into the rainy London gloom and walked the quarter mile to the mosque.

The moment he entered, feeling the peace of the mosque slip around him like a welcoming cloak, Sharii felt a contentment he thought he had lost forever. He moved inside, taking his place among the gathered congregation and kneeling. His loneliness had been washed away by the gentle murmuring of the imam as he read from the holy book. Sharii reached out with his heart and asked God for reassurance. When he'd experienced the warmth that came with awareness, the tears fell from his eyes and he wept with the joy of belonging.

In the days that followed, Sharii returned to the mosque as often as he could, taking growing comfort from the serenity of the holy place. It was a return to his roots. His faith. And the longer he spent within those sacred walls, the more certain he became that he had done the right thing in leaving Iraq and denying his previous allegiance to the evil that had been the Hussein regime.

Something deep within him urged Sharii to document everything he knew about Khariza and his group. During his time working within the tight circle Khariza had created, Sharii had heard many things. He knew faces. Names. There were contacts Khariza often called, many of them outside Iraq, people with whom he had strong ties, people who could, if the time came, help

Khariza and his group. A secret network of people and places. The murmuring about a possible American-led strike against Iraq had been in the cards for months. Khariza and his group had many meetings in those months and Sharii had attended a number of them. At the time he was concerned with his own part—dealing with finance and associated matters. He'd often sat on the periphery of the meetings. Answering questions when they were directed at him, sometimes offering advice. Then there would be nothing for him to do but sit in silence while other business was discussed. His agile mind absorbed facts and figures, names and places. They were retained in some distant, half-conscious memory bank, present yet never summoned for recall.

Until now, as Sharii sat with pen and pad, bringing back all those meetings and transcribing the ebb and flow of conversation. Fragments, perhaps, but his agile mind began to sort and collate until he had written down a cohesive narrative of things Razan Khariza and his group had proposed in those frantic times before the day the Americans had launched their first strikes against Iraq.

With his thoughts down on paper, Sharii fell back into his mundane routine again.

He had been using a local café to eat in when he needed to leave the flat. Shortly after he'd started to visit the mosque he accidentally overheard a news report on the television on the counter of the café. The report stated that a well-known investigative journalist had been found murdered in his London apartment. The report also stated that the journalist had been working on a series of articles about the possible where-abouts of ex-Hussein regime members. Photographs had been found in his apartment, in an envelope mailed in San Remo, Italy, where the journalist had last been working. The report suggested the journalist had mailed the prints to himself for security. Claiming a "scoop," the report went on to say it had copies of the photographs. They were then flashed on the screen and Sharii found himself staring at men he had hoped never to see again.

The final one was of someone even the reporter said had been claimed was dead.

Razan Khariza.

Not dead, but alive, well and looking extremely healthy.

Sharii had sat in stunned silence long after the report was over. He had eventually stumbled from the café, wandering the busy street, realizing that whatever brief moments of peace he had found inside the mosque had been blown away by what he had just seen.

His suspicions about Khariza had proved to be accurate. There was little satisfaction in that small victory.

He had returned to his flat, locking the door, and had spent the rest of the day with his gaze fixed firmly on the faded pattern on the wallpaper.

If Khariza was alive, he would be looking for Sharii. If there was anyone alive who might be able to help with the secret bank accounts, as far as Khariza was concerned, it was Ibn el Sharii. Which meant Sharii's freedom, if it could be called that, was coming to an end.

Khariza's influence was far-reaching. He had already settled with the unfortunate journalist who had stumbled on his existence. Sharii saw himself next on the list.

It was at that point he began to think about something he had done shortly after settling in London. He had packaged up the two disks, along with a note explaining how important they were and that they must not be disclosed to anyone, and that he would explain when he came to collect them, and had mailed them to his sister in the north of England. Now, with conclusive proof that Khariza was still alive, Sharii realized the danger he had put his sister in. Unwittingly he had drawn her into his own troubles. And with Khariza emerging from the shadows, that danger would be of the most vicious and painful kind conceived.

He knew he needed to go to her to retrieve the disks and move as far away from her as he could. It was too late telling himself he shouldn't have sent the disks to her. It had been done. All he could do now was to try to undo that error before it was too late.

He had gone to the mosque again that evening, hoping he could ease his anguish and clear his mind for what lay ahead.

And that was where a Mossad agent recognized him, approached him and, when he'd heard what had happened, moved Sharii to a safe location while arrangements were made to keep him out of harm's way.

KHARIZA'S SHOCK at what Sharii had done had been instant and had left him stunned. When the effect of the virus had become evident, the access codes to the accounts corrupting in front of his eyes, Khariza had ranted at his operator, demanding the man do something. He'd refused to believe there was nothing that could be done. He'd stood and watched the list break up and vanish, and was helpless. It had taken no more than a minute or so, ignoring the frantic keyboarding of the operator. The blank screen had mocked him and for a time Khariza had remained immobile, unable to react. Hours later, after his computer people had confirmed that the access codes were irretrievably gone, he had calmed to the point where he was able to accept the fact. He was, if nothing else, a man capable of accepting something that could not be changed, so he did just that. But his mind was working on solutions even then. He was sure there was something he had missed. It took the revelation that Sharii was the guilty party when the video tapes came to light to make Khariza realize all was not yet lost.

"Sharii has been located in London. We are moving to detain him even as I speak."

Abdul Wafiq, small and slender, balancing his coffee cup on one crossed knee, leaned forward. "Will the loss of the arms shipment from Santa Lorca have consequences?"

"At this stage it is more of an irritant. To be honest, the capture of Rasheed concerns me more. Weapons can be replaced. Someone like Rasheed cannot."

Wafiq inclined his head in agreement.

"Any loss of a brother is sad. At this time it is something we could do without. Rasheed also has a great deal of knowledge concerning our aims. If that should…"

"That is one thing we do not have to be worried about. Rasheed will die before he allows himself to betray us."

"I understand that, Razan. My thoughts were along the lines that we have lost his input. Rasheed brought enlightenment and expertise to our meetings."

"Then we must work harder to compensate for his loss."

"I have some information from the training camp," one of the others said.

He was Tarik Bader. A formidable figure, especially when he wore his military uniform, Bader still impressed with his powerful presence. Due to a wounding in a confrontation with an anti-Saddam Hussein group, Bader had been struck in the face with a knife. It had left him with a scar down his left cheek and the loss of his vision in his eye. He had worn an eye patch ever since.

"Give us your report, Tarik."

"The input of volunteers has risen again. A new group arrived at the camp in Chechen three days ago and are settling in well. Training is proving to be useful. We already have a number of people proficient with the operation of the explosives."

"At least it's better news than we have been getting lately," Saeed Hassan, the third member of Khariza's group, said. "Razan, we need to push forward with the arming of our groups in Iraq. Until they are supplied with enough weapons it makes it difficult to control those areas we are weakest in."

"In a few days we will have the means to fly in a supply of arms for a delivery to the camp in Chechen. It has taken a little longer than expected to acquire the correct aircraft, and the location of someone to fly the plane has taken longer."

"We have someone now?"

"Yes. One of our Algerian brothers. A good man by all accounts. He was taught by the French."

Amer Khaliz, who had remained silent so far, raised the next topic.

"The nuclear devices?"

"Our friends in North Korea assure me they are almost complete. When I am able to transfer the appropriate funds, they will be available. And the other main armament will also follow once payment is made. And I hope that will be soon."

Wafiq made an angry sound. "We are being denied our chance because of that damned coward, Sharii. Nothing will happen until we recover those account codes."

"I am aware of that, Abdul. The matter is being dealt with."

"Is there no way around this?" Khaliz asked. "No way of financing by other means? Cannot the Koreans supply us and let us pay later?"

Khariza found himself smiling.

"Did I say something amusing?" Khaliz asked.

"It struck me that you sounded just like an American, my brother. Is that not the way they run their economy? Buy now—pay later?"

There was a ripple of laughter from the assembled group. Even Khaliz managed a weak smile.

"If I even thought I had been tainted by the Americans I would wash out my mouth with soap."

"Listen to me, friends, I understand your frustrations. Sharii did us a great disservice when he stole those codes and left his virus in the computer system. It destroyed our link to the banks and denied us the money we need so badly. If we are unable to gain access to that money, our plans will be of little use to us. But we have not lost everything yet. We must keep our faith. God will not desert us. Our day *will* come. As for the North Koreans, they are only doing what any good businessman would do. Their need for hard cash is as strong as ours for the weapons they can supply. If they allow us to take the weapons and we fail to pay, their loss is doubled.

"We will let our people loose in London. Allow them to hunt down Sharii. And we will continue to send weapons to our people in America, give them the time to prepare for what is to come. Saeed, I want you to increase the unrest across our region. Encourage the strikes against every target they can. Especially between the Palestinians and the Israelis. Agitate. Create mistrust. Find every weakness and exploit it. If the streets must run red with blood, then let it be so."

CHAPTER FOUR

London, England

"How come we don't get to ride like this every mission?" Hawkins asked.

"Because most trips we're flying to some godforsaken place, weighed down with equipment and probably jumping out at thirty thousand feet."

Hawkins nodded, stretching his frame out in the comfortable seat. "I could get to like this, boss."

"Don't get too comfy. The way this thing flies we'll be touching down before they get round to serving us any bloody drinks."

McCarter peered out the side window. They were already at altitude and well over the Atlantic, the Gulfstream C-20F cruising smoothly and silently. They were due to touch down at RAF Lakenheath. Their ride was being provided by the U.S. Air Force's high priority unit, which explained the VIP standard. The C-20F had been assigned to McCarter and Hawkins via special dispensation from the President himself.

One of the cabin crew appeared from the rear of the aircraft. "Can I get you anything, gentlemen?"

"I could go for a cup of coffee," Hawkins said.

"And you, sir?"

"You have any Coke?" McCarter asked. "I mean, the genuine article. Not some pansy substitute."

"Bottle or can?"

"Bottle. Hey, is it chilled?"

The crewman smiled. "Would we serve it any other way?"

Minutes later McCarter and Hawkins were enjoying their respective drinks. The Briton was well suited with his Coke Classic. The bottle had condensation frosting on the glass.

"If the Iraqis get wind of this guy we're looking for, his life isn't going to be peaceful for very long," Hawkins said.

McCarter lowered his bottle. "They get wind of him, the poor sod is in deep trouble."

"If Sharon managed to locate him so easily, the opposition could do the same."

"Exactly, T.J., my boy."

EVERYTHING WAS READY for them. The moment the U.S. aircraft landed, a car came out to meet them. McCarter and Hawkins stepped out of the climate-controlled atmosphere of the jet into a damp U.K. day, carrying their belongings in leather carryalls. The car, a dark blue Chrysler Neon, rolled to a stop. The driver was a young USAF sergeant. The name tag on his jacket read: Denning.

"Good morning, gentlemen," he said. "Have a good flight?"

McCarter jerked a thumb in the direction of the Gulf-stream. "In that? What do you think?"

Denning smiled. He began to speak, but his words were drowned as an F-15E Strike Eagle burned its way into the sky. The jet fighter was part of the U.S.'s 48th Fighter Wing based at Lakenheath. Three more F-15s followed the first, climbing with breathtaking speed. The rumble of their passing remained after the jets had become tiny specks in the gray sky.

McCarter glanced across the wide spread of the base. There was a great deal of activity going on. A number of the fighter aircraft were moving along the feeder strips toward the main runways.

"We come at a busy time, Sergeant?"

"The base is on alert in case unrest in the Middle East gets any worse. But I guess you people know all about that."

They climbed into the car and the sergeant drove them across the apron to a low building set slightly apart from the main complex. They pulled up outside.

"Car's all fueled up. Documents are in the side pocket, sir," Denning said, handing McCarter the keys. He indicated the building. "Direct phone line via satel-lite as requested."

"Thanks," Hawkins said.

They watched as Denning walked away.

"So polite," Hawkins remarked.

"For a bloke who probably wonders who the hell we are and why we rate so much clout—very polite."

They took their bags inside the building. It was basic, but McCarter had no intention of spending too much time here. It was simply a base for them to take off from.

There was a plain wooden desk, USAF issue, that held a telephone. The Phoenix Force commandos used the desk to dump their carryalls so they could get at their personal weapons. McCarter had his 9 mm Browning Hi-Power; Hawkins, the Beretta 92-F. They slipped off their jackets and donned shoulder rigs, checking that the handguns were locked and loaded. They each carried a couple of spare magazines for the weapons. McCarter took a pair of identical cell phones and handed one to Hawkins. They were Triband models, capable of sending and receiving calls from any location.

"Better let Hal know we've arrived," the Briton said.

He used the telephone on the desk to dial the number that would connect them to Stony Man via the satellite link. Barbara Price answered.

"Is the boss there?"

"No. He had to go to see the President. Things are happening. More problems in the Middle East. A minister in the Iraqi government was assassinated a couple of hours ago. He had just stepped out of his house in Baghdad and took a bullet in the head. From what we've been able to learn, it looks like a sniper shot. This was no suicide attack. The guy was deliberately targeted. He was one of the moderate Iraqi politicians. He had no patience with the agitators or the hard-line pro-Hussein opposition."

"Lakenheath looks like it's on standby in case things start heating up."

Price sighed. "We've had reports of similar shows in Israel. Tanks are patrolling the Gaza Strip. There have already been a number of demonstrations. The Israelis are holding back for the time being, but things are looking increasingly fragile. Every news program is hitting the TV screens with rolling reports."

"We're moving out to meet up with Sharon. Contact from now on can be through our cell phones. Let Hal know we're up and running."

"Talk to you later."

McCarter put down the phone.

"You set?"

Hawkins nodded.

They took their bags with them and placed them in the trunk. McCarter held up the keys.

"Feel lucky?"

"Driving on the wrong side of the road? I'll let you take this one, boss."

"No spirit of adventure. That's the problem with you colonials."

"Yeah, whatever." Hawkins grinned.

They left the sprawling airbase, McCarter pushing the Neon along the A1065, heading for the A-11 and eventually the M-11 motorway. They had seventy miles to cover before they could link up with Ben Sharon. The

roads were busy, McCarter driving as fast as the conditions permitted. His driving skills proved useful as he
edged by slower vehicles, gaining ground as the miles
slid by. He was able to speed up when they reached the
M-11, ignoring the sudden shower of rain that turned
the motorway into a glistening strip, fine spray misting
the air from beneath the wheels of other vehicles.

"You always drive this fast?" Hawkins asked after a
prolonged silence.

"Hell, chum, this isn't fast."

"My mistake," Hawkins said. "If you see anyone
selling worry beads, stop so I can buy a couple of sets."

The M-11 gave way to the M-25, the circular route
that ringed London. The M-25 had been built with the
intention of easing traffic around the capital, but it was
prone to long holdups, with long tailbacks of stationary
vehicles. The M-25 had been rechristened the largest car
park in the U.K.

McCarter headed west, his destination one of the service stations that allowed for gassing up and refresh-
ments. This was where Sharon would be waiting for them.

"They serve strong liquor here?" Hawkins asked as
McCarter eased the car into a parking slot.

"My driving that bad?"

"Let's say jumping at thirty thousand feet with no
chute would offer better odds."

McCarter tossed the keys to his younger partner.

"Go fill up," he said. "I'll find Ben."

McCarter recognized the Israeli easily when he did
find him. Sharon's dark good looks made him stand out

in any crowd. He was tall and leanly muscular. His clothing was sober, dark pants and shirt and a light brown leather jacket. He moved forward as he spotted McCarter, reaching out to take the Briton's hand.

"You made good time," Sharon said.

"The way things are going, time is something we don't have a lot of."

"Tell me." Sharon paused. "I was sorry to hear about Yakov. He will be missed. I liked that man a lot."

This was Sharon's first contact with McCarter since the death of the Israeli former commander of Phoenix Force. In the past he had worked closely with the commandos on active missions. He and Katz had always maintained a close working relationship, passing information back and forth. Sharon's Mossad connections had proved useful on many occasions, as they were now.

McCarter could see that Sharon's concern was genuine. As Phoenix Force had lost a irreplaceable comrade, Sharon had lost someone he considered a true friend.

The Briton nodded. Time still hadn't diminished the feelings and the respect he held for Katz. It would be a long time, if ever, before the loss faded.

"What's the drill, Ben?"

"We go from here to north London. It's where we tracked our man."

"So how long have you been in town?" McCarter asked.

Sharon smiled. "Long enough to know I'm missing home. But this needs doing. I've been trailing this group for a while now. Trying to get a feel for what they're planning."

"And?"

"Khariza is determined to get back into Iraq and into the government. He has friends from the old regime still there. He has contacts and they have some money to buy what they need. Up to a point. They still need to get their hands on the bulk of the money that was salted away by Hussein and his faithful during the last couple of decades. Until they do, they're having to put the big events on hold."

"Did you read the report on Rasheed?"

"Pure example of what we've been concerned about. Khariza's group are going to go all-out to buy in weapons. Until they break out the big money, all they'll be able to do is buy small arms. But they can still do a lot of harm with those."

"Sharii. What's his story?"

"Sharii has been on the move since he got out of Iraq," Sharon said. "Once he broke from the party he knew his life was over unless he kept one step ahead. One, he knew too much. Two, the fedayeen don't take kindly to being betrayed, and as far as they are concerned that is exactly what he did when he wiped those access codes from the computer system.

"He tried to keep out of the spotlight in Holland. Eventually he made it to London. When Sharii settled in London, he stayed low profile. If he hadn't started attending a local mosque, one of our undercover people might not have spotted him at a prayer meeting. He seemed relieved when our man approached him and told him we could help. It now appears he has a sister living in the north of England. This is what he told us when he talked to our contact man. We didn't know anything about her until that meeting. Sharii is scared the fedayeen might find out about her and use her to draw him out. There's something they don't realize yet. The backup disks he made holding the access codes—he sent them to his sister for safekeeping. He's decided that wasn't such a smart thing now his regime friends are after him. He wants to get to her to retrieve them."

"Ben, can he give us any deeper background on Khariza? What the bloke is up to?"

"Sharii was pretty close to the inner circle of Khariza's when it came to finance. He was able to sit in on meetings and give his advice on how to arrange payments, hide money. When they murdered his brother they expected him to toe the line. What it actually did was to make him step over. He decided to get out before he was next."

McCarter's face revealed his suspicion. "Tell me, Ben, is he genuine?"

"That's exactly the way I felt when I first heard," Sharon said. "We did some background checking and Sharii *is* a wanted man. What he did hurt Khariza's plans badly. They want him so they can pull him apart and try to get their missing account codes back."

"You don't think he's playing games with us all."

"Why would he? It wouldn't get him much. We looked at it from every angle. Look, the guy wants some kind of sanctuary. A safe place to live. He knows what the fedayeen can do and he doesn't like it. He sees Khariza on the loose and he knows the man isn't going to sit back and forget Iraq."

McCarter stared out across the busy parking area. He found it hard to accept what Sharon was telling him. It wasn't that he didn't trust the Israeli. Sharon had always been straight with Phoenix Force when they had worked together before. The Briton trusted the Mossad agent. It was the so-called contact he doubted.

He realized he was being a little paranoid, but put it down to the job. The kind of work Stony Man undertook left little time for instant trust and believing without rock-solid confirmation. It wasn't paranoia. Just a healthy attitude toward sudden changes of heart. Switching loyalties did happen. McCarter accepted that. He also knew this particular enemy, and they weren't noted for casting aside their beliefs so easily. Extremists such as the fedayeen were, by nature, ultraloyal to the cause. Loyal to the death. Cutting themselves free from what they lived and breathed for was a drastic move. And McCarter had to see it from that angle, and be fully convinced otherwise before he walked into the line of fire.

"I understand your reluctance," Sharon said. "I'm going into this with both eyes wide open until I know better. On the other hand, we can't pass up the chance."

McCarter nodded. "Let's hope you're right, Ben. If not we're both bloody fools who need their heads examined."

"I haven't been to the new location yet," the Israeli

said. He showed McCarter the address written on a slip of paper. "You know how to get there?"

"I know," McCarter said.

"Easy to get to?"

"Getting in isn't the problem."

"Tough area?"

"Sort of place where even the kids walk around tooled up."

"Translate."

"'Tooled up' is an old criminal expression. Means going around carrying a weapon. Gun. Knife."

"Sounds like most places I end up in."

McCarter grinned. "Ben, don't play the old woman with me. You wouldn't know what to do in polite society."

"Must be why I feel comfortable in your company."

"Okay, let's go find my partner and we can get this circus on the road."

McCARTER DROVE, using his knowledge of the city to get them across London to the area where Sharon's contact was hiding. Hawkins followed behind in the Neon, sometimes struggling to keep up with the Briton. McCarter cut him no slack. It would keep the younger man on his toes.

Less than an hour later McCarter eased Sharon's Ford into a parking slot a street away from the building where the Mossad had Sharii housed. McCarter climbed out of the vehicle and waited until Sharon joined him. Hawkins pulled up behind.

Sharon checked the address again and indicated a building across the street.

"That's the one."

The area was edging toward shabbiness. The long stretch of road was lined with three-story buildings, a mix of businesses and residential: video stores and all-night provisions convenience stores, ethnic restaurants catering for a wide range of tastes. Even from their position across the street McCarter and Sharon could pick up the food aromas vying for attention.

"Up market doesn't seem to be the word here," Hawkins said.

McCarter breathed in deeply. "Just smell that," he said. "Now I know I'm back in London."

"The entrance is down the side of the Greek restaurant," Sharon told them.

"Let's get in there, Ben. Sooner we control things, the better."

They crossed the road and walked down the alley flanking the restaurant.

McCarter caught Hawkins's eye. "Watch our backs."

"You got it."

"Using the local patois, are *you* two tooled up?" the Mossad agent asked.

McCarter grinned. "Always."

The Briton pushed his jacket aside and slid his 9 mm Browning Hi-Power pistol from its shoulder rig. He held the weapon down at his side, the barrel parallel with his leg. Hawkins eased his Beretta from its shoulder rig.

"Let's do it," he said.

Midway along the alley, stone steps, with an iron rail on the open side, led up to a door on the second floor. A plastic number was screwed to the door. Toward the rear of the alley were a number of large, wheeled garbage bins. Hawkins remained at the bottom of the steps, covering McCarter and Sharon. As they reached the top of the steps McCarter scowled. He pointed at the door and Sharon saw that it was ajar.

Sharon reached inside his jacket and eased out a SIG-Sauer P-226. Glancing across at McCarter, the Mossad agent nodded.

McCarter stretched out his left hand and gently eased the door open, pushing it away from him. He followed the widening gap, using every advantage he could gain. The Briton lowered his body height to reduce his target area, crouching, the muzzle of the Hi-Power tracking ahead as he peered along the passage the opening door exposed. Sharon was leaning forward slightly to one side, double-checking where McCarter had already scanned.

A hunched figure was on the floor a few feet along the passage, hands pressed to a stomach wound that was leaking blood between his fingers. As the door swung open, the wounded man turned his head and saw McCarter and Sharon. His eyes widened in recognition when he saw Sharon. Despite his wound, he raised one bloody hand extending four fingers, then indicated the far end of the passage.

McCarter picked up the low murmur of voices coming from that direction. He was about to warn Sharon when he caught a flicker of movement at the far end of the shadowed passage. The shadow moved from left to right. A sudden surge of voices alerted the Phoenix Force commander.

From somewhere inside the flat came a sudden, unexpected cry of pain. More voices. Urgent. Insistent. A harsh torrent of words.

"Damn!" Sharon said, and pushed by McCarter.

The Briton followed Sharon along the passage, and being behind the Mossad agent, he was able to pick up on the armed figure stepping into view. The man was stocky, dark, and he was brandishing a stubby SMG, the muzzle already tracking Sharon's moving figure. McCarter didn't hesitate. He brought up the Browning, snapping off two quick shots that caught the gunner in the left shoulder. The 9 mm slugs cored in, tearing a bloody chunk out of the man's shoulder, spinning him in a half circle. A spray of flesh and splintered bone erupted from the exit wound, blood spreading in a red spray as the guy went down in a moaning heap. McCarter hit him again, a single shot to the head that took the man out for good.

Sharon had continued running, reaching the end of the passage and only just managing to haul to a halt before he exposed himself. As he flattened against the wall a second armed man appeared from the junction of the corridor. He was moving to check out what had happened. He had a cell phone to his ear and was speaking rapidly in Arabic. The moment he saw Sharon he opened his mouth to yell. The Israeli used his SIG-Sauer to club the man across the side of the head, repeating the blows until the gunner fell to his knees, a weak hand trying to ward off the Israeli. Blood was streaming down the side of his face, spilling out over his coat collar. Sharon snatched the SMG from the man's other hand. Spotting the cell phone, Sharon bent and snatched it from the man's fingers, slipping it into a pocket.

"Bastards got here first," Sharon yelled. "They'll…"

McCarter eased past the Israeli, putting his head around the corner to get a look at what lay in front of them. The angle of the corridor opened onto a large living room that had sliding doors at the far end that opened onto a balcony. The first thing McCarter saw was a man on his knees in the center of the room, head down and dripping blood on the carpet. There were two other men, armed, one standing over the kneeling man, the other staring around the room as if he was looking for a way out. The armed men were talking to each other and neither was listening to what his partner was saying. It was obvious that they hadn't expected to be disturbed. The sudden appearance of McCarter and Sharon had thrown them. The condition might only be temporary, but it presented McCarter and Sharon with a narrow window of opportunity.

The Briton tapped the Mossad agent on the shoulder.

"Now!" He didn't wait because their window was closing fast.

One of the gunmen was bringing his SMG around to aim the muzzle at the newcomers.

McCarter stepped clear of the wall, his Browning leveling even as he moved. He caught the gunman in his sights and triggered two fast shots. The slugs impacted against the side of the man's skull, burned through his brain and emerged out the other side with enough force to detach a large chunk of bone. The shooter stumbled sideways, then fell, his body shutting off as a large percentage of his brain came away with the bone casing. He hit the carpeted floor a deadweight, all resistance gone from his body. The impact geysered bloody debris across the carpet.

Moving slightly to one side of the Briton, Sharon angled his SIG-Sauer in the direction of the second gunman and fired the second he had target lock. The P-226 spat out a volley of 9 mm slugs that hit the target in the chest, shattering bone and puncturing lungs. The man toppled backward, arms and legs flailing as he lost all coordination. He hit the floor on his buttocks, the impact rippling up his arm and jerking his finger against the trigger of his SMG. It stuttered briefly, sending a burst of gun fire into the kneeling man, slamming him facedown on the carpet.

McCarter left him to Sharon. The Briton was more concerned with making sure none of the opposition still had weapons. Even a wounded man could put up a fight. Knowing these extremists as he did, McCarter decided he wasn't going to allow them the option of trying again. He moved to each man, clearing guns and searching them for additional weapons.

"How is he?" McCarter asked.

Sharon didn't answer. He was on his knees beside the man McCarter presumed was Sharii, desperately trying to stem the blood streaming from the man's upper chest and shoulder wound. The Israeli's hands were already red.

McCarter pulled his cell phone and hit a speed-dial number. It was a number Stony Man had negotiated through the British government that gave Phoenix Force access to a medical service used by the U.K. security services. He was connected quickly and ordered medical backup. He gave the location.

"No time for bloody questions. Just get that help here now. This is priority. If it wasn't, I wouldn't have this number, would I?"

Behind McCarter the man Sharon had pistol-whipped had crawled into view. He was pushing against the wall at his back, trying to get himself in a sitting position. Pushing to his own feet, McCarter crossed the room to stand over the man.

"Planning on going somewhere, chum?"

The man stared up at the Briton with a gleam of anger in his dark eyes.

"If I had my gun, I would kill you where you stand."

McCarter smiled. "That might even be funny if it wasn't so bloody pathetic. Listen, mate, you had your chance and blew it. So your next move will be to a nice quiet cell. You're going to have to answer some questions. If you think we're bad, wait until you meet the blokes who are going to be asking those questions."

"You think I am afraid of your torturers? We were told what would happen if we were captured. The things you would do to us. It will make no difference. It will not stop us. More of us will come. They are waiting for the chance to come here and be allowed to sacrifice themselves."

"And what's that for? Just exactly what is it you jokers are trying to prove? That you can kill yourselves by the dozen? Haven't you people got real lives to live instead of this bloody waste."

"We do these things because we choose to."

"Because Razan Khariza tells you to. You buggers want to keep the war going. More killing. More suffering. All so Khariza can get his hands on stolen money."

"No. Khariza wants to free Iraq. Give it back to the people."

"My mistake," McCarter said. "I forgot he's such a humanitarian. He take lessons from Saddam?"

"You people have no idea what we die for."

"Right. So you dead and me left alive is pushing your cause to the front?" McCarter couldn't resist a smile. "I see a flaw in your argument. A big, bloody flaw."

"And what is that?"

"It won't achieve a damn thing. People *will* die. On both sides. But in the end everything will be the same. It's self-defeating. All you'll do is make us more defiant. You can blow things up till eternity plus one. We'll bury our dead. We'll grieve. And then we'll just rebuild and carry on. You think you're the only ones with perseverance? If you think we don't have the stomach for this fight, then you've been given a bum steer. So where's the gain for you in that? Tell me, because I am bloody curious."

"We will achieve immortality in paradise. Our sacrifice will repay us a thousand times."

"So you're telling me all this is just so you get to live happy ever after? Bit extreme, isn't it? Are you sure you've got it right?"

McCarter glanced at Sharon. "I give up."

T.J. HAWKINS HEARD the crackle of gunfire coming from the flat. He resisted the urge to go check what had happened. Until he had made certain the area was safe, it was his responsibility to stay alert.

As he rounded the end of the building, Hawkins heard the sound of a car engine starting. He moved behind one of the trash bins, trying to ignore the stale smell from the dumped leftovers. He stayed there as a dark-colored Toyota Avensis rolled into view. As it cruised by him, Hawkins saw two men in the front seat arguing heatedly. The passenger seemed to want to go. He kept gesturing to the driver, shaking his head. The car stopped at the bottom of the steps.

The driver made a sharp gesture and shoved his door open, climbing out. He ran around to the bottom of the steps, pulling a handgun from inside his jacket as he turned to look at his partner, holding out his free hand, beckoning the man.

The passenger turned to open his own door.

Hawkins knew his time was up. If he waited any longer, these two backup men would be up to the flat.

He stepped out from the cover of the garbage bin, his 92-F already rising to target the man on the steps.

"Put the gun down," Hawkins yelled.

The driver became aware of the American's presence. His reaction was predictable. He brought his pistol into action, swinging the muzzle to line up on Hawkins.

The driver's weapon had almost settled on Hawkins when the Phoenix Force commando pulled the trigger. Two fast shots caught the man in the chest and knocked him off the first step. He thumped back against the brick wall, his pistol bouncing from his hand as he went down, moaning at the pain spreading across his chest.

Hawkins had been moving forward as he fired, bringing himself down the side of the car. He could see the passenger struggling to pull his own weapon and exit the car at the same time.

The passenger shouldered the door open and half fell out, attempting to bring his weapon on track. He fired, more in panic than anger, the bullet flying wild. Before he could gather himself, Hawkins was on him. He slammed his foot against the car door, kicking it shut against the man's upper body. The inner frame bounced off the guy's skull. His gun fired again as his finger jerked against the trigger. The bullet struck the concrete at Hawkins's feet, whining off at an angle. The Phoenix Force commando used the barrel of the Beretta to hit the man's gun hand. The sound of breaking bone was audible. As the pistol fell from the man's hand, Hawkins reached down, caught hold of him by the collar of his jacket and dragged him bodily from the car. Swinging the guy around, Hawkins yanked him upright, then slashed the Beretta across the side of the man's jaw. The man sagged to his knees, blood dripping from the gash the Beretta had opened.

Hawkins stepped back, covering both men. He pulled out his cell phone and hit the number that would connect him with McCarter. When the Briton answered, Hawkins gave him a brief rundown on what had happened.

"You okay?"

"I'm fine. Just a little fracas down here."

"Keep an eye on them," McCarter said. "We have a situation up here."

"Is Sharii there?"

"Yes, but he's been hurt. T.J., I've called for medical backup. They should be on site soon."

"No problem. Hey, I always thought London was such a quiet place."

"T.J., you think Texas is tough? One day I'll take you on a *real* tour of this town."

HALF AN HOUR LATER the area had been cordoned off after a horde of security personnel appeared. The black-clad response squad, fully equipped with body armor, helmets and SMGs, swarmed over the alley and the building. There might have been confusion if McCarter hadn't contacted Brognola before they'd arrived. The big Fed had it all in hand, getting through to the appropriate department in the U.K., and by the time the response squad arrived they had their orders to cooperate fully with McCarter—cover name Jack Coyle—and with icy reserve that was what they did.

"I'm Greg Henning," the response team leader announced, ignoring McCarter's offered hand.

"I washed it this morning," the Phoenix Force Leader said casually.

"Oh, a comic."

"If you want. But at least I have good manners. Is downright rudeness something they teach you buggers, or are you just a miserable sod all the time?"

Henning's cheeks darkened with anger. "Who the fu—"

"I'm someone who just shot a couple of people a while ago. So did my partner over there. So go easy on me, Mr. Henning, I'm not in the most stable condition at the moment."

McCarter turned and left the man standing. He crossed over to where Sharon was watching the Mossad agent being placed in the ambulance that would take both him and Sharii to the secure medical facility just outside London.

"How is he, Ben?"

"They managed to stop the blood. He was knifed pretty badly. But they believe he'll pull through."

"You know him?"

"I worked with him a few times. He has a family back in Haifa. Two young children. I haven't identified the other two yet."

McCarter squeezed the Israeli's shoulder. "I'm sorry about your people."

"Sharii has bullets in his upper chest and shoulder. Before that those bastards had worked him over pretty hard. His face is all broken up. They snapped some fingers, too."

"Did he say anything to you?"

"He was angry they found him, especially after we said we'd look after him. Dammit, he trusted us and we let him down."

"Don't blame yourself, Ben. There's no such thing as total security. Sounds good on paper, but we all know how life screws things up. You cover all the bases, then something happens that turns it upside down. We know Khariza's people have been looking for Sharii."

"We should have had it covered."

"You did. But Khariza's people had, as well. They got lucky and traced Sharii here. How? Maybe they laid out such good bonuses somebody talked. Maybe they have smart people out on the street, too."

"We need to move pretty fast. Khariza's men kept asking Sharii about the disk copies he made. He tried to bluff it, but they told him they had him on surveillance cameras back in Iraq. They know what he did. It gives Khariza an added incentive now. He'll want those disks. They searched the flat but couldn't find anything. They kept at him and Sharii let something slip about his sister. Khariza will figure it out."

"Do we know where this sister lives?"

Sharon nodded. "Sharii gave me her location. It might give us an advantage. Khariza is going to have to do it via databases, so he might be behind us timewise. But he *will* find her."

"We need to get a move on, then," McCarter said.

"I can help you with that."

McCarter turned and found himself face-to-face with the response team leader, Henning.

"Mr. Coyle, I apologize for my attitude. You were right, I was a miserable sod. Out of order. No excuses."

Henning put out his hand and McCarter took it immediately.

"We all have bad days," McCarter said. "Sometimes I think I have more than most. Now about this help?"

LESS THAN AN HOUR LATER McCarter, Hawkins and Sharon were on board a SA-341 Gazelle helicopter, piloted by Henning himself. The French-inspired machine, originally the first ever to feature a Fenestron tail rotor, was one of three belonging to Henning's antiterrorist squad. The chopper was equipped with weapons pods that held HS missiles. It also carried an M-134, 7.62 mm, General Electric minigun, fitted into a traversing nose pod. Henning had explained that the M-134, fitted to all three of the special helicopters, were unusual in that the ordnance wasn't the norm in the U.K.

"The response team is relatively new," Henning explained. "We were formed after 9/11. A reaction to the new situation."

"You seen much action?" Hawkins asked.

"Some. More since the Iraq war. A lot of bloody false alarms, but we've had our moments."

"You might have seen some action today if we hadn't jumped in," McCarter said, glancing across at Henning.

"Don't get me wrong," Henning said. "I'm in no hurry to get my head shot off."

"Sensible kind of bloke," McCarter said. "My kind of man."

"These people we're going after," Henning said. "Iraqis still hanging on to the old regime's way?"

"They're doing their best to stir the pot," McCarter said.

Henning glanced at the on-screen computer map. Their course had been fed into the computer from Henning's HQ, following McCarter's data input on the location of Sharii's sister.

"If we meet up with any of these Iraqis?" Henning asked. "What I mean is…"

"No bloody quarter is the answer, Gregory, my old mate. You saw the way they operated back at the house. No question about it. We're in a bloody war situation here. It's just that it spilled over from Baghdad and settled in the U.K. These boys want to play rough, then that's the way it's going to be."

Henning squared his shoulders, reaching out to adjust a setting.

"Fine by me," he said.

"Fighting talk," Hawkins said in a slow drawl.

"Don't mind him," McCarter stated. "He comes from Texas and can't get the Alamo out of his system."

"Let me take him down the East End at throwing-out time on a Saturday night," Henning said. "When the locals fall out of the pubs, they don't take prisoners."

"They really that rowdy?" Hawkins asked and failed to understand why both McCarter and Henning burst out laughing.

CHAPTER FIVE

Nuevo Laredo, Mexico

Rosario Blancanales stepped out of the cantina and made his way across the street. He took his time, pacing himself to the mood of the day. Hurrying would only have made him stand out. This was no place to go around as if life was ending and there was a lot to do. Blancanales was in Nuevo Laredo for a reason. Right then he didn't want to tip his hand to any opposition by stepping out of line, which meant staying in the background and not attracting any attention.

He reached the dusty Oldsmobile parked at the curb on the opposite side of the street and opened the driver's door. It was hot inside the car, the air heavy with the smell of plastic and metal. Blancanales settled himself, turning on the engine. He sat for a moment considering his next move. The man he had come to meet hadn't shown up. Blancanales considered that to be something to worry about. Able Team's contact, Tomas Barranca, had stressed the importance of the meeting, implying that it couldn't be delayed. Now Barranca had failed to make the meeting, which was out of step with what he had said. Blancanales didn't like it when arrangements fell through. It made him nervous.

Blancanales took out his cell phone and made a call. It was answered by Carl Lyons, Able Team's commander. When he heard what his teammate had to report, Lyons's response was a curt grunt of annoyance.

"That it?" Blancanales said.

"What do you want, Pol, a round of applause?"

"Something a little more than a grunt would go down well."

"Feeling a little delicate, are we? Too much local beverage? Maybe we can't handle it like we used to."

"*We* are likely to kick your monkey butt when *we* get back."

"So where do we go from here?"

"Only option is to make a house call."

"Fine if we knew how to get to Barranca's place. Aaron's file forgot to give directions."

"I'm heading there now."

"Should I ask how you found that out?"

"I just used a little charm on the guy who runs the bar. He knows Barranca. I convinced him I needed to see the guy bad. I'm only passing through and I had some family business to handle for his brother up in Taos."

"Barranca have a brother in Taos?"

"Yes. Barranca told me when he called to set up the

meet. I told you the guy was worried. He wanted to talk, so we talked. People skills, Carl, you remember those, don't you?"

"Getting close," Lyons muttered.

Blancanales grinned at the cell phone. Sometimes it was so easy to wind Lyons up it wasn't as satisfying as it had been when the Ironman stayed sharp.

"Follow me in, but don't get too close in case I'm being tailed. The way things are going, I don't trust anyone in this damn town. Including that bartender. He could have been setting me up instead of giving me information."

"Sad for someone to lose their trust in human nature at such an early age."

Blancanales broke the connection. He turned the Oldsmobile around and drove off. He kept checking his rearview mirror and after a couple of minutes he spotted the Ford that his partners were using. It stayed well behind him, allowing a couple of other cars to push into the space. Blancanales watched these vehicles, wondering if his suspicions had been correct. Then one of them turned off onto another street, leaving only a battered, peeling pickup truck behind him. The back of the pickup was loaded with wire-mesh boxes holding live chickens. The load was high and secured by thin ropes. It swayed from side to side as the driver drove along the uneven road.

It took Blancanales almost half an hour to reach the area where Barranca lived. It was on the outskirts, where property values had to have been at an all-time low. The houses lining the street were wooden, not in the best condition, and the locality seemed to be a dumping ground for a large percentage of Nuevo Laredo's abandoned automobiles. A number of them had been burned out. Blancanales drove by one that was still smoking, presumably from the previous night.

According to the information he'd been given, Barranca's house stood at the far end of the street, separated from its neighbor by a wooden fence. When the fence came into view Blancanales drove by, checking out the house. He felt satisfied enough to turn around and drive back, easing the Oldsmobile up onto the dirt parking area. There was a car already there. A bright red Pontiac, some years old, with Mexican plates. House and car matched the description Kurtzman had supplied.

Blancanales switched off the engine and sat studying the house. It looked to be larger than any of the others on the street, but still had the same dilapidated appearance. Blancanales called Lyons on his cell phone.

"You see me?"

"Yeah."

"I'm going in."

"Okay."

"I'll leave the phone open."

Blancanales exited the Oldsmobile and made his way to the entrance to the house. It was on the left side. He reached under his loose shirt and made sure his Beretta pistol was available. He paused at the step, checking to see if there was a bell. Nothing. Blancanales knocked on the wooden frame. No response. It was quiet. Too quiet. Blancanales moved along the side of the house until he located a window. He peered around the edge of the wood frame and looked in on the open living area. It was neatly furnished. Everything looked to be in its place.

Except for the naked arm poking out from behind a leather sofa. The arm was extremely bloody and some of the fingers on the hand looked to be bent into unnatural positions. Blancanales pulled back from the window, taking a breath. Then he drew his Beretta and spoke into his cell phone.

"You better get up here. And stay sharp, guys."

Blancanales moved back to the door. He tried the handle and felt it give. When he pushed, the door swung open. He eased off the Beretta's safety and waited to one side of the door until Lyons and Schwarz appeared.

"What?" Lyons asked.

"Looks like a body on the floor inside the living room."

Lyons and Schwarz took up covering positions as Blancanales went in. He moved to the left, flat against the wall, tracking the area with the Beretta. Once he had confirmed the room was safe, he moved on. He didn't check behind him because he knew his partners would be there, covering him as he ventured farther into the house. He couldn't see them, but the whisper of sounds they made reached his ears. Blancanales's faith in Lyons and Schwarz was strong enough to give him that degree of confidence.

The leather sofa he had seen through the window was

hiding the naked body of a man. Blancanales saw the face first and, despite the severe beating he had taken, Tomas Barranca was still recognizable. In addition to the facial beating, Barranca had been cruelly tortured with a knife. His tormentor had obviously known what he was doing. Barranca had been mutilated both above and below the waist. There was a wide pool of dark blood spreading out from the body.

Blancanales crouched beside Barranca. He didn't have to touch him to know he was dead. The skin had already started to take on the pallor of death. Flies were starting to hover over the corpse, and Blancanales could almost taste the sickly sweet taint of decay.

"If he knew this was what they might do to him, I can understand why he was scared."

Lyons stood looking down at Barranca. "Did he give you anything?"

"Only that the new man he'd seen was an Arab. His words."

"I guess you don't see many around Nuevo Laredo," Schwarz said.

"What do you think?" Lyons asked. "One of Khariza's people?"

"Could be." Blancanales stood, putting his gun away. "The guy was shopping around for weapons, and this is a good area for buyers."

"So why this?" Schwarz asked.

"Barranca asked for a meet because something about the guy scared him. He had a feeling he was after more than just personal weapons."

"He isn't going to tell us now."

Blancanales crossed the room and stopped beside Barranca's work desk. It held a computer, scanner and printer. Papers were strewn across the desk and more littered the floor around an overflowing waste bin.

The computer was switched off. Blancanales checked that it was connected to the electrical outlet and switched it on. As it powered up, he went through the papers on the desk. He couldn't find anything to suggest why Barranca's visitors had needed to kill him. He sat at the desk and stared at the monitor. He used the mouse to open the Documents window. It was empty. He checked the desk for disks. There were none. Someone had cleared Barranca's supply. Blancanales tapped his fingers against the desktop in frustration. If the disks were gone, anything Barranca might have put down was lost. He stared at the screen again, eyes flicking across the various icons until he spotted the one labeled Recycle Bin. The icon showed the bin held discarded items. Blancanales clicked on the icon and opened the window. There were two items showing. He moved the pointer to Restore All Items and sent them to the Documents file. Returning to the Documents file, Blancanales opened each item and studied it. One of the files was in Spanish. The second was in some kind of machine code.

"What have you got?" Lyons asked.

Blancanales shrugged. He was reading the Spanish text document.

"It's some kind of report. Barranca says he'd noticed considerable interest in weapons purchase among the local dealers. Automatic pistols, assault rifles and SMGs. Requests for rocket launchers, grenades. Explosives. He'd picked up on talk about buyers contacting or asking for contact with anyone ready to deal. Mention of bigger ordnance. Ground-to-air missiles. A big order for those. Lot of interest shown from Central America. The talk is of someone who wants to move the ordnance to the U.S. border regions. Money no object. Something here about shipping to the West Coast region. Other consignments to the Gulf Coast as far along as Corpus Christi."

"Anything about the buyers? Who they are?"

"Yeah. Here. Barranca keeps using the phrase Arab-type people."

"Could be Khariza," Schwarz said. "Easier for them to buy in Central America."

"Ties in with Phoenix and that broker down in Santa Lorca," Lyons said. "There any names we can move on?"

"Only a couple. Luiz Santos. We already know he's involved. And Philo Vance."

"Vance? I know that son of a bitch. He works out of Vegas. He'll buy and sell anything as long as it makes him a buck. He's handled weapons in the past. Has some out-of-state contacts, too."

Blancanales turned back to the computer and used the mouse to connect the internal modem. Then he opened the e-mail facility. He tapped in the e-mail address that would be accessed by Kurtzman, typed a message about the names they had found and the files he was sending, attached the files and hit the send button. A couple of minutes later he received an acknowledgment.

"If anyone can unravel that text code, Bear can."

Aaron Kurtzman was a computer genius, a man who could break the most complex codes with ease. He had an affinity with the cyberworld second to none, but made the worst coffee on the planet.

Satisfied the data was in safe hands, Blancanales emptied the Recycle Bin.

"What now?" Schwarz asked.

"Let's go see if we can smoke out Luiz Santos."

THEY HAD A LOCATION for Santos. He worked out of a meat-packing plant on the edge of Nuevo Laredo that supplied specialist products to the catering trade in the local area and to establishments over the border. The man was known in the area but as with most of his kind, Santos had connections. According to his file, he was suspected of illegal business but it had never been proven. His influence ran high in the local law enforcement agencies. The honest cops had never made any kind of charge stick because Santos bought and paid for people who ran interference all along the line. Nothing ever got past the initial crime sheet. Reports were lost. Witnesses vanished or lost their memories. It had also been known for stubborn individuals to turn up dead. A couple of the local cops had suffered the same fate when they'd persisted in trying to push for a conviction.

Able Team wasn't open to bribes, and they didn't

play by any rules, local or otherwise. Intimidation wasn't in their book, either.

Stony Man had provided them with identification sheets for Santos and his principal lieutenants, along with photographs for them to memorize.

The packing plant was a working business. It made a good profit, though that would be small when compared to the turnover of Santos's illegitimate enterprises. The plant covered a large area, fenced off.

"Must be a lot of meat burglaries around here to warrant all that security," Blancanales murmured as Able Team did a drive by.

The chain-link fence and high gates were complimented by a gatehouse, where a couple of security men wearing side arms checked people and vehicles in and out.

"Could be a hard nut to crack," Schwarz observed as the plant fell behind them.

"If it's hard, there's only one way to do it," Lyons said.

"And that is?"

Lyons stared at Blancanales over the top of his dark glasses. "No crap. We wait until dark then go over the fence and make things happen."

"That little speech just wiped out years of strategic planning and feasibility studies," Blancanales said.

"The way it goes is this. The background of this mission, and any others involving this guy Khariza, are all running on a time limit. Agreed?"

There were nods all around.

"So we don't have time for screwing around. Assessing whether we should or shouldn't. Checking the wind factor is going to eat up time we don't have. If Khariza and his bunch are planning chaos, it might happen anytime. So we have to make the play, and if that means going over the wall and making noise, we do it."

"When you explain it so beautifully," Schwarz said, "who am I to argue?"

Blancanales sighed. "Reduced to basic street talk I guess you are saying let's go kick some ass."

"I thought you'd never get it."

THEY HAD USED the Oldsmobile, picking up their combat gear from their motel, and making the run to the packing plant by a route that brought them in along a narrow dirt road that ran parallel to the rear of the site. Schwarz rolled the car into a dry gully about a quarter mile from the plant, cut the engine, and Able Team exited the vehicle and assembled at the rear.

They had donned blacksuits and dark baseball caps. Lyons wore his holstered .357 Magnum Colt Python while Blancanales and Schwarz carried 9 mm Beretta 92-Fs. Their primary weapons were the M-16 A-2s. Lyons's rifle had an underslung M-203 grenade launcher and he carried a number of 40 mm loads for the weapon on his body harness. The other team members had fragmentation and incendiary grenades. Each man had a sheathed combat knife on his belt. For communication purposes they wore lightweight Tac-Com units. Before leaving the car the trio had smeared combat cosmetics on hands and faces.

"Set?" Lyons asked.

Blancanales and Schwarz nodded. "Let's do it."

They eased out of the gully and cut off across the moonlit scrubland. They moved quickly, silently, the only mark of their passing the soft puffs of dust from their booted feet. Lyons called a halt when they reached the halfway point, giving them the chance to rest while they checked out the plant.

"Looks quiet," Blancanales said. He was eyeing the building on the far side of the fence. "Vehicles parked up. Security lights across the loading bays. I can't see many people around."

"Hey, Carl, might not be any ass to kick," Schwarz said.

"Always got you pair," Lyons replied. "C'mon, let's move."

They closed on the perimeter fence, taking the last stretch flat to the ground and reassembling at the base of the barrier. They took time studying the plant. The complex of buildings used for the meat processing were scattered around the site in a random fashion. Directly ahead of them were the loading bays, with trucks backed up to the ramps. None of the shutter doors used to move the meat out onto the ramps was open.

"I hear a truck engine," Schwarz said.

The others picked up the sound.

"Maybe a special delivery being loaded—or unloaded," Lyons said.

He took a look up at the top of the fence to see if he could spot any sensor wires. He saw nothing.

"No cameras," Blancanales reported.

"Let's see if it's our lucky night," Lyons suggested.

"What a decisive guy, Pol. No wonder they made him boss."

"That's the thing about democracy. It allows all kinds to reach the top," Blancanales said.

Lyons ignored them. He slung his M-16 and reached out to grip the chain fence. Using his powerful muscles, he climbed the fence at a rate that had Blancanales and Schwarz throwing each other glances.

"Now that is just showing off," Blancanales said.

"Yeah," his partner said. "Go ahead, Pol, show him he isn't the only fit guy in this team."

Lyons had swung over the top of the fence. He hung from his hands before dropping lightly to the ground, then unslung his rifle and crouched at the base of the fence.

Blancanales followed Lyons's example, a little slower, but he managed to join him without breaking too much of a sweat. They both covered the area as Schwarz brought up the rear, finally dropping to the ground beside them.

"Yeah," he said to no one in particular.

They moved through the shadows, reaching the cover of a line of industrial waste bins. The sickly sweet smell of decaying meat hung around the containers.

Lyons scanned the way ahead. "We can use the loading bay for first cover before we reach the end of the building," he said, indicating the position. "Pol, you go first. I'll stay here so Gadgets can follow."

They made another sweep, checking that the area

was clear, before Blancanales moved out. Once he broke cover he moved quickly, knowing that his partners were covering him and would warn him if there were any problems. He reached the long loading bay and crouched at the base, his back flat against the concrete siding. Once he had the area covered, he spoke quietly into his Tac-Com unit. Seconds later Schwarz rounded the end of the garbage bins, crouching as he cut across the open space and made for Blancanales's position.

"Cover Carl," Blancanales said. "I'll take this side."

The moment Lyons received the all-clear, he swung around the garbage bins and crossed to the loading bay.

"That engine we heard," Blancanales said. "Parked around the other side of that storage building. I hear voices, as well."

"Let's do it," Lyons said.

They used the same formation as before. Blancanales first, Lyons covering Schwarz, then Ironman making the final run.

Flat against the end wall, they edged to the corner, giving themselves the chance to observe what was taking place. Lyons, crouching, peered around the corner.

There was a refrigerated truck near the open doors of a storage building, the rear doors open. Inside the chilled interior of the vehicle he could see hanging beef carcasses and plastic trays of prepared meat, curls of white mist swirling around the meat. The load held less interest for Lyons than the foot-deep false floor section set beneath the freezer compartment. A metal plate had been removed so that the compartment was fully exposed. Men were exiting the storage building, carrying plastic-wrapped packages. The packages were being slid into the compartment. Each package was secured to the next by the knotted ends, then pushed deep into the false floor by a couple of men using long poles. The size and shape of the packages told Lyons all he needed to know.

Automatic rifles. Illumination from the lights on the building walls allowed Lyons to identify the weapons through the clear plastic—AK-74 assault rifles. Flatter packages held magazines for the 5.45 mm loads.

Lyons counted three armed Mexicans standing watch over the loading. A little way off he could see three more men standing beside a long black car.

One was Luiz Santos. The big guy next to him was a bodyguard. Lyons could tell by the man's stance and the way he constantly checked the area around his employer.

The third member of the group, slender and dark, his face adorned by a thick mustache that made him a leaner Saddam Hussein, was in conversation with Santos. The Mexican appeared to be in a generous mood as he smiled and replied to his companion.

Lyons pulled back. "Meat in the freezer, weapons stored in a compartment underneath the main body."

"How are we going to handle this?" Blancanales asked.

Lyons turned to stare at him. "Say what?"

"We don't know if those weapons are heading for the U.S., and if they are, where they are going?"

"I think he's saying if we take these guys on we could end up with nothing," Schwarz said.

"I understand," Lyons snapped. "Only way we can do this is to let the truck go then follow it."

"There's a second way," Blancanales said. "One of us trails the truck. The others stay here and wait until it leaves, then move on this place. See if they can pick up anything from Santos and his people."

Lyons considered the option.

"Makes sense," Schwarz said. "Gives us two chances."

"Okay. Pol, you stay. Gadgets, you get back to the car and follow the truck. We can keep in touch using the cell phones."

Schwarz nodded. He turned and left the others, making his way back to where they had entered the compound, keeping to the dark shadows and watching for any roving security people. There didn't seem to be any additional guards around. He scaled the fence and retraced his steps back to where he had left the Oldsmobile. He stowed his weapons and Tac-Com unit in the nylon carryall in the trunk and changed back into civilian clothing, using a removal cream to clean off the camou paint from his face and hands. He started the car and drove back along the road they had come in on until he located an intersection that gave him access to the strip that ran alongside the packing plant. He killed the lights and sat waiting. He could see the main gates of the plant from where he was parked.

His cell phone rang.

"The truck is getting ready to leave," Lyons said.

"I'm in position."

"Good."

"You guys take care."

Schwarz cut the connection. A couple of minutes later he saw the truck roll out of the gates and turn right. It vanished ahead of him, its taillights winking through the darkness. Schwarz gave it a good start before he eased the car back onto the dusty road. He drove steadily, passing the plant and settling down for the drive.

Schwarz figured it would take around half an hour to reach the border crossing, if that was where they were heading. He considered contacting Stony Man and asking for help getting through the checkpoint. If the guards decided to inspect his car and opened the trunk, it was going to take some explaining away of the weapons he had stored there.

Schwarz decided he was going to have to take a chance. It was fine getting Stony Man to use its clout to allow him through without formalities, the downside was the possibility of border guards being on Santos's payroll. Any order for them to stand down at Schwarz's presence might warn any bought officials, giving them the chance to alert Santos's vehicle. Schwarz figured he was going to have to bluff it out. If he *was* discovered, then he might have to call home so they could bail him out.

He kept the truck in sight as it made its way through to the border crossing bridge. There was a steady stream of freight moving back and forth between Mexico and the U.S. at this time of night. Schwarz stayed three vehicles behind the truck. The driver chose to move across to a particular gate. When he stopped, Schwarz saw a

Mexican customs agent step out of his booth and pause to talk to the driver. After a couple of minutes the customs agent wandered around the truck, peering underneath, checking randomly. Then he returned to speak to the driver again, waving him through. The truck pulled away and Schwarz watched as it took the bridge.

It took him almost ten minutes to reach the checkpoint. As he slowed his approach, Schwarz saw the same Mexican watching him from inside the booth. The man strolled out as Schwarz braked. He ignored the documents Schwarz held out and walked around the car, then stopped beside Schwarz's door.

"Nice car," the Mexican said as he took Schwarz's documents. "Did you enjoy your stay in Mexico?"

"Very informative," Schwarz said.

"That is good, señor. Please come again."

A couple of minutes later Schwarz was back in the U.S., trying to figure out just what the heck had taken place.

He took out his cell phone and called Stony Man. He was routed to the Computer Room and Carmen Delahunt. After explaining Able Team's current status he gave her details of the truck and where it was at that moment. He also gave her the name of the customs agent who had seen him through the border crossing—the man's name had been on his uniform shirt.

"Gonzalez? Is that it, Gadgets?"

"I know it's not much, but I'm sure you can narrow it down to a customs agent working the Nuevo Laredo bridge crossing tonight. If you get anything, patch it through to the Mexican authorities in the vicinity and tell them this guy might be worth checking out. The feeling I've got tells me he's taking from Luiz Santos."

"I'll run a make on him and let you know if anything comes up."

"Carl and Pol will call you if they have anything to report. Until then keep phone silence. No calls that might give them away."

"Understood."

The conversation over, Schwarz put his foot down as he went after the truck. He spotted it a short time later.

Computer Room, Stony Man Farm

CARMEN DELAHUNT TURNED away from her monitor, easing her shoulders as she leaned back in her seat.

"I never realized how many people there are with the name Gonzalez in the Nuevo Laredo area."

Aaron Kurtzman, who had been totally absorbed with the machine code Able Team had sent him, suddenly pushed his wheelchair back from his workstation and rolled across the room to where his infamous coffeepot was gently simmering. He poured himself a mug, then turned to face the team.

"Cracked it," he said. He wasn't bragging. Simply stating a fact.

"And I have your Gonzalez, Carmen. Barranca had been working on names and locations. Meetings. Even bank records. That guy was no slouch when it came to amassing statistics."

Kurtzman returned to his monitor and transferred the data to one of the large wall screens. He scrolled through the readable text he had translated from Barranca's machine code.

"Hector Gonzalez. Works the border crossing. Barranca has him linked with a guy named Manuel Sottero. Sottero is a known associate of our main man Santos."

"Confirms Gadgets's suspicions," Delahunt said.

"Better call and update him. Gonzalez being linked to Santos could change the situation. Gadgets needs to know."

Delahunt nodded and reached for her telephone, tapping in Schwarz's speed-dial number. The number failed to connect. Delahunt tried again. Nothing. Schwarz's cell phone was dead.

"Problems?" Kurtzman asked.

"Can't get a response. Nothing."

Kurtzman tried the number from his station. "Damn."

"You think Gadgets might be in trouble?"

"Could be."

Texas

THE TRUCK HAD CUT OFF across country after Laredo, leaving Interstate 35 and picking up U.S. 83. It drove steadily, fast but within the posted speed limits. Schwarz stayed well behind. There wasn't a great deal of traffic, so he maintained a decent distance from the vehicle.

They had been driving for close to two hours when the truck slowed and made a right turn onto an unpaved road. Schwarz slowed until he was almost stationary.

Once he turned off the main highway and fell in behind the truck, he would be committing himself fully. There would be no turning back. If Able's Team's suspicions concerning Luiz Santos proved correct and the weapons inside the truck were destined for some kind of terrorist action, then risk didn't even enter into the matter. It was something that had to be done.

Cutting the Oldsmobile's lights, Schwarz turned the car onto the side road, feeling the tires sink into the dusty ruts. The Oldsmobile, built for urban roads, swayed and rolled as it negotiated the undulating track. Schwarz gripped the wheel, easing the big car in the wake of the truck. He still kept a good distance between himself and the vehicle he was following, using the truck's rear lights to maintain visual contact.

Schwarz heard, then saw, the large 4x4 that emerged from somewhere beyond the edge of the track. When the spots mounted on the 4x4's roof blazed on, filling the rear of the Oldsmobile with stark light, Schwarz realized he had been tagged.

The Able Team commando reached for his Beretta, placing it beside him on the seat. He was at a disadvantage. The car he was driving wouldn't get far if he turned off the rutted road. The terrain on either side was rough and treacherous. Too much for the low-slung Oldsmobile to handle. The 4x4 would outrun him with ease.

Up ahead the refrigerated truck had stopped. Schwarz decided he was only fooling himself keeping his headlights off, so he flicked the switch and turned them on. He saw two dark figures emerging from the cab of the truck, moving to the rear.

The sound of the 4x4's engine revving warned Schwarz something was about to happen. It occurred before he had time to react. The 4x4 surged forward, the solid crash-bar mounted at the front slamming into the Oldsmobile's rear, the impact driving the car forward. Schwarz had to fight the wheel as it whipsawed from side to side. A second impact almost threw him off his seat. He had to reach out and grab the Beretta before it slid to the floor. He jammed it behind his belt. Grabbing the wheel again, he hit the gas pedal. The thought struck him he wasn't going to go far in the cumbersome Oldsmobile, but he had to attempt some form of resistance before... The 4x4 crashed against the car for the third time, coming in at an angle. The driver had picked up speed and the impact threw Schwarz across the seat. He heard metal creak and felt glass shower over him as a window shattered. The driver of the 4x4 kept up the pressure, shoving the Oldsmobile off the track, lifting the driver's side wheels off the ground.

Schwarz struggled to right himself, rapidly realizing he was losing the battle. He yanked the Beretta from his belt, braced his feet against the tilted floor of the car and peered through the windshield. The two figures from the truck were close now. They carried stubby SMGs.

The 4x4 pulled back and the Oldsmobile dropped onto all four wheels. The dazzling lights, still directed at the car, blinded Schwarz.

"Get out of the car. Hands where we can see them. Leave the gun behind."

The voice was hard, commanding. A man used to issuing orders. A military background?

And it was American.

It was one of those superfluous thoughts that often intruded in the middle of a difficult situation.

Schwarz ran through his options. It didn't take long.

He shoved open his door and threw out the Beretta. As it hit the ground, one of the men from the truck moved forward to pick it up. He stood by as Schwarz stepped out of the car.

"Smart fucker," the man said. His accent was Mexican. He moved then, slamming the barrel of his SMG across the side of Schwarz's face. The impact knocked Schwarz back against the side of the car. Pain flared and he felt blood coursing down his face, dripping onto his shirt.

"Who is he?" someone demanded.

Schwarz recognized the voice as belonging to the man who had ordered him out of the car. The American. The man had climbed out of the 4x4 and moved forward so he could study Schwarz closely.

The man who had struck Schwarz said, "A cop? Probably some nosy federal agent. We should do him now."

"Uh-uh. We need to know who he's working with. How much he's found out." He paused. "Put him in the back of the truck. Let him cool off for a while." He laughed at his own joke.

The man with the SMG looked over his shoulder to where his partner stood. "Cover him while I check him over. You," he said to Schwarz, "turn around. Hands on the roof. Breath out of turn and I'll hurt you."

Schwarz didn't doubt the man's sincerity. He faced the Oldsmobile and assumed the standard position for being frisked. The man knew what he was doing. His hands were thorough. He found Schwarz's cell phone and his wallet. He passed them to the 4x4 man.

He methodically stripped down the phone, throwing the parts in all directions. The power pack was crushed under his boot. The SIM card snapped and discarded.

SMG Man sniggered. "ET ain't phoning home tonight." He spun Schwarz around to face him. The Able Team commando held the man's hostile stare. "I don't like this bastard."

The American glanced up from Schwarz's wallet. "Bet you wont be on his Christmas card list, either."

SMG Man hit Schwarz again, driving his weapon into Schwarz's stomach, then cracking it across his face. Schwarz felt a numbing blow across his cheek.

"Okay. Enough games, Sottero. Get him in that truck. And lock it up good and hard. Come on, let's move. We've a schedule to meet. I don't want to miss it."

"What about his car?"

"By the time it's found we'll be long gone."

"We could burn it."

"And advertise where we are? Just get him in the freezer and let's go."

Schwarz was prodded into motion. He did what he was told because he had no option. By the time they reached the truck, SMG Man's Mexican partner, Sottero, had the back door of the freezer open.

"Get in," he said. "Just do it. Go be a side of beef, gringo."

Schwarz hauled himself up on the metal step and went inside the freezer unit. As he moved, he felt the chill wrap around him. Before he could even turn, the door swung shut, thudding into position. Schwarz was left in total darkness and freezing cold.

CHAPTER SIX

Santos Packing Plant

Carl Lyons gave the truck a five-minute start before he signaled to Blancanales. They eased forward, M-16s up and ready. Prior to moving out, Lyons had armed the M-203 launcher with an M-576 round. This was in effect a canister filled with buckshot, a deadly projectile for use in close-quarter combat situations.

Santos and his group had remained outdoors for a short time before making their way inside the storage building. The loading crew, dismissed, had climbed into a battered pickup that had left the site. One of Santos's men had followed them to the gate to let them through before locking it again. This same man stayed outside, lounging casually near the door to the storage building, an M-4 carbine hanging from his hands. He was standing with his back toward Lyons as the Able Team commander moved in.

Lyons slung his M-16 and eased his combat knife from its sheath. There was no hesitation as he stepped up behind the unsuspecting guard and clamped his big left hand over the Mexican's mouth. The knife in Lyons's hand flashed briefly in the light as it made its single deep cut across the guard's throat. The man began to jerk and kick, uncontrolled resistance to the injury caused by Lyons's blade. Maintaining his grip, The Able Team leader dragged the guard away from the door and pulled him down on the ground, still keeping his hand over the man's mouth until the guard stopped moving. Lyons cleaned the blade of his knife on the dead man's shirt, sheathed it and unslung his M-16.

"Go," he said.

They moved in quickly, not wanting to lose any advantage, reaching the open door to the storage building and peering inside. Large freezer units comprised the far end of the building. Before that section the main area was taken up by metal storage racks that held boxes and cartons. Large metal and plastic barrels stood on the floor. Parked just inside the main door were two bright yellow forklifts.

While Santos and his buyer stood at a workbench, the bodyguard a little to one side, the other two guards had put aside their weapons and were packing more weapons into plastic bags and storing them inside flat containers.

Santos was turning his attention to a black attaché case. The case was laid flat on the bench, the lid open. He peered inside, nodding in satisfaction at what he saw.

"I've seen enough of this cozy crap," Lyons rumbled into his Tac-Com microphone.

He stepped inside the open doorway, covering the group ahead with his rifle. Blancanales moved in on the opposite side of the door so they were well clear of each other.

"Let's hope you all understand English," Lyons said loudly, "because I'll shoot the first man to move."

Santos said something in Spanish.

Blancanales, who spoke the language fluently, made no show of understanding. He spoke quietly into his Tac-Com unit. "Santos told them to take us down."

No one moved. Lyons stepped forward, the muzzle of his M-16 tracking back and forth between the five men.

"Anyone with a gun I want to see it. *Now*."

Blancanales moved forward a few feet, keeping his distance from Lyons and putting himself where he could effectively cover the two packers who were casting furtive glances between themselves.

Dammit, they were going to do something.

Turning his head slightly so his mouth wasn't visible, Blancanales spoke softly into his microphone.

"The two packers. Watch them close."

"Don't make me ask again," Lyons called loudly. "Weapons out now."

One of the packers had edged forward a few inches. He stopped, but his eyes were turned in the direction of his SMG that was lying on the edge of the workbench.

"Okay, that's enough," Blancanales yelled, jerking

his M-16 in the direction of the packer who had been moving. "You, don't move."

Only then did Blancanales realize he had been suckered. It wasn't the man who had deliberately moved who made the attempt. It was his partner, on the edge of Blancanales's vision, who snatched a handgun from where it had been tucked in his belt at his back.

As the pistol swung at him, Blancanales yelled a warning to Lyons, then pulled the muzzle of his rifle at the man with the pistol.

The M-16 crackled, loud inside the building, and the would-be shooter caught the burst in his chest. He spun in a half circle, his trigger finger pulling back on his handgun, sending a single shot that missed his own partner by a fraction. The guy ducked forward, reaching out for his own SMG. His fingers came within a hairbreadth of contacting the weapon before Blancanales followed up with a second burst that cleaved through the front of the target's skull, pared the top off in a sudden splash of red, and dropped him to the concrete floor.

The moment Blancanales engaged the packers, Santos's bodyguard stepped in front of his employer and the buyer. The bulky Mexican dragged a large pistol from under his coat and drew down on Lyons, firing as he moved. The weapon was heavy-caliber and, when he heard the loud blast, Lyons recognized a .45 Colt automatic. He felt the powerful slug ripple the air close to his cheek and returned fire, loosing off the M-576 buckshot round from the M-203 grenade launcher.

The spray of buckshot caught the bodyguard in his midsection, tearing at flesh and bone and almost cutting the guy in two. As the guard's scream of agony was drowned in the echoing detonation of the charge, Lyons saw Santos and his buyer pulling back, recoiling from the overshoot. The buckshot tore at their clothing and seared flesh. The buyer went down on his knees, one hand at the side of his face where blood was streaming through his fingers. Yet the man still managed to drag a handgun from his pocket, bringing the weapon around in Lyons's direction.

The Able Team leader had already changed position, crouching as he dropped the muzzle of his M-16 and triggered a burst that hit the buyer in the chest, flipping him onto his back. The gun slipped from his fingers as the man clutched his chest.

Santos, erupting with a torrent of abuse, scooped up the .45 the bodyguard had dropped and began firing in Lyons's direction. The Able Team commando felt one of the heavy bullets tear at the fabric of his blacksuit's left shoulder. He returned fire, his burst catching Santos in the throat. The Mexican toppled over, blood erupting from his wound. He hit the concrete floor with a heavy thump, legs kicking wildly. He was clawing at his ruined throat, gargling sounds coming from his bloody lips until Lyons punched another round into his head. Santos's body jerked, turning half over as he died, blood spattering the concrete from his shattered skull.

Blancanales moved quickly around the workbench to pick up weapons and check out the two packers. The one he had hit in the chest was still alive, breathing in short gasps, blood bubbling around his mouth. He stared up at Blancanales without any kind of recognition in his eyes and before the American could even kneel to check him closely, the man died.

"Clear over here," Blancanales said. He pushed to his feet and joined Lyons, who was moving weapons from the floor around the downed men.

"Why can't people just come quietly when you point a gun at them?" Lyons asked.

Blancanales shrugged. "Beats the hell out of me."

"Cover me," Lyons said as he knelt beside the buyer.

"I know you understand English," he said. "Where are those guns heading?"

The buyer, sucking in hard breaths, simply gave a thin smile, shaking his head from side to side.

"I should have expected that."

Lyons went through the man's pockets. An expensive wallet was stuffed with U.S. currency. There were various credit cards, a couple of business cards and some receipts. Lyons zipped the wallet away in a blacksuit pocket. The only other thing he found was a slim cell phone and a passport. It was a U.K. passport, the photograph inside identifying the owner as Jafir Rasifi. It had him down as a U.K. citizen. He showed phone and passport to Blancanales.

"Might tell us something."

Lyons pushed to his feet, pocketing the objects as he crossed to the workbench and inspected the weapons the packers had been bagging and storing in the containers. They were AK-74s, identical to the weapons that had been stored in the truck's false floor.

"I wonder what else Santos has stowed away," Lyons said.

He took a quick tour of the building. There was nothing in the floor to suggest an underground location for weapons. The only other structure within the building was the large meat location room. Lyons crossed over and hauled the large door wide. As it opened, lights came on inside the room. Soft tendrils of vapor curled from the open door. Lyons could feel the cool temperature inside.

"I'll take a look," Lyons said over his shoulder.

"Okay. Hey."

"What?"

"Stay cool."

Lyons stepped inside the meat locker. The interior held metal bars from which were hung sides of beef. He moved back and forth, checking the room. The walls were smooth. Grilled vents high up the walls blew in the chilled air and he could hear the whir of the fans.

He found what he was looking for after a couple of minutes. Metal grilles made from heavy-gauge aluminum comprised the floor. As he moved back and forth across the room Lyons noticed that one square of the grille sections wasn't sitting as neatly as the others. He knelt beside it, reached down and hooked his fingers between the bars and lifted. The four-foot square panel lifted without resistance. Lyons pulled it fully clear and slid it aside. He found himself staring down into a cutaway, with layers of boxes and cartons in sight. Lyons reached in and caught hold of a strap on a box. He heaved the box into the clear, seating it beside him on the floor. He freed the clasps on the lid and flipped it open.

More AK-74s. Lyons stared down into the cutaway and made out a number of similar boxes. The smaller ones he decided had to be ammunition. He sat on his heels, pushing the baseball cap to the back of his head.

The Mexican connection was coming up with the goods. All Lyons needed to know now was where they were heading. That was where Schwarz would come in.

Lyons pushed to his feet and went back to where Blancanales was waiting. "Back there," he said. "More guns and ammo."

"We're not going to get anything from these guys," Blancanales said.

"I know, I know. What was I supposed to do? Sweet talk them out of shooting?"

Blancanales shrugged. There wasn't much he could say in light of the two men he'd fatally shot.

Lyons pulled out his cell phone and called Stony Man. He got Brognola himself.

"We have a situation down here. You need to call in someone from the Mexican authorities. Isn't there a U.S.-Mexican task force looking into the trafficking business? A team from Justice? Leo Turrin is involved. He can make this thing run. Let them know there are fatalities, including Santos and a guy named Jafir Rasifi. Had a U.K. passport. I've got that now with the guy's wallet and cell phone. There's also a substantial weapons cache. AK-74s and ammunition in the meat locker. We need to get out of here before any locals show up.

We'll take Santos's car and leave it at the motel when we pick ours up. When we get to the crossing we'll need some kind of official clearance so we don't have to screw around. Soon as we're over the border we need to pick up Gadgets's trail. Did he call?"

"While you take a breath, I'll bring you to speed," the big Fed said. "I'll arrange an escort for you at the bridge crossing. All I can tell you about Gadgets is that he called in to let us know he was following the truck from the Santos plant. He tracked it along I-35 and then onto U.S. 83. We haven't heard any more from him, Carl. Last time we tried to contact him his cell phone didn't respond. No signal. Nada."

Lyons waited a few heartbeats before he spoke. "Have someone waiting for at the crossing. I want to pass over Rasifi's stuff. Have it flown back to you priority."

"You going after Gadgets?"

"We need to locate him and that truckload of guns. Damn, this has gone belly-up on us."

"Easy, Carl. It's early days."

"Yeah? Hal, how long does it take to pull a trigger?"

Texas

BROGNOLA HAD WORKED his end of the deal. The Able Team pair were cleared to cross the bridge by officials from both the U.S. and Mexico. Everything was done quickly, without delay, and Lyons wondered just what had been said to get them such priority. A courier from Stony Man was there to meet them when Lyons and Blancanales completed their trip across the bridge and into Texas. Lyons dropped the cell phone, the passport and the wallet they had taken from Jafir Rasifi into the secure bag the courier held out. The courier got back in his car and drove away, heading for Laredo International Airport, where a Learjet waited to fly him back to Virginia.

Blancanales was behind the wheel of the Ford, waiting. Once Lyons was back in the car, Blancanales moved off. They had a map of the area and Lyons traced the route Schwarz had described.

"Isn't much to go on. I-35, then onto U.S. 83. That's one hell of a long route," he said.

"Hey, there's a gas station," Blancanales said. "I'll fill up before we get too far out."

While Blancanales gassed up the Ford, Lyons took himself clear of the station and called Stony Man again.

"Barb, how soon can the Air National Guard get that spotter plane up for us?"

"They said in the next couple of hours, as soon as it gets light. They'll have a better chance of spotting anything then."

Lyons felt like yelling they weren't doing enough. The problem was everyone *was* doing everything they could. It just didn't seem enough as far as Lyons was concerned. Especially with one of his team having disappeared.

Stony Man Farm, Virginia

"CARL, WE DO WHAT we can do. If we could make it lighter sooner I'd throw the switch myself. But we can't. Do you think you're the only one worried about Gadgets?"

"I guess."

"That was a reluctant yes."

"Best you're going to get."

"Right now we're running some checks on Philo Vance and Manuel Sottero. See if we can tie them up with any of the other names we're collecting."

"We'll keep in touch."

"Do that. We're here 24/7, Carl."

Price put down the phone.

"The Ironman getting tetchy?" Kurtzman asked.

"You know Carl. Always the hard way."

Kurtzman rolled his chair away from his workstation, crossed to the coffeepot and filled his mug. "Heads up, people," he said.

The full team was there, and they left what they were doing at Kurtzman's call.

"I know you're pulling out all the stops, but I'm going to ask you pull even harder. Able and Phoenix are trying to make sense of all this damn stuff. Right now they're coming up against brick walls. So we need to throw them something. Anything. Let's do it, people."

BARBARA PRICE EMERGED from the washroom, turning down the corridor on her way back to the Computer Room. She had taken a few minutes to splash cold water on her face. She had been on her feet for so long she had lost track of time and, despite numerous cups of coffee, she had reached the point where she needed a time-out.

As she neared the doors to the Communication Center one of them opened and a familiar figure stepped into the corridor, a thick folder tucked under one arm.

"Hi, Erika," Price said.

Erika Dukas, the Farm's newest recruit, swung her head around and smiled in recognition.

Just under Price's height, Dukas was a strikingly attractive young woman. In her late twenties, she had thick, slightly curly dark hair that reached her shoulders. Brown eyes, bright and barely concealing a touch of mischief, peered over the top of reading glasses perched on her nose. Her smiling mouth was full-lipped and mobile. She wore a cream, open-necked shirt, dark slacks and flat-heeled leather shoes.

"I was just on my way to the inner sanctum," she said.

Price chuckled. "Facing The Bear in his den?"

"Well, if my findings are what he wants, he might not bite my head off."

"Have you completed the translation?"

Dukas nodded, indicating the file she was carrying.

Erika Dukas was an accomplished, if not the most accomplished, linguist Price had ever come across. She had been at the NSA at the same time Price had been there. Even then Dukas had outshone her colleagues in the linguistic section. Already able to speak, translate and fully understand French, Arabic, in all its dialects and subdialects, Japanese, Cantonese and Spanish, Dukas was now progressing with German and Greek. She learned quickly, picking up languages with an ease that was the envy of her colleagues. Her high learning rate gave her an affinity with the written and spoken word, allowing her to assimilate new languages and grasp the root core with ease.

Price had remembered the young woman during a conversation with Hal Brognola and Aaron Kurtzman. They had been debating the need for an expert linguist for the Comm Center. Someone with an in-depth ability to be able to translate foreign languages and take the linguistic capabilities of the department to a higher level. Price had no hesitation in recommending Dukas. After the discreet security investigations into her background, Brognola had asked Price to make the preliminary approach. When she'd spoken to Dukas and told her she had been selected for a position in the ultracovert organization that Price herself worked for, the young woman had said yes without hesitation. She had missed Price when she had moved from the NSA, and as far as Dukas was concerned if it was good enough for Barbara Price, then it was fine by her.

Erika Dukas fit into Stony Man without a hitch. Once she'd accepted the position, it was explained to her that she couldn't talk about the SOG to anyone, and she'd sworn an oath. Her initial tour around the Farm, above and below ground, had fascinated Dukas. The nature of the SOG, its anonymity and its direct responsibility to the President himself, leaving a deep impression.

She had been with the SOG three weeks when Kamal Rasheed's organizer had been passed over to the Comm Center for analysis and translation. It had landed on Dukas's desk and she'd immediately set to working on the Arabic script that filled many of its pages. It had taken her only a short time to realize that the translation would be a challenge even to *her* skills.

Over the centuries Arabic script had developed and spread to a number of Arab nations. With the expansion came subtle changes, brought about by individual nationalities. Local area dialects introduced more vocal and written changes.

Within the Arabic alphabet, the twenty-eight letter forms alter shape depending on their position within a word, others retain the shape but are given a different meaning by the addition of dots in and around the letter. As Dukas immersed herself in the elegant curves and swoops of Rasheed's flowing script, slowly starting to see a semblance of awareness, she'd been forced to go back to previous sections as the narrative became lost in the translation. It had taken her most of the first day before the truth dawned. Rasheed was using an obscure form of the Riq'a script form and was making very subtle changes within that style to produce a coded narrative.

When the words finally began to make sense, Dukas would return to the beginning again, using her acquired code-breaking knowledge. From that point she was able to start the painstaking, literal translation, typing it directly into her computer system. Even now she would come to a dead stop when she reached an entry that briefly defied even her linguistic ability. It seemed that Rasheed wasn't averse to breaking his own rules and introducing yet another dialect string. She had to admit the man knew Arabic in all its forms. Dukas was no slouch herself and proved it by finally breaking through Rasheed's literary astuteness.

She'd remained at her workstation until all but a few pages of Rasheed's input had been deciphered and safely loaded in her computer, sustaining herself through the long hours by sheer determination. She was driven by not allowing Kamal Rasheed to beat her and also by the knowledge that the information in the organizer was important to the Stony Man combat teams.

On completion of the task she'd sat back, stretching her spine and scrubbing her hands through her mass of dark hair. Glancing at her monitor, she'd picked up on the time and date, realizing just how long she had been at her station. She needed rest but had dreaded that that would have to wait until she presented her findings to Kurtzman.

She printed off the data. The document ran to nine pages and though she hadn't spent too much time taking in the English version, there were some facts and figures that did stand out. It struck Dukas, more than anything that had been explained before, that Stony Man *did* deal with life-threatening situations. It also made her aware of how important it was to get the data across to the Computer Room.

Barbara Price led the way to the Computer Room, letting Dukas enter in ahead of her.

The full cyberteam was there, as well as Hal Brognola. They all turned as Dukas appeared.

The full impact of all those eyes focusing on her made Dukas hesitate for a microsecond. Then she felt Price's hand against her shoulder, heard the whispered words, "Go and show them I was right about you, girl."

Brognola was the first to respond to her appearance.

He could see she was slightly taken aback at the confrontation with the full cyberteam complement.

"Erika, we're hoping you have something for us."

Dukas nodded. She held up the file. "Sorry it took so long. Rasheed used some complicated Arabic written dialects. He created his own code, jumping between alternate script forms. It had me fooled for a while."

"All very interesting, but did you break the code, Miss Dukas?" Kurtzman asked with his usual brusqueness.

"Yes, I did, *Mr.* Kurtzman," Dukas responded with equal sharpness, her moment of awkwardness evaporating. "If I recall, it's the reason I was offered the job. Because I'm good at it. They *tell* me you're the same with computers."

There was a momentary silence. At the back of the room Akira Tokaido cleared his throat.

Kurtzman abruptly spun his wheelchair from his workstation, rolling it across the room until he was directly in front of Dukas. He raised his head to meet her stubborn gaze, his eyes searching her face for any sign of weakness. He found none.

The silence stretched, then Kurtzman stuck out his huge right hand.

"Miss Dukas. *Erika.* How about a cup of coffee?"

"He must like her," Carmen Delahunt whispered to Hunt Wethers. "He doesn't offer his coffee to just anyone."

"I know," Wethers replied. "One small blessing in a troubled world."

Behind them Tokaido gave a sigh of admiration. "Is she cool, or what? Talking to The Bear like that."

Delahunt glanced over her shoulder at the younger man, smiling at the expression on his face.

"I do believe our boy is smitten."

Kurtzman wheeled across to his infamous coffeepot and picked up a clean mug, poured a generous amount, and returned to hand it to Dukas. His eyes were fixed on her face as she took a swallow. She savored the hot, black brew, not a flicker of an expression showing until she raised the mug in Kurtzman's direction.

"Now *that* is coffee," she said.

Kurtzman had a mile-wide grin on his face. "Always said it needed an expert to appreciate it."

No one noticed Dukas's quiet moment as she turned to the Computer Room conference table and caught Barbara Price's eye, or the whispered, "I owe you for letting me know about the coffee."

Dukas placed her file on the table and spread the printed sheets out so they could all be seen.

"I have all this on my computer," she said, "so it can be downloaded on any of your machines."

"Does it give us any pointers?" Brognola asked.

"First, Rasheed has a number of locations within mainland U.S.A. Each location has a name and telephone number. The location seems to be the important part of the notation, so I'm taking a guess they could be sites where weapons are hidden. I'm only theorizing here, you understand. This isn't my field of expertise."

"Erika, you're doing just fine," Brognola said.

"Thank you, sir."

"Just one thing. The name is Hal. The queen of England hasn't given me a knighthood yet, so drop the sir."

"Sounds good, though," Price said. "Sir Hal of Stony Man."

"Barb," Brognola warned.

She smiled. "Okay, Hal."

"We'll run checks on those locations," Kurtzman said. "See what they turn up."

"This next section had me struggling," Dukas continued, warming to her subject now. "Until I broke through the padding. In brief, this is a shopping list. Weapons from small arms all the way up to and including ground-to-air missile systems. This section has ticks next to the items, so I'm assuming he has taken delivery of those. Or they've been located. Here he has communication equipment, tracking systems. Footnotes on this page also detail a contact in North Korea, a man named Sun Yang Ho. There's reference to a meeting in a Hong Kong hotel with someone from a company called Chang Li Ltd. of Kowloon, a man named Kim Yeo."

"Hunt, take this Korean and Hong Kong stuff," Kurtzman said. "Run it through the databases."

Wethers nodded.

"I'm on it."

"Carmen, the location list."

"Erika?" Brognola said.

"There were names I think you already know about. Abe Keen, the murdered journalist. Ibn el Sharii. I found references to possible attacks in Turkey, Kurdish-held territory in Iraq and suggestions concerning sabotage on Kurdish oil fields. There's more. Some of the entries tended to ramble on a little. Rasheed's personal thoughts. I think he was using this as a journal as well as for information he needed to remember."

Carmen Delahunt interrupted them. "I think you should all take a look at this."

On one of the wall-mounted TV screens the CNN logo was rolling aside to show images that were being beamed in from Israel, according to the captions and the voice-over.

Merkava battle tanks were traversing dusty streets, their turrets swinging back and forth. Smoke hung in the air in the background. The crackle of small arms fire could be heard behind the urgent voice of the news anchor as he described the action by the Israeli army as retaliation to terrorist attacks on Israeli patrols. There were shots of bodies lying in the streets, a burned-out truck. The tank closest to the camera swung around, its 120 mm cannon locking on to some distant target before it fired. The camera swung in a fast pan, trying to keep up with the shell and picked up just as it exploded against a building. Clouds of dust and smoke mushroomed into the air. The thump of the detonation drowned out all other sound for few seconds. Debris flew from the point of impact.

"This attack is just another incident in the ongoing hostilities that have struck the West Bank over the past few days. Deaths have occurred on both sides. Three Israeli soldiers were killed in a sniper attack, followed by further incidents in which two more Israelis were wounded during a gun battle with suspected Hamas members. Each side is blaming the other. The only odd note here is that both sides seem genuinely surprised by the attacks. Ever since the American peace initiative, which was put into operations months ago, the lull in attacks from both sides seemed to indicate a real attempt at building some solid foundations for a lasting settlement. The question is why would either side suddenly start the shooting war all over again."

"Good question," Delahunt said as she muted the sound. "Do we believe what we're seeing is the real thing? Or is it someone trying to stir up trouble? Especially following on from the information we've picked up."

"Thanks, Carmen. That's a talking point for later, Barb," Brognola said.

"Fine. Now let's get back to Erika's report."

"Rasheed has some kind of timetable, dates for deliveries, drop off points in Iraq. Some are located in Israel outside Tel Aviv and a camp in Chechnya. And there were a few references that I translated but couldn't figure out. Like here. He mentions MOAB. It seemed to ring a bell, but I couldn't put my finger on it. But according to Rasheed the delivery of this MOAB was imminent."

"Would that be Massive Ordnance Air Burst?" Tokaido asked. "MOAB. The bomb that replaced the

Daisy Cutter? The Air Force tested it just before the Iraq war and threatened to use it but never did."

"Where did they test it?" Dukas asked.

"Air Armament Center at Eglin AFB in Florida."

"Exactly what Rasheed has noted here," Dukas said.

Brognola glanced across at Price.

"Are you thinking the same?" she asked.

"Let's find out."

Brognola turned to Kurtzman. The man was way ahead of him, swinging his wheelchair back to his workstation where he started to hit the keys, sending out his probing electronic fingers to do some backdoor investigations.

"What's he doing?" Dukas asked.

"Hacking into the military database, specifically the Air Force to see if they're missing any of those MOAB bombs," Price told her.

"You can't be serious. Weapons don't go missing that easily. Do they?"

"It has been known," Brognola said. "The news seldom gets out if something major happens. No point panicking the public. More importantly so that the service that lost the weapon don't get red faces."

"Are these MOAB weapons some kind of nuclear device?"

"No," Tokaido said. He moved up to the table. "These are conventional bombs, not nukes. No radiation. They're filled with a mix of TNT and aluminum powder. When they detonate, the mix is in the form of a fine mist. It spreads, then detonates. This is close to the ground. It creates a massive fireball. It would incinerate everything within a defined radius. The Daisy Cutter, the first version, was used to clear jungle so that an instant helicopter landing zone was created. Then the notion came that it could be used to kill the enemy, as well, a virtual firestorm that just ate up everything and everyone in its path. The MOAB is just an updated version. It's much larger at twenty-one thousand pounds of ordnance. The threat of that being used over Iraq, say on a city, had one hell of a physiological effect."

Dukas was envisioning the effect on a crowded city in America.

"You're not saying Khariza would do that?"

"We're certain he has something in mind for the U.S.," Brognola said. "If he did get his hands on one of these MOAB units and managed to detonate it over a heavily populated area, imagine the damage it could do, not to mention the aftereffects."

"According to the stats I read," Tokaido said, "this MOAB creates a high-pressure wave, then a near vacuum. It would cause lung and eye rupture. As the blast area expands, the effects would lesson, but there would still be injuries."

"Add-on effects in a city would be from debris, fire hazards. Power stoppages," Brognola said.

Kurtzman swung his chair around.

"Hal," he said, "he didn't get his hands on *one*. There are two MOAB bombs missing from Eglin AFB."

"That's all we need. Khariza's group getting their hands on a couple of MOABs," Brognola said. "Any detail on how it happened and when?"

"I'm checking that now," Kurtzman said. "The Air Force is trying to keep this low key. Nothing to the media. Only information between key sections of the AF. I'd lay odds, Hal, they haven't even told the Man."

"Keep looking," Brognola said.

He turned back to Dukas. "I hardly dare ask what else you've turned up, Erika."

"I'll go through it all. Then I need to get back so I can decipher the last few pages. I thought you needed to see the bulk of the translation first. Now I have a couple of other items that are puzzling me. Reference a couple of times to a date—April 9. Rasheed had it written down a couple of times, always emphasized. Circled."

Brognola glanced around the table, over his shoulder, seeking a response.

"If it refers to some incident, we're already running out of time," he said. "April 9 is close."

"The other item is this," Dukas said. She pointed to a name. "Rod McAdam. He has it with a question mark beside it."

Brognola looked up. Before he could say anything Kurtzman raised a hand and waved it around.

"I heard. Run it through the system. Okay, I'm on it."

Brognola smiled. "You'll get used to him," he said to Dukas.

She eyed him over her reading glasses. "Oh, don't worry. The coffee got me into his club. I'm way ahead of you."

Brognola realized there was a great deal more to Erika Dukas than showed outwardly. He liked her style.

And her confidence. She was already proving to be a valuable addition to the Stony Man team.

BROGNOLA MADE HIS WAY back to his office in the farm house. Tokaido had sent him the information on the MOAB weapon and it was on his monitor now. The big Fed sat scrolling through the data, which made chilling reading.

The MOAB was the latest incarnation of the weapon that had started life as the Daisy Cutter. The latest version even had smart-bomb capabilities. Once dropped from a carrier aircraft it would be guided by satellite and its detonation set for around six feet off the ground. It had never been used in action. During the Iraq war the threat had been broadcast, along with video footage, showing the MOAB's capability. That had been a psychological attack, simply showing to the enemy what the U.S. could do if it wanted. The hostilities were over before the MOAB needed to be used—if it ever would have been.

Brognola had no doubt that if Khariza had MOABs under his command he *would* use them. The man and his followers seemed determined to cause some death and destruction on the U.S. mainland. If he was able to reach the weapon-ready condition, Khariza would press the button.

CHAPTER SEVEN

San Remo, Italy

Calvin James walked outside and stood beside the pool, turning to look at the villa.

The deserted villa.

Razan Khariza and his group were long gone. The spacious villa was empty, and nothing had been left behind. Khariza had been extremely thorough.

James glanced up as he heard footsteps to see Rafael Encizo coming around the side of the villa. The Cuban shook his head before James even asked the question.

"Nothing in the garage except tire marks on the floor."

"Talk about batting zero," James said.

"Khariza is pretty good at covering his tracks, Cal. It's why he's stayed on the loose for so long."

"Hey, you two, I think we might have something."

James and Encizo saw Gary Manning standing in the open doorway, holding something in his hand.

"You remember the Hitchcock movie *Psycho?*"

"Don't tell me you found Khariza's mother preserved in the cellar," James said.

Manning smiled. "When Marion Crane's boyfriend and her sister are looking for her in the Bates's Motel, what did they find in the bathroom?"

"Beats me," Encizo said.

"*He* finds a scrap of paper in the toilet bowl with figures on it."

"Uh-huh. And the answer is?"

Manning showed the torn section of a piece of notepaper in his hand.

"It's blank," Encizo said.

"It has the impression of writing on it. I had a look around. There's a writing pad on the nightstand beside one of the beds. This matches the sheet torn off it."

"Are you saying someone wrote something on the pad, took it, then tore off the next sheet because of the impression?"

"Trying to be thorough. Maybe because they were in a hurry they tossed this in the toilet and flushed it away. *Thought* they had flushed it away."

"Can you make out what the impression says?" James asked.

"It's a number," Manning said. He held up the paper and angled it until the light picked out the numbers. He read them out as James jotted them down. "What do you think?"

"Looks like a phone number to me," James said. He held up the written number so Encizo could see it. "Rafe?"

"I'd go for that."

Manning took out his Tri-Band cell phone and hit the button for Stony Man.

Computer Room, Annex, Stony Man Farm

AARON KURTZMAN READ the number back to Manning.

"Okay. I'll run it through the system. I'll call you back soon as I have anything."

"Anything come up on those other searches you were making?"

"Khariza has a longtime buddy called Radic Zehlivic, an Albanian Muslim. They went to school in the U.K. Zehlivic has made himself a fortune playing the stock markets. He's quite a wheeler-dealer. Dark horse kind of character who doesn't form attachments easily. But the friends he does have he keeps. Has a reputation as a ladies' man. Played the field until he recently got married to a much younger woman. French girl called Monique Cadot. Zehlivic seems happy to let her play around and spend money. New York. Paris. Rome. The usual circuit."

"Was Zehlivic involved in Khariza's disappearance from Iraq?"

"Let me get back to my searches and I might be able to answer that."

"Okay."

Manning signed off.

Kurtzman turned to his monitor and tapped in key words and phrases, then sat back while his deep data banks began to scan for answers. He had entered a wide-ranging set of parameters, asking for anything that might involved Khariza, Zehlivic, known terrorist organizations and locations. He had included vague references that would allow the searching computers to pull in the loosest data and tie it in to his general request. Kurtzman's program, developed by the Stony Man Farm cyberteam, based on previous experience at tying together the most flimsy information scraps, was now one of the most useful pieces of data-gathering they had. Kurtzman himself was often surprised at some of the things it dredged up.

The first response concerned the number he had typed in. It was a cell phone number, and the number belonged to Radic Zehlivic. As Kurtzman watched, the computer threw up a call-receive list going back a couple of months. He transferred the list to Carmen Delahunt's computer and asked for a rundown on the numbers.

"Give Gary a call and tell him who we have for the cell phone number. Run a make on Zehlivic and see if there's anything we can give Gary."

On his return to his own monitor Kurtzman found another result.

The listening satellite system, Echelon, had analyzed and identified voice patterns in calls from Zehlivic to Razan Khariza over a period of weeks. The connection that led to Khariza hadn't been recognized at first. There were only a few recorded examples of his voice, taken before his alleged death, and no one had been looking for him with any dedication until key phrases were picked up. Then a definite isolation of the other party on Zehlivic's caller was initiated and Khariza had eventually been identified. There were also conversation snatches between Khariza and Zoltan Dushinov a Chechen Muslim. Dushinov wanted total autonomy for the region. He had no love for Mother Russia or her politics. He saw Chechnya as a separate state, capable of running its own affairs without interference. He ran his part of the country like his own fiefdom, fairly free of Russian control. It was an isolated area, lacking in amenities for the greater part, and the Russians had neither the men, equipment, nor the heart for long-term engagement with Dushinov and his stubborn, experienced fighters. The Russians had branded Dushinov as a terrorist.

There had been rumors Dushinov had been allowing fellow Muslims to hide out in Chechnya. Providing them with a camp where they could plan future activities in their ongoing battle with the West. Kurtzman was sure other intelligence agencies had been picking up these exchanges. No one had taken any action. Long-term analysis and agency deliberations as to whether action should or shouldn't be taken simply exacerbated the problem.

The detailed information on the individuals had rested within the Echelon data banks while other priorities were looked at. Echelon, for all its propaganda, wasn't infallible, nor could it pick up every snatch of information and readily identify it. There was still a long way to go before the system became fully cognizant with every form of communication transmission, and there were still times when it failed to live up to its reputation. Despite this, it had become a useful listening post for what were termed hostile transmissions.

Kurtzman, using another of his back-door programs, took a sneak peek at agency databases, running a check on whether they had recorded any of the details his probing had unearthed. He found indications that confirmed agency filtration of the Echelon data had been acknowledged, but only banked for further evaluation. The computer wizard sighed in frustration. Sometimes he failed to understand the policy of some agencies when they sat on information he thought should have been acted on straightaway.

He was about to exit when he spotted something that spiked his curiosity. Data on the calls between Khariza and Dushinov had been intercepted by a CIA agent and pulled out of the main data bank and placed in a restricted file. From what Kurtzman could see, the data had been lifted out of the general CIA information stream and isolated before sent to the main distribution list. In essence, someone had seen the data and had removed it before anyone at CIA could read it. Kurtzman stored the data in a separate file of his own before he closed his program.

He took a mug of coffee and sat back, studying his monitor, a frown furrowing his brow as he wondered why.

The CIA keeping secrets from itself?

On reflection he knew it wouldn't be the first time someone had a separate agenda from the Agency's own policies. But considering the implications of the people and possible actions they might be involved in, he found this particular piece of deception worrisome.

Kurtzman set the search looking for any name that might be attached to the CIA reference. He put it on a background file and left it to run. If a connection was eventually found, it would alert him.

"Zehlivic owns an oceangoing motor vessel called *Petra*," Delahunt said. "Guess where he likes to drop anchor?"

"Please tell me it's San Remo."

"I just ran a check through the San Remo local coast guard computer. The *Petra* was in San Remo harbor for a couple of days around the time Abe Keen was taking his photographs. She left soon after. According to the coast guard data the *Petra* was moving up the coast on a cruise. No final destination or duration given."

"Coincidence? Zehlivic is around when his friend Khariza returns from the dead, and he leaves just after Khariza is spotted by Abe Keen. What does that suggest to you?"

"More than a lucky chance."

"What are these guys up to?"

"You want me to expand the searches?" Delahunt asked. "We know Khariza is on the hunt for weapons. Recruiting, as well. It looks like he's after the big money now, so he must be looking to buy more than just small arms."

"If Khariza has been pushing weapons into the U.S., he must be working on something. Let's go for broke. Every connection we can make. Look for anything. Buying. Stealing. Mix and match. Tie it in with the data from Erika's translation notes, those locations she came up with. We need a handle on this thing because right now we don't have a clear idea what's going on. Call Hunt and Akira. Tell them their coffee break is over. I want them back in here now. We need a full crew on this."

Wethers and Tokaido had taken their first break since the breaking of Kamal Rasheed's notes in his organizer. The Computer Room had been on full steam following Erika Dukas's revelations and slowly small data bits were starting to come together. Aware that despite their enthusiasm his team needed breaks, Kurtzman had sent out Delahunt first, then Wethers and Tokaido. The pair had been gone for just twenty minutes, but if the need arose, Kurtzman would cancel Christmas to get the job done.

Delahunt picked up her phone to make the call that would bring Huntington Wethers and Akira Tokaido back to the Computer Room.

While Delahunt put out her call, Kurtzman made a link with the SARS satellite. This was a piece of Canadian equipment Kurtzman had used before. The SARS, working on C-band technology on a 5.6 cm wavelength, provided sharp, detailed feedback utilizing microwave signals. Brognola had used presidential clout to get priority access to the satellite at short notice. And it also helped that Kurtzman had connections at the SARS facility. He watched as the satellite came online, its orbit taking it across southern France and Italy, out across the Ligurian Sea. Kurtzman led the image across Corsica and Sardinia, sweeping south, then off to the east into the Tyrrhenian Sea skirting Corsica and into the Mediterranean. Kurtzman tapped in the coordinates that would realign SARS so that it turned its electronic eye along the Italian coastal area initially. If he failed to find what he seeking, he could expand the parameters so that the satellite encompassed a greater spread.

He was looking for the *Petra.* The SARS capability, utilizing its powerful imagery, gave Kurtzman added flexibility as he brought vessels into sharp relief, scanning configurations and angling in to check names. He spent the next twenty minutes tracing an imaginary line along the coast, taking the satellite out at least thirty miles from land. He had asked SARS to work in a grid search, so that no area was overlooked. The satellite swept back and forth, locking on whenever a vessel was located so that Kurtzman could make a detailed pass before moving on. The entire operation was being digitally recorded for later examination if required.

It was at the latter end of the twenty-minute period when Kurtzman made his catch. The satellite focused in on a motor vessel that was almost out of Kurtzman's thirty-mile area scan. As the SARS' eye locked on the image and Kurtzman asked for close detail, the orbiting satellite altered its degree of travel, bringing the vessel into sharp relief. With a little more judicious manipulation Kurtzman was rewarded with an image of the name across the stern.

Petra.

Kurtzman logged the time, position and course of the vessel, realizing it was heading out in a southerly direction, away from land, toward the Mediterranean.

"Get me Gary, Carmen."

San Remo, Italy

"BEST WE CAN DO is keep tracking that boat until it makes a call," Kurtzman said. "I'll make another sweep before we lose the window, see if I can identify anyone on board. Nothing else I can do until they make a move."

"Okay," Manning said. "Let's hope they're not booked for a long cruise."

He cut the connection, turning back to the others and raising his shoulders in a shrug of resignation. There wasn't much they could now but wait. Manning found himself hoping that McCarter and Hawkins were getting better results.

Cumbria, Northern England

"THIS IS SOME green country," Hawkins said as the Gazelle swooped in across the Cumbrian landscape. Interspersed with the undulating landscape were stretches of gleaming water, the lakes that gave the area its name: the Lake District.

It was an area of natural beauty, a tourist attraction that brought thousands flocking each summer. This early in the year there weren't as many tourists, but at this moment in time there *were* visitors to this particular stretch of the countryside, though not the kind Cumbria would make welcome.

Henning glanced at the GPS unit installed in the chopper and tapped McCarter on the shoulder.

"Coming up," he said.

McCarter glanced at the screen. They were no more than a quarter mile from their target.

IBN EL SHARII'S SISTER, Haruni, lived in a converted farmhouse. Since her move to the U.K. nearly eight years earlier, Haruni had stayed in London for six months before moving up to Cumbria with her then partner. He wrote and she was an accomplished artist, with a deep love of pottery. They had bought the old farm between them. He had set up his study where he could write. Haruni had converted one of the downstairs rooms into a pottery studio and had devoted herself to designing and creating her pottery. She combined the artistry of her home country with that of her new one.

Slowly, over the next few years, she'd begun to produce examples of exquisite and colorful objects. She'd put her pottery in local exhibitions at first, then gone farther afield, her name becoming known. Her work had sold well and Haruni had been able to open her studio to visitors. During the summer tourist periods, her studio was never short of visitors.

Unfortunately her partner failed to acknowledge her success. His writing career hadn't taken off. Haruni's success eventually came between them. He'd begun to drink, become jealous, and one day packed his bags and left. Haruni had received two letters from him. One asking if she wanted to buy his share of the farmhouse. She did, becoming the sole owner. The second letter, some months later, informed her he had just gotten married and was leaving for Australia. Haruni was never quite sure why he'd felt the need to tell her. She was over him. Happy on her own and busy with her growing business.

Her happiness was always tinged with sadness because both her brothers had stayed in Iraq. She had always refused to accept the Hussein regime. It was the reason she had left the country. Despite her denial of the regime, she'd maintained what contact she could with her brothers, hoping one day they might have a change of heart and join her.

Then she'd received news that her elder brother had been murdered by the regime. When the American-led invasion began she feared she would never hear from Ibn ever again. But then she had received the package from him, a brief telephone call, telling her keep the package hidden until he contacted her again.

MCCARTER TOOK a look around the area as Henning swung the Gazelle in a wide curve that would bring them in at the rear of the farmhouse. According to the local area map, Henning had pulled up via the onboard police computer, the house stood on a large section of land, with hills surrounding it, overlooking one of the area's minor lakes. A narrow, winding track led from the main road that ran parallel with the lake. There were wooded sections to the northeast and to the south of the farm.

"Is that the farm?" Sharon said.

They all followed his finger.

"That's it," Henning said. "Lake over to the west. Woods to the northeast and south."

"And bloody visitors," McCarter said. "Two SUVs. Something tells me they haven't come to look at pottery."

"How the hell did they get here so fast?" Henning asked. He put the chopper in a steep dive, heading directly for the farmhouse.

"Figure it out," Sharon said. "You must know there

are Islamic terrorist cells in the U.K. It's the same everywhere. Since the Iraq war, they've been put on alert in
case a strike is called for. It's why your unit was formed.
To combat instances like this. All Khariza had to do was
get his commander in the U.K. to call up a local unit,
give them their orders and send them out."

"Lock and load, lads," McCarter said. "Remember
why we're here. We need to get hold of those disks
Sharii sent to his sister, and we need to keep her alive
if possible. I don't think she deserves to get caught up
in this if we can prevent it."

As Henning dropped the Gazelle with dizzying
speed, the pair of SUVs roared to the top of the track,
dust billowing in their wake. The lead vehicle cut across
the lawn that fronted the farmhouse, smashing through
a flower bed and demolishing a display of clay pots. The
SUV bounced from the grass onto the stone-paved area
fronting the house and came to a rubber-burning stop.

Doors flew open and four armed figures jumped out,
rushing toward the house.

Aware of the approaching Gazelle, one of them
turned and raised his weapon, loosing of a burst of autofire. A number of the slugs clanged against the chopper's landing struts.

"Bastard," Henning said. "I had to sign for this machine."

He swung the Gazelle around and reached across to
activate the M-134 minigun. His finger touched the firing button and the six-barrel machine gun let fly a short

burst. The Gazelle vibrated under the power of the electrically driven weapon.

The shooter who had turned on the chopper vanished in a haze of earth and stones as the burst hit the ground first, then enveloped him in dozens of 7.62 mm slugs. The concentrated impact of the rounds shredded the man, turning the dust cloud red. As the Gazelle overshot the stricken figure it toppled to the ground, reduced to bloody, steaming rags and tattered flesh.

Henning arced the chopper around to face the farmhouse. The moment the machine was on the ground McCarter, with Hawkins and Sharon close behind, stormed out of the cabin. They hit the ground running, pistols out and ready as they confronted the invading force.

The second SUV had bolted to the rear of the farmhouse, crashing through anything in its way. It came to a bouncing stop and its armed crew, five of them, exited the vehicle and made for the rear of the house.

"Five heading for the back of the house," McCarter yelled, waving wildly at Hawkins and Sharon. They turned and ran around the side, following the five-man crew.

McCarter had business of his own to handle, as he saw two more shooters emerge from the first SUV. One was working the cocking bolt of his weapon as he hit the ground. The Briton took him out with a double tap to the side of the head that bounced the guy off the side of the SUV, leaving a bloody print on the paintwork. As the dead man hit the ground, McCarter sank to one knee, his Hi-Power held in two hands as he tracked the other shooter. This one had paused to take aim at Mc-

Carter, but the Phoenix Force leader was still faster, calm even in a combat situation. He fired twice while the other guy was still leveling his gun. McCarter's 9 mm slugs hit the man in the chest, over the heart, and he went down in an ungainly heap, jerking in a final fight for life. He had lost that fight by the time McCarter paused beside him and snatched up the unfired Heckler & Koch MP-5, a weapon the Stony Man soldier was well versed in. The 9 mm submachine gun felt comfortable in his hands. He noted that it was fitted with the 30-round magazine, with a second one taped to it for speedy reloading. McCarter snapped back the bolt, cocked the weapon and turned to move in on the trio who had first exited the SUV.

He sprinted toward the direction of the farmhouse front door, spotting the last man as he made to run inside. McCarter raised the MP-5 and triggered a burst that smashed into the target's back, severing his spine and dropping him, screaming, to fall across the step. McCarter kept moving, silenced the yelling man with a short burst to the back of the skull, then went in through the open door full-tilt.

He took in the open room, heard the crash of feet as they thundered across the wooden floor, and spotted one of the hitters as he paused at the foot of the stairs leading to the upper floor. The man turned, his face etched with rage when he saw the Briton wasn't who he had expected. McCarter hit him with a savage burst that slammed him against the wall, blood geysering from a ravaged throat. The man coughed, spitting more blood as he struggled to return fire. McCarter fired a second time, stitching the guy across the chest, dropping him on the stairs.

A woman screamed. There was a crash of breaking crockery and someone yelled in anger. McCarter followed the sound, heard a man yelling in Arabic, then the sound of an MP-5 on full-auto drowned all other noise. Without breaking his stride, the Stony Man commando went through the door ahead of him and into the wide, beamed-ceilinged kitchen. Smashed crockery lay on the floor, as did overturned chairs. At the open door leading outside, one of the raiders, his back to McCarter, was firing his SMG and yelling. McCarter didn't know whether it was from rage or adrenaline.

The Briton's entry into the kitchen was less than silent as he trod on broken crockery and kicked a smashed chair out of the way, stumbling briefly as he regained his balance.

The shooter at the door turned without warning and brought his MP-5 with him, mouthing something at McCarter the Briton failed to understand. All McCarter saw was the muzzle of the MP-5 tracking in on him. He began to pull his own weapon online. Something slammed into him from behind, knocking him aside. As he stumbled, McCarter heard the heavy boom of a shotgun. Out the corner of his eye McCarter saw the shooter's chest blown open by the triple shots that sent the shotgun charges into him. Bloody chunks flew from the ravaged torso and the shooter was driven back against the door frame where he hung for a second before crashing to the kitchen floor in a bloody, lacerated heap.

"You okay?" someone asked.

McCarter glanced around, into the face of Greg Henning. The antiterrorist cop was cradling a Franchi SPAS-12 combat shotgun. The 8-round semiauto weapon had a powerful delivery. The Briton nodded in Henning's direction, then heard a crackle of gunfire coming from the rear of the farmhouse.

HAWKINS AND SHARON heard the gunfire as they ran around to the rear of the farmhouse. They passed the SUV, its doors wide open and the last of the five-man crew disappearing around the edge of the building.

Hawkins flattened against the wall, peering around the corner, and saw the five armed men spreading out around the paved area. The Phoenix Force pro dropped to a crouch, extending his Beretta as the tail-end man turned, the muzzle of his MP-5 rising. They locked eyes and there was a moment when the other guy hesitated. Hawkins didn't know why and it made no difference. He triggered the Beretta and the pair of 9 mm slugs punched into the target's left shoulder. A dark chunk flew out from the back of the man's shoulder, blood following. The would-be shooter twisted, seeking a way out, the MP-5 dropping from his hands as he clutched at his shoulder. It was his last living act. Ben Sharon, leaning over Hawkins's crouched figure, delivered a single shot from his P-226 that cored through the guy's skull.

Ahead of the pair the remaining four hitters were converging on the back door. The crackle of autofire could be heard from inside the house.

A woman ran out the rear door. She was dark-haired, slim and had a brown envelope clutched to her chest. Before she was aware she had run directly into the path of the lead crew member. He was tall, lean, his head shaved. He was wearing a long leather coat. The man caught hold of the woman, turning her so he had her back to him. One arm circled her neck, pulling her close. His right hand, gripping a Glock pistol, turned the muzzle so it pressed against the side of her skull.

"Oh, great," Hawkins murmured.

"I will kill her. Make no mistake," Leather Coat said in clear English.

McCarter and Henning appeared at the kitchen door.

Leather Coat backed up, his armed crew spreading out to cover McCarter and company.

"This isn't going to happen," McCarter said, stepping out into the open, his MP-5 directed at Leather Coat and the woman hostage.

"He will kill her," Sharon called.

"You know him?" Hawkins asked.

Sharon nodded. "His name is Barak, Khariza's trained dog. He's an assassin and a sick son of a bitch. We know him."

Barak had moved farther across the paved area. One of his crew moved in closer and snatched the package from the woman's hands. He opened the package and showed Barak the disks.

"So?" Barak said. "Do we kill each other now? Let this woman die, too?"

"It could happen," McCarter replied.

The Briton kept his MP-5 trained on Barak and Sharii's sister.

"Somehow I do not think you have solved my problem," Barak said. "It seems I will have to do it myself." He lowered his head, his lips moving. After a few moments he looked up, a smile edging his lips.

McCarter realized the man had been speaking into a compact radio unit attached to the collar of his coat.

Calling in reinforcements?

His question was answered seconds later when the rising throb of rotors reached his ears. It was coming from somewhere behind Barak, beyond the farm outbuildings. The sound rose to a roar as a helicopter swept into view, sweeping in over the outbuilding roof. A Sikorsky S-76, it hovered, black and menacing, the side door open to reveal a swivel-mounted machine gun that arced around to cover McCarter and his group.

"One word, you all die here and now," Barak said, and McCarter had no doubt he meant every word.

The chopper sank to within a few feet of the ground.

"Boss?"

McCarter glanced at Hawkins. He knew the unasked question. His gaze flicked back to Haruni, still in Barak's threatening embrace, and he knew there was no way he could endanger the young woman's life. One brother dead. Sharii in hospital with life-threatening wounds.

Barak sensed the Briton's hesitation. He knew he had won, but he was wise enough not to let it show. Mocking his adversary at this point might just tip him over the edge and push him to do something reckless. The Iraqi snapped orders to his crew and they all backed away, converging around the S-76, one by one climbing inside until only Barak and his hostage were left. Barak worked his way onto the floor of the helicopter, willing hands pulling him and the woman inside.

The helicopter began to rise. Haruni was being held in the open hatch, fear showing on her face. McCarter lowered his MP-5, letting out a snort of frustration.

"He'll kill her now," Sharon said. "Once they're out of range they'll get rid of her. We missed our chance, dammit."

Barak's chopper swung over the crest of the hills behind the farm and vanished from sight. The echo of its engine could still be heard.

"Let me go after them," Henning said. He turned to face McCarter.

"No way you could do that without them spotting you."

"I could get air control to track them on radar. At least we can get an idea where they're heading."

"Do it," McCarter said.

Henning headed for the Gazelle.

McCarter slumped against the wall of the house. He fought back the urge to let it all out. To yell and curse at the way the odds had gone against them, but there had been no other way. He didn't care about Sharon's disappointment. The day he let himself act like the animals they were fighting against was the day he was finished.

He had been forced into making a tactical decision. Whether to attack, putting himself, his own people and Haruni in the firing line, or to stand off and let the Iraqi and his team go. He had chosen the latter because Barak's team had had the superior firepower at that given moment and when the shooting started they would have outgunned McCarter's people. The odds had been too great in Barak's favor. McCarter couldn't have exposed his people to those odds. There was no doubt in his mind that to have gone against Barak would have been nothing less than a wasteful gesture. The Briton's reckless nature, held down now by his position of command over Phoenix Force, might once have led him into doing something off the wall. Now he was able keep the urge to grandstand under control.

Even so, all he could register was the fact they had been that close to getting their hands on the disks and now that chance had slipped away from them.

He took out his cell phone to call Stony Man to let them know what had happened. It was not a call he was looking forward to.

Stony Man Farm, Virginia

"DAVID, DON'T BEAT YOURSELF up about it. You had to make a call. You did, and that's an end to it. I'm not going to chew you out because you chose not to sacrifice people just to complete your mission."

"We nearly had the bloody disks, Hal. They were no more than thirty feet away."

"And if you'd gone ahead? Could you guarantee you would have got the disks? No answer there, David, because you might all have been dead. If not, there would have been heavy casualties. I'd rather have my people alive."

McCarter couldn't answer that.

"Listen, get yourselves back to London. We've had the translation of Rasheed's organizer. It's given us some indication where Khariza might be doing his negotiating with a North Korean named Sun Yang Ho. We have a point of contact in Hong Kong. Guy called Kim Yeo. We need some backup on this. Is Mei Anna still in London?"

"Last time I spoke to her she was."

"Maybe she can arrange a meet with some of her people in Hong Kong. They might be able to help with this Kim Yeo."

"Worth a try." McCarter paused. "Hal?"

"I'm still here."

"Thanks, mate."

This time the silence was at Brognola's end of the

line. "None needed. David, I want live people who know when to back off. Not dead hotheads."

"Hey, I used to be that hothead."

"I said that to Katz when he put you up for his job."

"What did he say?"

"I'll tell you when you finish this mission."

"Bloody hell, Hal, why not now?"

"I don't want you crying into that cell phone. You know how much they cost?"

CHAPTER EIGHT

Texas

Hermann Schwarz lost track of time after the first half hour. The ride in the freezer compartment of the moving truck was uneven, and he was thrown from side to side as the vehicle went over bumps or swerved. He couldn't be certain whether they were simply travelling across hard country or the driver was just playing games with his passenger. Whatever the reason, Schwarz had no choice in the matter. He could have sat, feet braced against one of the metal frames that ran the length of the interior, and rode out the trip. That notion was discarded the moment he had developed it. The low temperature inside the compartment meant he would have frozen solid if he'd just sat immobile. His only chance at surviving was to keep moving. Schwarz knew he had to keep his body warm enough to avoid letting the freezing temperature weaken him. Once he gave up and let himself fall into a stupor, there would be no waking up.

Schwarz kept on the move, around and round the freezer compartment. To the door end, then back to the front. He moved as fast as he could, working his arms as well as his legs. He thrust his hands deep into the pockets of his jacket. He tried to ignore the rise and fall of the truck floor and to keep his momentum up. There were times he failed and fell, banging himself against the aluminum side, other times slamming into the swaying beef carcasses hanging from the curved hooks on the rails bisecting the interior of the compartment. His body was soon aching from the bruising it received when he did come into violent contact with the unyielding objects.

One fall slammed him face-first against the metal side of the compartment. Schwarz felt a sharp pain in his left cheek as the flesh was cut. He felt warm blood start to ooze from the wound. It slid down his cheek and wet his lips, some getting into his mouth. The brassy taste of the blood made him angry. Schwarz pushed to his feet and continued his endless movement. He wasn't going to give in.

It wasn't on the cards. He had been through too much to end up dead and frozen. If the bastards sitting in the cab of the truck thought they were going to find him frozen to the floor like an oversize ice-cream treat, they were in for a damned surprise.

It was a struggle of mind over matter. His body wanted to slow down, to rest and let the seductive cloak of the cold lull him into immobility. In his mind

Schwarz was telling himself his only chance was to stay on his feet, on the move, and to hell with the sadistic sons of bitches who had locked him in this freezing hell.

He tramped up and down the length of the compartment, becoming so used to the routine that he soon found he didn't need to worry about walking into the end panel or the door. He knew when he had reached the limit, turning automatically and retracing his steps back the other way.

Come on, Hermann, this is easy. It's just a little cold air. Nothing to worry about. You've been in worse situations than this. He couldn't think what those other situations might have been, but that wasn't the point of the exercise. He needed to keep his mind focused.

He felt the truck slow. The swaying eased off as the truck came to a stop. Schwarz rounded on the door end of the compartment. He couldn't hear anything. The construction of the insulated freezer compartment acted as efficient soundproofing.

Schwarz made his way to the door and waited. There was movement and the doors swung open. Car lights a little way off illuminated the interior of the freezer. To one side Schwarz could see the American. The man was watching as the Mexican, Sottero, approached to rear of the truck and stood directly in front of Schwarz, a taunting smirk on his face.

"Hey, *cabron*, get your chilled ass out of the truck."

Schwarz took the first step to climbing down out of

the truck, staring into Sottero's grinning face. He never knew what made him do what he did next, and later he realized how close he had come to placing himself on the edge, but at the time it just felt like the right and proper thing to do.

"Come on, gringo, I don't have all fuckin' night to wait for—"

Schwarz drove his right foot into Sottero's face. He had already raised his foot to take a step down, so it was no effort to swing it back a little more, then put every ounce of rage into the kick. The blow landed hard, crushing Sottero's nose flat to his face, splitting his lips wide open and loosening a number of teeth. Sottero staggered back, blood squirting from his mangled nose, streaming down his face and soaking his shirtfront. The Mexican went down on his knees, screaming in pain, reaching up to clutch both hands to his injuries. Blood began to well from between his fingers.

From the side of the truck other figures moved into the light, weapons rattling as they covered Schwarz as he walked down the metal steps of the truck and stood waiting.

"Back off," the American said. He walked up to Schwarz. Glanced down at the moaning, bloody-faced Sottero. "For a man in your current position, that might be considered a reckless thing to do."

Schwarz, shivering in the chill Texas air, managed a shrug. "Seemed the right thing from my angle. He was getting to me."

The American smiled. He ran a hand over his

cropped hair. "Yeah, well, he's that kind of guy. But he probably won't see it that way."

"Right now Sottero doesn't even rate on my scale."

The American gestured to one of the waiting gunners. "Get him in the plane."

One of the men bent over Sottero and helped him to his feet. The Mexican was still moaning, head down, blood stringing from between his fingers. The gunner led him away.

"Over here," the American said to Schwarz.

When Schwarz neared him, the American reached out and gripped his arms. His hands were pulled together and he felt the cold bite of plastic cuffs being looped over his wrists, pulled tight.

"Am I safe, or do I do your feet?" the American asked dryly.

Schwarz didn't reply. The American escorted him away from the truck. As they tramped across the rough ground, Schwarz saw that the thin light of early dawn was just pushing its way in from the east. He made out flat, desolate country. A scattering of rocks, clumps of brush. Nothing much else to see.

Apart from the Beechcraft King Air aircraft waiting on a crude landing strip. The twin turboprop engines were turning.

"Let's move it, hotshot," the American said, pushing Schwarz ahead of him.

They reached the plane and Schwarz was ushered inside. The gunner who had taken Sottero held his SMG on Schwarz as he was taken to one of the seats. The seat belt was pulled into place over Schwarz's arms and buckled.

"I'll watch him," the American said. "Go help with those guns. Tell the others to make it quick."

"Sottero's up front."

The American nodded.

When they were alone, the American leaned against the seat across from Schwarz. "The flight might be smooth, but it's going to get rough at the other end. You get my meaning?"

"I didn't expect cookies and a glass of milk."

"The people we're supplying tend to get a tad upset if they think they're up against it."

"What do they expect? Buying guns to kill Americans. Not exactly the best way to make friends."

"If you're trying to appeal to my patriotic side save your fuckin' breath. I gave that crap the heave-ho a long time ago. These days I go where business takes me. If the assholes in Washington screw around with foreign governments, they got to have their heads up their collective ass if they don't expect shit to happen."

"*Shit* in this case could be more than just a few guns being used."

The American took a breath to consider his reply. "The way things are going, we'll all go down together one day. You understand what I'm saying? It's going to happen one way or another. I did my time. Wore the uniform. Even got the medals. For what? Most of my buddies dead. Or sent home with half their bodies missing. The fuckin' government doesn't give a shit. Too many mothers busy hatching their own plans.

Building empires. Selling out to the enemy. The CIA with its own agenda. Spooks running wild all over. Making deals with regimes the grunts have spilled blood taking out. Trying to get their own people in place. Every agency, the military and the government. They all have the big plan. And each one is certain theirs is the best. You know something, pal? The whole world is in a mess. Tying itself in knots. There's only one way to survive. Look out for yourself before the other guy screws you." The American leaned forward, an amiable grin on his face. "Sottero? I've been waiting for something like that to happen to him. The guy is a jerk-off."

He turned away and moved along the aircraft.

TWENTY MINUTES LATER the Beechcraft was in the air. Schwarz, peering through the side window, studied the sky and tried to work out which way they were heading. With the sunrise taking place he figured they were flying west. It was the best he could do under the circumstances. If he was correct, they were still in Texas. He looked down at the terrain below them. No urban sprawls. Just open, desolate country. A couple of times he caught the gleam of water as they passed over meandering water courses.

"I could draw you a map," the American said.

He had moved up to stand beside Schwarz's seat. Without warning, he leaned over and unbuckled the seat belt.

"I don't think you're going very far."

Schwarz had taken note of the armed men who had come on board once the smuggled weapons had been brought onto the plane. They were spaced out along the compartment. He relaxed, letting the warmth inside the plane permeate every inch of his body. The chill from his time in the freezer was slowing ebbing away. It was taking time. Schwarz flexed his muscles, working at the stiffness that had invaded his body. He wanted to be ready for whatever lay in wait when they reached their destination. He was working on what he would do once he broke away from his captors. Not if, but when. Schwarz worked on a positive plane. He saw no profit in being pessimistic. Once he allowed himself to accept defeat, the game was already closing. He had to work on the assumption that at some time ahead he would see a chance—and take it. Now wasn't the time, but when they reached wherever they were going a window, however slim, might present itself and he would take it.

He glanced up and met the American's stare. "Not the time," Schwarz said.

"Damned if I didn't know you were going to say that."

"Like you told me. Every man for himself."

"Hell, yeah. The American Way."

Left alone again, Schwarz found himself wondering what the rest of Able Team was doing. Knowing Lyons and Blancanales, they wouldn't be sitting on their butts with their heads in their hands.

En Route, Texas

LYONS PEERED through the windshield of the Ford as it bumped its way along the dusty track. He was sweating a little because the air-conditioning unit in the car kept cutting out. When it did, the air inside the vehicle became oppressive. He couldn't open a window because all that did was to let in the fine, choking dust billowing up from under the wheels. Lyons had tried banging the unit with his hand but that had failed to achieve anything. He decided to call the unit names and again achieved nothing. So he sat back and sweated until Blancanales switched the unit off, left it a few minutes, then turned it on again. When cool air started to circulate, Lyons said something uncomplimentary under his breath.

"Was that aimed at me or the air conditioner?" his partner asked.

"Now I know why I don't like Texas," Lyons said, ignoring the question. "It's hot. It's dusty and it's miles from anywhere."

"I don't understand the last part. *What* is miles from anywhere?"

"You name it and it is."

Blancanales shook his head. There were times Lyons's thinking bordered on the surreal. This was one of them. He decided for his own sanity not to take it any further.

"You see that damn spotter plane?"

Blancanales took a look. He picked up the single-engine spotter plane from the Texas Air National Guard that had been assigned to locate the Santos truck. They had been following it for the past couple of hours, first along U.S. 83 and then onto the rutted, dusty back road that headed into the silent, near desolate landscape of southwest Texas. They had located the Oldsmobile that Schwarz had been driving. It had been damaged from some kind of impact, the rear and one side stoved in.

The car had been pushed off the track. When they had taken a look, the vehicle was empty. There was no sign of Schwarz except for the scattered pieces of his cell phone. It didn't take much figuring to work out that he had been taken prisoner.

All they could do was continue to follow the tracks left by the truck and a second vehicle.

"He's still up there."

As Blancanales spoke, the Military Band radio they had been loaned crackled and the pilot from the spotter plane came on.

"I see the truck. She's a mile and a half ahead. You keep on this road you'll come in sight. I done a fly-by and there's a 4x4 there, too. Didn't see any folk around."

Blancanales glanced across at his partner. Lyons's jaw muscles were clenched tight, bunched hard under his skin as he digested the pilot's report.

"Damn," Lyons said. "They've changed transport. Met someone to pass over the guns and moved on." He slammed his fist against the closed window.

Blancanales picked up the handset and keyed the transmit button.

"Hey, Sarge, did you see any sign of anything heading away from the area? Tracks? Tire marks? Over."

The radio crackled. "Saw some kind of leveled section. Looks like somebody fashioned a cut-price landing strip. Bet those boys had a plane come in and pick them up. Over."

"They use light aircraft out here like we use cars in the city," Blancanales said. "And I'll bet local air traffic control can't pick up on every damn flight that comes and goes. Most of these guys just hop in and fly by the seat of their pants."

"You're a great help," Lyons said.

"Anything else I can do for you guys?" the spotter pilot asked.

"I guess we're done here, Sarge. Listen, thanks for your assist. Pass it on to your base commander. Much appreciated. Over."

"If you need anything else, give us a call. Hope you find your buddy. What I can do is have local air traffic control see if they can find any trace of this plane. But don't hold your breath, guys."

"Any help is appreciated, Sarge. Over."

"Take care now. Over and out."

Blancanales saw the plane waggle its wings before sweeping in a wide turn that put it back on course for its base.

"Looks like it's down to us, *buddy*," Blancanales said lightly.

"You can cut out the Lone Ranger-Tonto crap," Lyons snapped. "Now let's find that damned truck."

LYONS PROWLED around the abandoned truck and 4x4 like some big cat. He was in silent mode, searching for anything that might give a clue as to where Schwarz was. Blancanales left him to it. There was no point telling Lyons there was nothing to find. All that would have got Blancanales would have been an angry rebuttal. So he did his own survey of the scene, which simply confirmed the fact that the area was clean.

One truck, the back open to expose the beef hanging

inside to the hot Texas sun. The freezer unit had been turned off when the truck had been abandoned. The temperature had risen, and now the sides of beef were dripping greasy water onto the truck floor. The false floor sections had been pulled out and the weapons removed. Next the 4x4. It was new, with the plastic covers still on the seats and less than three hundred miles on the clock. There were no plates on it. Very smart, Blancanales thought. No ownership to trace. No documentation. The interior of the 4x4 was as clean as the moment it had rolled off the line. A stolen vehicle for a once-only trip. Used and abandoned.

He used his cell phone to call Stony Man Farm and give them the news. Barbara Price listened, then advised she would contact local law enforcement agencies to check the vehicles over.

"Let them pick up the pieces. It's their jurisdiction, anyway." She spoke to someone then came back to Blancanales. "Jack touched down at Laughlin Airbase about an hour ago. He should have the Lady in the air by now so he'll be calling to make a rendezvous to pick you guys up."

Lyons appeared at Blancanales's side. "Have they got anything we can move on?"

Blancanales asked the question.

"I think we have," Price said.

Stony Man Farm, Virginia

CARMEN DELAHUNT had been evaluating information about Radic Zehlivic. She had the man's statistics on both her screens, dividing her attention between them.

"Everything else apart, Zehlivic is a clever guy," she said as Barbara Price leaned over her shoulder to take a look. "He started from nothing and built his empire over a ten-year period. Never put a foot wrong anywhere, and always comes out on top every deal he makes."

"Lucky or clever?"

"I'd say clever. He moved into areas most everyone else shied away from, took chances. He seems to have an instinct for picking the right deals. I guess he did his homework before he stepped in. It paid off and still is. The man has a good head on his shoulders for business."

"Not so smart where women are concerned."

Delahunt smiled. "That's the only area where he's lost out. A string of failed relationships. They all cost him. But as far as Zehlivic was concerned it was pocket change. Now look here. Three years ago his luck changed. He married for the second time, a French model, half his age, but they seem to have made it last. Still together, when she isn't traveling or spending his money. Plenty of coverage of her in the gossip columns. Paris. London. The U.S., mainly the West Coast. Seems she enjoys the climate. And especially San Francisco."

"What's this?" Price asked. She pointed to a number of photographs and an article in a San Francisco newspaper. Zehlivic's young, blond wife performing some kind of ceremony outside a store. A bookstore named Cadot's Nest.

"Cadot's Nest?" Price asked.

"Monique Cadot. Her family name."

"Hey."

Hunt Wethers's call alerted both Price and Delahunt.

"Hunt?" Price asked.

"The name of that bookstore in 'Frisco?"

"Cadot's Nest."

"Yes, yes, yes," Wethers chanted. He transferred his monitor screen to one of the wall screens, highlighting sections.

"Cross-referencing all the intel we've pulled in from various sources. Cell phones, Barranca's data. Jafir Rasifi's wallet. There are connections starting to show." He highlighted one section of data and magnified it. It was a credit card slip. "Rasifi paid for a room at a motel in a place called Bucklow, Texas. The credit card used at the Bucklow Star Motel was issued to a Cadot's Nest. Until you mentioned the name Cadot, I didn't make a connection. Zehlivic must have used his wife's own name when he set up the company. Everything is in her name. He's covered himself by using the bookstore for activities he doesn't want broadcast."

"Simple but effective," Kurtzman said, wheeling himself across to stare up at the wall screen. "Not the first time that's been done. Hunt, check to see what brought Rasifi to a place like Bucklow, Texas."

Kurtzman brought up a map of the area once he had established Bucklow's location. It was in Bucklow County, in the Big Bend country of West Texas, near the rising slopes of the Davis Mountains. The area had driven a wide swathe of industry in the mid-1800s, from cattle to horse breeding, lumber from the forested slopes of the mountains. Back in the 1920s there had been a few oil finds. They had petered out just as quickly, leaving Bucklow County with its core businesses—beef production, and farming to a degree.

Kurtzman went through the town's back history, trying to establish why this isolated community in West Texas had been chosen as Jafir Rasifi's destination.

The thought also occurred to him that this was where the illegal weapons had been heading. Rasifi had been the buyer. The abandoned truck had been stripped of its cargo that had been put aboard a plane that had taken off out in the middle of nowhere for...?

Kurtzman stared at the monitor, his brow furrowed as he read and reread what he had in front of him. It was possible he was completely wrong, that the contraband guns hadn't been taken to Bucklow. That Rasifi's visit to the town had had nothing to do with where the weapons had gone.

He banged his fist against the edge of his workstation. He refused to accept that the two pieces of information didn't go together. It was too much of a coincidence.

Rasifi, Bucklow.

There had to be a connection.

"Come on, people, we should be able to get this damn thing together."

"Try this," Wethers called.

Wethers had done some further searching and come up with a checking account for Cadot's Nest. He found that the company had leased a wood-chipping mill, situated a few miles outside Bucklow for twelve months. The full amount had been paid up front.

"The Cadot account hadn't been used for months after the initial payments. Then we have a number of transactions over the past couple of weeks. One for car rental. Fuel. Then the motel charge."

"What would Cadot's Nest want with a wood-chipping mill?" Delahunt asked.

"Maybe the same reason we have one," Tokaido said. "As cover for something else."

"A place to hide illegal weapons?" Delahunt said. "Maybe even distribute them in the company trucks."

"Makes some kind of sense," Tokaido added.

Wethers swung his chair around, his expression hard. "Aaron, you've been checking Bucklow's history. Does it give a date when it was finally established as a proper community?"

Kurtzman tapped his keyboard. The whole of the Computer Room turned to look at the wall monitor that mirrored what he had on his screen.

"There," Kurtzman said. "Bucklow was recognized as a township 150 years ago."

"See the date?" Wethers said.

"April 9," Price read out loud.

"The date referred to in Rasheed's organizer," Wethers said. "The date we couldn't put our finger on for certain."

"How were we to know it meant Bucklow's?" Price argued.

"We were looking for the same date, different meaning," Wethers replied. "The one we should have known. April 9—the day designated by the new Iraqi governing council when they first met. They chose the day

Baghdad fell to U.S. forces. What's known as Saddam Hussein's Downfall Day."

Tokaido let out a slow breath. "Now it makes all kinds of sense," he said. "But for the wrong reasons."

"And the wrong time," Delahunt said. "Today is April 9."

Aboard: Dragon Slayer

LYONS, BLANCANALES and Grimaldi listened to the information Price gave them over the combat chopper's radio linkup.

"I hate to bring this up," Blancanales said, "but there's the matter of the two missing MOAB devices."

"Don't you think we haven't been working on that?"

"Working on it isn't going to help Gadgets if he's in the vicinity when it goes off," Lyons snapped back.

"You know for sure?"

"April 9. It's a special date for the Iraqis. Bucklow is celebrating its birthday. That means a lot of people in town. If I was Khariza I'd go for it. A perfect time to make my point. Jesus, do you need a goddam picture?"

Grimaldi checked his instruments. "Heads up, guys, we're homing in now. Bucklow is five minutes flying time ahead."

"Jack, can't you boost this thing any faster?"

"She's on full throttle, Carl. You want faster, get out and push."

Grimaldi scanned his instrument readouts. He could feel *Dragon Slayer* pushing hard, the powerful turbines howling as they burned out the power that thrust the helicopter to its maximum. The Stony Man pilot had no concerns about the chopper maintaining its performance. The sleek black machine was kept at its peak performance level by thorough and meticulous servicing after every outing. Any suspect part, program, no matter how small, was picked up on and the offending item replaced. Grimaldi was always involved in the mechanical or electronic checks. He had the final word on whether the aircraft had passed the inspection and repair standard required. Grimaldi saw no problem with that. After all, he was the man who flew *Dragon Slayer,* so he figured he had more right than anyone to see that the chopper was in prime condition each time he sat behind the controls.

"Can't we get through to the sheriff's department?" Lyons persisted. "Or don't they have one?"

"We're trying," Price said. "We haven't been able to raise anyone yet."

Wood-Chipping Mill, Bucklow County

SCHWARZ OPENED HIS EYES to a world full of pain. The effects from his time in the freezer unit faded to nothing compared to the physical beating he had taken at the hands of his captors. He hurt from head to toe. It felt as if every inch of his body had been punched, kicked, beaten. His face was a bloody, battered mask. He could taste it in his mouth where the inside of his cheeks had been driven against his teeth. The left side of his face had taken the worst and it was swollen badly. His eye was almost closed. Each time he took a breath, pain stabbed at his lungs from bruised ribs.

The only consolation he derived from his condition was that he was still alive. He had to be. If he had been dead there wouldn't have been such pain. Or so he kept telling himself.

For the moment his tormentors had left him alone. He had been warned that when they returned he had better have answers to the questions they had been asking.

Where is Jafir Rasifi?

Who do you work for?

What have you learned about our operations within the U.S.?

How many of you are there?

Where are you based?

Who betrayed us?

Each question punctuated by a barrage of blows. Not the subtlest of interrogations. Schwarz had realized there was a degree of agitation behind the questions, as if his captors were short on time and needed his answers quickly. Which only made his resistance stronger.

One of Schwarz's interrogators was the Mexican, Sottero. Schwarz didn't fail to notice the man's suffering. Sottero's face looked extremely sore from the full-on kick Schwarz had delivered. Sottero's punches were fuelled by rage and though many landed, his coordination was poor. He put a great deal of effort into his work but his blows had less impact than Sottero imagined.

There were a number of interrogators. In the time before his questioning got under way, Schwarz was able to satisfy his curiosity about his captors. There were two more Mexicans. The American who had spoken to Schwarz on the plane had a couple of partners. The man in charge, Schwarz had no problem identifying. He had seen the man's face in one of the photographs during the initial Stony Man briefing. Schwarz couldn't put a name to the face, but he knew the Iraqi was one of Razan Khariza's people.

This one asked the questions. His voice was gentle, well modulated. He never once raised it. There was a persuasive quality to it. This man was well used to interrogation.

The only thing he lacked was an in-depth knowledge of the man he was questioning.

He didn't know Hermann Schwarz at all. If he had, he might have saved himself some wasted time.

The sudden end to the interrogation left Schwarz semiconscious and not a little curious as to why it had ended so abruptly.

By the time he was able to focus his attention on his surroundings, taking in the untidy office, furnished with out-of-date wooden desks and chairs, the wall hung with fading calendars and charts describing the benefits of chipped wood, Schwarz realized he was entirely alone. His captors had left him tied to one of the office chairs. If he hadn't been secured to the chair, he would have fallen from it.

Schwarz didn't dwell on his injuries for too long. He had no idea why he had been left alone, nor did he know how long the situation might last. So he needed to do something to reverse his position.

He tested the rope that held him to the chair. It had been expertly tied, around his body and his wrists, holding him firmly in place. Schwarz checked out how secure he was held. There was some movement. Not a great deal. It was going to take him some time to loosen the rope.

Turning his head, Schwarz was able to look out through the glass partition that composed the upper section of the office's outer wall. Beyond was a walkway that overlooked the mill's operation section below. The machinery he could see wasn't in use, nor could he see any employees. The plant looked to be deserted.

At the far side of the building, large wooden doors stood open. A group of people were standing on the loading dock. Schwarz recognized his captors. They were gathered together staring out beyond the building, and it looked as though they were waiting for something.

Schwarz checked out the rest of his close surroundings. He failed to see anything in the office that might prove useful in helping him to free himself.

He braced his feet on the floor and raised himself as much as he could, lifting the chair off the floor. Then he banged the chair down hard on the rear legs. The impact jarred through his body. Schwarz felt the chair give a fraction. He repeated the action a number of times, putting all his strength into the moves. He checked the group standing outside the mill doors. The sound didn't seem to have reached them. Schwarz increased his escape attempt, encouraged by the fact he couldn't be heard. He felt a slackening in the rope around his body.

When he tested the chair, he felt it sagging to one side. He continued to bang the chair against the office floor. Sweat began to trickle down his face, stinging his cut and bruised skin. It soaked through his shirt, but he ignored the discomfort.

The chair had taken on a distinct twist and the more Schwarz strained against the rope, the more the chair began to sag.

Schwarz took another glance through the window, checking out the gathered group.

And saw the Mexican, Sottero, walking back inside, cutting across the floor of the mill.

"Son of a bitch," Schwarz said through swollen, bleeding lips.

He pushed to his feet again, finding the rope's slackness allowed him to stand almost upright. With a final effort he slammed the weakened chair down hard. He heard wood splinter, felt the binding rope go completely slack, and went down on the floor hard. The impact drove the breath from his aching lungs. Schwarz coughed harshly, sucking air into his lungs. He lay, hurt and stiff, willing himself to get to his feet because he could hear Sottero stamping his way up the wooden stairs leading to the office. He fought himself free of the tangled rope, rolled to his side and dragged himself to his knees.

He was in that position when Sottero appeared in the office doorway. The Mexican took in the sight of the American free and on his knees and mumbled a curse.

He reached under his leather jacket for the pistol he had tucked into his waistband.

Schwarz sucked in a ragged breath, summoning every ounce of strength he possessed, and pushed himself upright, launching himself at Sottero. As he came up off the floor, the Able Team commando closed his right hand over one of the splintered chair legs, gripping it tight and pushed it forward as he lunged across the office. His left hand smacked against Sottero's upper chest, driving the Mexican back against the door frame, pinning his gun hand behind his back. Sottero opened his mouth to yell the instant before the slivered end of the chair leg smacked into the soft flesh under his jaw. There was a soft, wet sound as the length of wood penetrated the Mexican's throat, emerging just below his ear and severing the jugular vein on its way out. Blood began to spurt from the wounds, cascading down the man's front. Any sound he might have been about to make was cut off, leaving Sottero capable of little more than gurgling moans.

Schwarz maintained his grip on the chair leg, keeping up the pressure. He ignored the rush of warm blood that drenched his hand and spilled across his shirt. He held Sottero's panicked stare, as the man struggled wildly until massive blood loss took its toll and his movements slowed, became weaker and finally stopped. Sottero became a deadweight. Schwarz pushed his hand under the Mexican's coat and located the pistol. He freed it, then stepped back and let Sottero drop to the floor.

Schwarz moved back, leaning his weight on the edge of the closest desk. He stayed there until the waves of nausea eased off. If anything, he was hurting more now then when he had been tied to the chair. He checked the handgun, a P-226. Schwarz checked the clip, snapped it back in place and cocked the weapon. He took a quick glance out the window and saw that the group was still in the same position. Moving to where Sottero lay, Schwarz went through the man's pockets. He found two extra clips for the pistol.

He also found a cell phone. Schwarz switched it on, waited until it powered up, then checked the signal. It was there but weak. Schwarz tapped in the Stony Man number and offered a prayer there was enough signal to transmit to the satellite link. The connection seemed to take forever. Schwarz spotted a water cooler against the wall. As he neared it, he could hear the unit humming softly. He snatched up a plastic cup and filled it. He took a long swallow of the blessed chilled water. It had never tasted better. He took a second cup and splashed it over his aching face. A third he downed in a single gulp, then turned and went to the window to run another check on the opposition.

They were still there, though they had moved farther out from the door.

His attention was drawn to the connection being made. He heard distant sounds. A voice he couldn't recognize. He identified himself, his swollen jaw making talk difficult. As he spoke he moved around the office, trying to locate a stronger signal spot. He stepped out of the office and the volume on the cell phone suddenly rose.

"Gadgets? That you?"

Now he could recognize Brognola's voice. "Yeah. Hal, I might not have much time."

"Where the hell are you?"

"Somewhere in Texas as far as I can work out. I'm in some plant. Looks like a wood-chip mill of some kind."

Someone on an extension broke in. "Bucklow? Bucklow, Texas?" It was Kurtzman. "Gadgets, we think it's where stolen MOAB bombs may be stored. It's likely Khariza's people have them. We also believe at least one of those bombs may be detonated in or around Bucklow. Today. April 9."

Schwarz tried to absorb all the information.

"I could—"

"Gadgets, Pol and Ironman are on their way to your location. We figured out what was going on and sent them in *Dragon Slayer* to try to intercept."

Barbara Price broke in. "They should be over your location any time now, Gadgets."

"And me still not up and about," Schwarz muttered.

"What was that?"

"Nothing. Just let them know I'm down here. I don't want flyboy dropping his heat-seekers on me."

Aboard: Dragon Slayer

"GADGETS IS DOWN THERE." Grimaldi repeated the message he had just received over his headset. "Inside the mill building."

Lyons glanced up from checking the Franchi SPAS-15, 12-gauge shotgun he had pulled from the arms locker. The SPAS-15 was the next generation of Franchi combat shotguns. Instead of the under barrel loading tube of the SPAS-12, this model had a 6-round magazine just forward of the trigger, making for faster reloading. Lyons clicked in a full magazine, slipped an extra one into a pocket of his blacksuit and cocked the weapon.

"About time he showed up."

"Here comes Daddy Care Bear," Blancanales said.

Grimaldi flew over the wood-chip mill. There were a number of panel trucks parked behind the building. A quarter of a mile away a Beechcraft turboprop aircraft stood at the end of a flattened landing strip. As the combat chopper swooped past the main building, the occupants could see a group of men on the loading dock. They appeared to be staring in the direction of Bucklow town.

Grimaldi took *Dragon Slayer* in toward it.

"Something tells me we're running out of time," Blancanales said. He checked his watch. "Almost noon."

"That supposed to mean something?" Lyons asked.

"I just read through that data Bear sent us about Bucklow's April 9 celebration. They're holding it on the town picnic ground. The whole town and the surrounding neighborhood is expected to be there. Town band. School. Veterans. Up to a thousand people expected to turn up."

"Hey, they got the town sheriff on the line," Grimaldi said. "Patching him through."

He put the radio on the cabin speaker.

"Sheriff Cooper here. Now what the hell is going on? Who are you people?"

"We're a Justice Department team on our way to Bucklow," Lyons said. "We just flew in over the wood-chipping mill. No time to explain, Sheriff. You need to get your people away from the picnic ground. We have reason to believe there's a massive bomb somewhere near you. You have to evacuate the area. Now."

"You foolin' with me, boy? If you are I'll—"

"Sheriff, get your fucking town away from that picnic ground. Don't argue. Do it before—"

The whole area in front of *Dragon Slayer* was obscured by a brilliant white flare that stung their eyes. The flare might only have lasted for a few seconds, but to the men in the chopper it seemed longer. The white light was replaced by a huge ball of incandescent red-orange fire that grew in size with terrifying speed. It expanded outward and upward, encompassing a wide area. The huge mass of flame lashed across the surface of the landscape, devouring everything in its path. It seared and burned and turned to crumbling ash anything it touched. The terrible force of the fireball turned fertile earth to scorched ruin. Grass and wood and metal succumbed to the horrendous power of the fire. The Bucklow picnic ground and the massed people on it were obliterated in an instant. The celebrating crowds, unaware of what was happening, died in a millisecond. Flesh vanished and bone was destroyed in the hungry maw of living fire. The temperature rose to a degree high enough to buckle metal, ripping through the rows of parked vehicles and reducing them to red-hot hulks. Fuel tanks ignited, adding more fire to the already solid ball of horror.

Following the fireball came the rumbling thunder of the detonation. The sound crackled and increased, the heavy sound expanding in a ripple effect, sound and fury merging into one.

Dragon Slayer shuddered as she was hit by the edges of the shock waves. The chopper yawed, swinging out of control for long, dangerous seconds before Grimaldi pulled himself out of his daze and clamped down on the helicopter's wayward flight. His hands and feet worked the controls, swiftly bringing the aircraft back under his command.

"Oh, my God," Grimaldi whispered at the sight ahead of them.

A rising pall of smoke rose above the fire burst, curling and swelling to form a mushroom shape. The dust and debris sucked up into the superheated air began to fall back to earth. As the massive fireball began to shrink, having done its deadly work, a dark cloud formed over the scene of destruction.

"Hal, you there?"

"Carl, what's happened?"

"Listen hard, Hal. Massive explosion near Bucklow. I mean massive. Get the emergency services in the immediate vicinity to Bucklow. We need to get to the mill. Can't tell you much now. Just send those services in."

"We're on it," Price called.

"Carl, what does it look like over there?"

"Like Hell just dropped in and landed on Bucklow County."

Lyons racked the SPAS, pushing the first shell into the chamber.

"We making a house call?" Grimaldi asked.

"Damn right we are, Jack, and I've brought my calling card with me. Now get us on the ground before those bastards figure it's time to leave."

Wood-Chipping Mill

"JESUS," THE AMERICAN SAID. "You never said anything about that, Kerim."

The Iraqi glanced at the American mercenary, a thin smile on his serene face. "If I had told you the effect would not have been the same."

"I still might have wet myself."

Kerim glanced at his watch. "Wet or not, Ramsey, would you hurry that fool, Sottero. We need to leave now, before the authorities start looking for us."

Ramsey turned to look in the direction of the offices. He held his gaze for a moment, then shook his head.

"No, he couldn't have."

As the thought took hold, Ramsey stepped back inside the mill and made his way across the shop floor, making for the stairs that gave access to the upper floor.

Kerim gestured to the others. "The panel trucks are loaded and ready. Go now. Make your deliveries, collect your payments and move on. You will be contacted as soon as we receive more consignments."

The Mexicans and one of the Americans stepped down off the loading dock as *Dragon Slayer* dropped from the sky, Grimaldi making a powered landing that kicked up dust and wood chips from the open yard in front of the processing plant. The side hatch swung open on hydraulic rams, Carl Lyons, still in his blacksuit, jumped out and ran across the yard, his SPAS combat shotgun up and ready. Close behind was Blancanales, wielding an MP-5.

Lyons headed for the loading dock, while Blancanales cut away to catch up with the two Mexicans and the other American.

The American standing next to Kerim yanked his handgun from its hip holster. He swung around, leveling the weapon at Lyons.

Lyons kept on his line of attack, closing the gap quickly. The sight of the black-clad figure rushing in his direction unnerved the American mercenary long enough for Lyons to take the advantage.

The black muzzle of the SPAS tracked in on target, Lyons tripping the trigger. The 12-gauge load ripped tissue and bone from the mercenary's left shoulder, taking a wedge out of his upper arm, as well. The merc screamed as the blast ripped into him. Blood showered from the gaping wound, splashing across the side of Kerim's face. The Iraqi stepped back, revulsion etched across his features. He was in time to see the results of Lyons's second and third shots. The up-close impact tearing the target's chest and torso open and kicking him back across the loading dock.

Kerim, reaching inside his jacket for the Glock handgun he carried, turned to run for the open door at his back.

Lyons scrambled up on the dock. "Turn around, you bastard."

Kerim knew he couldn't outrun the shotgun. He turned, the Glock in his grasp under his jacket.

"Whatever you do to me is too late. The deed has been done and we have our revenge."

"Is this what it's all about? Revenge? Because we beat your asses and brought down that psycho Hussein?"

"He was our leader. What we did here today was the first strike in a new war."

The rage in Carl Lyons's eyes was a terrible thing to see. "Yeah? Well yours ends right now."

Kerim realized what the American meant. He put out his left hand as if it would stave off his adversary. His right began to pull out the Glock, and up to the moment when the first shot from the SPAS hit him, he believed he could make it.

Lyons triggered the SPAS, placing the remaining 12-gauge loads into Kerim's head and torso. The Iraqi went down hard, his body far removed from the living form it had been only seconds before. Trailing bloody debris in its wake the corpse came to rest against the front wall of the mill.

WITH THE SOUND of Lyons's shotgun in his ears, Blancanales rounded the end of the building, pausing briefly to assess the situation ahead of him.

The three men he was pursuing had begun to sepa-

rate as they'd raced along the end of the mill. One of
the Mexicans, yelling something to his partner, swung
round to fire a hasty shot from the handgun he produced. The shot came close and Blancanales came to a
dead stop, raised the MP-5 and laid a short burst into
the shooter. The 9 mm slugs cored in through the lower
back, severing the man's spine. He tumbled facedown,
screaming in agony at the pain. His partner turned to see
what had happened and in the short space of time he was
motionless Blancanales stitched him in the chest with
a second burst from the H&K, laying him flat out on the
ground. Blancanales moved on, pulling his Beretta and,
as he passed the back-shot man, hitting him with a double tap through the back of his skull.

The third man, the American, had vanished around
the end of the building. Blancanales flattened against the
wall, MP-5 up and ready.

He heard the sound of an engine bursting into life,
the sound rising as the driver hit the gas pedal. Blancanales heard the whine of tires as they fought to gain trac-
tion. He stepped around the end of the building and saw
the American staring at him from behind the windshield
of one of the panel trucks that had been visible from
Dragon Slayer. The truck was already moving, kicking
up a thick dust trail as the driver decided on the fast-get-
away tack. His judgment was out because the ground
under the truck was uneven and the overrevved vehicle
was bouncing as the wheels struggled to maintain an
even grip.

Blancanales raised the H&K. He took seconds to establish his target, then eased back on the trigger, holding the weapon steady while he laid a long burst in through the windshield. Glass shattered, sending broken shards back into the cab. The driver's face was turned bloody in seconds as the glass struck, followed by the stream of 9 mm slugs that tore at his throat and chest, punching ragged holes in him. Blancanales stepped aside as the panel truck swerved toward him then rolled in the opposite direction. The driver's foot had to still have been on the gas pedal. Instead of slowing, the truck roared past Blancanales, across the open ground until it came to a sudden, hard stop against a rusting, abandoned piece of machinery left on the edge of the area. The truck's engine burned to a steam-spouting stop, the driver's bloody upper body flopping loosely out of the open door. It hung head down, dripping blood across the step.

Blancanales moved to the rear of the panel truck. He yanked open the doors and peered inside. The load area held plain wood boxes and crates. The impact had thrown them across the floor and Blancanales pulled at the loosened top of one crate. Inside were M-16s. He checked other crates and found ammunition. Grenades. One box held a half dozen LAW rocket launchers. He also found cartons of C-12 explosive compound and packed in other cartons detonators and timers.

The sight of the weapons only reinforced Blancanales's thoughts about Khariza's followers. They *were* totally committed to causing as much suffering and death as they could on the American mainland.

The detonation of the MOAB device proved that without a shadow of doubt.

RAMSEY REACHED the stairs leading to the office and charged up two at a time. As he hit the top step and turned toward the office, he saw Sottero lying across the door opening. From the massive pool of blood spreading from under his head, Ramsey knew the Mexican had to be dead. The merc pulled his handgun, snapping back the slide. He stepped to the side, flat against the wall, and advanced in the direction of the door. He couldn't see anyone inside the office, but that didn't mean it was deserted. Ramsey did see the remains of the broken chair their prisoner had been tied to. He could see the coils of the rope that had held the man down.

Damn!

That was all they needed. A loose cannon running around when they needed to make a clean break.

The crash of breaking glass caught his attention and Ramsey turned, momentarily distracted. He saw an object fly through the air, out the side window of the office. It curved out of sight to fall to the mill floor below.

Ramsey swore, calling himself every kind of fool for being caught by the oldest trick in the book. A false move to call his attention from the main objective, and he had fallen for it like a recruit straight out of boot camp. He turned his attention back to the office door as a moving shape materialized there.

Too late.

Something punched him in the chest. A hard, debilitating blow that knocked him back a step. It was followed by a second punch. This one cored in deep, and Ramsey felt pain over his heart. A third shot, because now he heard the sharp cracks, and Ramsey felt his legs go out from under him. He sagged back against the wall, gun arm slipping to his side as the pistol became too heavy to hold.

The day turned shadowy around him. Sound seemed a long way off, as if coming down a long tunnel. Ramsey could hear his own breathing, harsh and labored. He sensed movement in front of him, concentrated his gaze and saw the battered, bloody features of the man they had taken captive. He was crouching in front of Ramsey. The guy had Sottero's P-226 in his right hand. He knew it was Sottero's because of the fancy scrollwork on the slide.

The man was speaking. His words were dulled by Ramsey's fading hearing. He did pick up the final question.

"Where's the other bomb?"

Ramsey shook his head. The truth was, he didn't know. The truth, too, was that he was going to be dead soon, and the twist was he didn't like the idea. But he had walked into this with his eyes open. Maybe his ears had been closed to what Kerim and his bunch had wanted to do because the money had been so tempting, and Ramsey wanted out of the whole shitty game. He just wanted his money so he could find somewhere quiet and peaceful. That had been a fucking great joke, too, because Razan Khariza wanted the whole world tearing at each other's throats like a pack of rabid hounds. The Iraqi wanted his pound of flesh and then some.

Ramsey stared up into the eyes of the man who had shot him. Schwarz stared right back, mouthing the question again.

"Where's the other bomb?"

"Ask Vance. Philo Vance…"

His words came out in a bubbling red froth. Ramsey felt a rising, paralyzing burning sensation that engulfed his chest. The silence became profound and the darkness closed in with frightening speed, engulfing Ramsey completely.

Hermann Schwarz pushed to his feet. He walked out of the office, favoring his bruised body and becoming more aware of his facial injuries with every passing moment.

The gunfire from outside the mill had died down. As Schwarz crossed the mill and stepped out onto the loading dock, he barely paused to look at the dead lying there.

Lyons stood in the yard, his gaze directed toward the heavy, mushroom cloud of smoke rising from the distant site of the bomb explosion.

"I can't believe the bastards actually did it," Schwarz said.

Lyons turned to look at him, taking in the condition of Schwarz's face, the blood soaking his shirt.

"Can you make it?"

"I'll make it for as long as it takes to find Philo Vance."

"Vance?"

"Someone told me he might know where the other MOAB is."

Grimaldi had left *Dragon Slayer*. He came across to join Lyons and saw Schwarz.

"Gadgets?"

Schwarz saw Blancanales coming around the end of the building.

"Before I have to repeat it too many times, I'm okay. I just need to take a minute." He sat on the edge of the loading dock, lowering his head into his hands. "Jack, just don't tell me any funny stories. I have a feeling it's going to hurt if I laugh."

"Okay, that's it," Grimaldi said. "Let's get him inside the Lady. I need to take a look at him."

Stony Man Farm, Virginia

"IT'S TERRIBLE," Barbara Price said from the Communications Room. "We have a feed from a local TV news crew. Carl, there's very little they can do. The area where the bomb detonated is just burned out. Emergency services haven't located a single survivor within the main blast area. From what we've been able to get from on-the-spot people, there's nothing left. First estimates are talking about eight to nine hundred people."

"We were still in the air when the bomb went off. The chopper was hit by the shock waves, and they kicked us around some."

"Hold on, Carl, there's something coming in."

Price turned to look at one of the wall monitors where a news flash had interrupted the main news. The voice-over announced that a tape had been received from a group claiming responsibility for the attack. The tape was run. It showed a solitary figure, seated in front of an Iraqi flag. The figure, clad in military fatigues, read from a prepared script.

"The attack on the American town of Bucklow, Texas, was carried out on the authority of the members of the Fedayeen Militia. We do not, and will not, recognize or surrender to the puppet government put in place by our enemies. The strike against Bucklow had a number of objectives. To pay back the U.S. for the unprovoked and cowardly attack on Iraq by letting the American people see how it is to suffer. We also wanted to show that Americans are not safe at home any longer. We have the means and the will to strike within your borders when and where we like. The American government is powerless to stop us. There will be more attacks. We have our people in place and we have the weapons. You in the West consider April 9 as the day Iraq fell to your outlaw forces. We of the fedayeen consider April 9 as Day One of the new war we now wage against America and her allies. Prepare yourselves. America's days are numbered."

CHAPTER NINE

Washington, D.C.

"Sit down, Hal," the President of the United States said.

Brognola sank into one of the chairs facing the President's desk. It was late. Too late in one sense of the word. Try as he might, Brognola was finding it hard to erase the images of Bucklow from his mind. Local and federal law had been on the scene for hours, assisted by units of the Texas National Guard, trying to establish some kind of sanity to a nightmarish scenario, and Brognola, along with the rest of the team at Stony Man, had been witness to the harrowing images sent to them via the closed-TV relay being shot by one of the federal teams.

The mill site had been closed off while teams went through it and examined the panel trucks loaded with illegal weapons. Locating these weapons was a bonus for the federal teams, though it had come at a price, with the death of Tomas Barranca.

Death had also come swiftly to the community of Bucklow. The hundreds who had died in the initial bomb burst had suffered only briefly before they'd ceased to exist. Others, on the perimeter of the sudden firestorm, hadn't been killed with as much mercy. There were dozens, now in hospitals, or on their way, with terrible burns. Others, farther out from the epicenter of the blast had lesser degree burns, but also injuries from flying debris. The death toll was still increasing as severely injured died while in transit to emergency departments. Others were on critical lists. Survivors had still to be told that whole generations of their families had been killed. Many would never be able to see their deceased relatives due to the severity of the burst. In many cases there was nothing left to identify. The explosion hadn't just killed, it had torn out the heart of Bucklow, devastating the whole community. Pinpointing the area as a monument to man and his lack of humanity. The dark cloud of smoke drifting over Bucklow bore mute testimony to the black soul of humankind at his worst.

The town itself hadn't escaped damage. The section of Bucklow closest to the blast had caught shock waves. Windows had been shattered, buildings scorched by the heat. Fires had been started where gas tanks had exploded, the flames spreading quickly in the dry Texas air. Bucklow's fire house, with a skeleton crew on duty, had responded with the only engine left in the building. The others had been at the picnic ground, having taken part in the celebratory parade.

"Have you been keeping track of current events?" the President asked.

"Hard not to," Brognola said. "Armed attacks against Americans in Iraq. Snipers, suicide bombers. Similar in Israel. Kuwait. It's like a damn plague. It all seems to have started at the same time."

"We're starting to get similar reports from here in the U.S. Six different locations so far. Two suicide bombers. One in Detroit. Another in Boston. Someone wearing an explosive device just walked into a restaurant and blew himself up. We have twelve dead in Detroit, eight in Boston. Just as many wounded. Luckily the death count has been small from those. I think the fact we raided locations with the speed we did took the edge off those kinds of attacks." The President stood and paced the Oval Office. "At least your intel allowed us to go for those locations. We've taken out over twelve of them. Found stored weapons and explosives. In some there were detailed plans of operations, where the targets were located and the best times to hit them."

"Any prisoners?"

"Right now we have twenty in custody. Three shot themselves rather than allowing themselves to be taken. I can't say that bothers me in the slightest, Hal. There are still sieges taking place in two of the locations. Atlanta and Casper."

"We've been expecting something like this ever since the World Trade Center disaster," Brognola said. "More after we went into Iraq. We've done everything we can to defend ourselves. We told ourselves it was going to happen. To be honest, Mr. President, it still comes as a hell of a shock."

"We have one thing that always works against us, Hal," the President said. "Despite all the precautions, the preparations, we're still a society that believes in freedom. We still let people in. We trust and we accept. And those bastards out there know that. They use our way of life against us. They preach their thoughts of hate against America and at the same time they use our openness to abuse us. Maybe it's time we started to hit back using their methods. It's time we stopped playing by the rule book our enemies discarded a long time ago."

"Mr. President, my people are ready to go after these people using whatever is necessary."

"Give me an update."

"Able Team is moving on a possible lead they received from a man involved with Jafir Rasifi. A man who is known to have dealt in illegal weapons. Philo Vance. He operates out of Las Vegas."

"Another American?"

"Yes, sir."

"I want this to passed to your teams, Hal, and I'll put it in writing if need be. Any American found to be consorting with Razan Khariza's group, comes under the hostile heading. If they think so little of this country they're prepared to sell her out for money, they can die for that betrayal. No mincing words on this, Hal. Clear and simple. They forfeit any and all considerations of mercy, clemency, whatever you want to call it. If anyone makes a fuss, just remind them about Bucklow, Texas." The President paused. "Now tell me where Phoenix Force is."

"They're working in two groups at the moment to give them more stretch. One section, along with Ben Sharon, has gone to Israel, following the final translation of Kamal Rasheed's organizer. The information looks as if it could match word Sharon received from an inside operative. He's in with an active fedayeen group, and he came up with information about an operation based in the Negev Desert. The second team is in Hong Kong, looking into the supply of weapons over there. We also have reason to believe that Khariza's group, now they have the access codes to the secret deposits, are increasing their overtures to the North Koreans."

"More than just a boatload of Kalashnikovs?"

Brognola nodded. "Way heavier than that, Sir."

The President sighed. "Pity Phoenix Force didn't manage to get their hands on those disks." He held up a hand. "I'm not criticizing, Hal. Your people were lucky to come out of that confrontation without casualties. McCarter's field decision was the right one."

"He'd be grateful to hear that, Mr. President."

"Did they locate the helicopter? Or the hostage?"

"By the time the helicopter was located, the passengers were long gone. They landed at an old RAF station on the northeast coast of England. Apparently a private jet took off from there. Last that was heard it had cut off across country and set course for somewhere in Europe. The flight had been preapproved so there was no reason for anyone to challenge it. It was later established the plane was refueled in Denmark before taking off again. After that, the trail became hazy. It looks as if Khariza's people paid for their flight to be left off the books. Khariza has loyal followers of his cause in surprising locations. That or the fact he's able to pay for assistance gets him what he wants."

"Any guesses what their destination might be?"

"Possibly the camp in Chechnya. The rebel leader, Zoltan Dushinov, has made it clear he backs the struggle of the fedayeen against the West. His Islamic background strengthens his cause. He hates the Russians. He hates the U.S. He loves his Iraqi brothers. What can I say, Sir?"

The President slumped back in his seat. "Get the word to the teams, Hal. I want these missions to proceed with extreme prejudice. Khariza and his damn Fedayeen Militia have decided to wage war on this country. So let's give them one, Hal. Give the bastards all the war they want. Understand? I want this made clear to Stony Man through all levels. We *are* on a war footing."

Hong Kong

DAVID MCCARTER HEARD the light tap on the door of his room. He crossed over and stood to one side of the door.

"Yes?"

"Henry Lee."

McCarter unlocked the door and opened it enough so he could check out his visitor. The man standing in the corridor was exactly as Mei Anna's photograph had shown him, except for the smart business suit, white shirt and maroon tie.

McCarter opened the door and let the man in. He locked the door behind Lee.

"I would only dress like this for Anna," Lee said, smiling as if he needed to apologize for his appearance.

"She has a way of getting people to do things they don't like."

Lee's smile widened. "Tell me about it. How is she?"

"Still on the mend. The wound from that bullet hit turned bad. She was ill for a long time, and it knocked the wind out of her sails. Took away a lot of her confidence."

Lee sighed. "That and the fact she had been driving herself for far too long. She was exhausted long before she took that bullet. But she refused to even consider taking time off. According to her, the Chinese Dragon never slept and it would swallow us whole if we let down our guard. Anna could be very poetic at times."

"Still is."

"You have become good friends?"

"I like to think so."

"It's time she had a friend, *Mr. Ryan.* Anna explained your problem."

"Can you help?"

Lee nodded. He reached inside his jacket and produced a number of photographs. He showed them to McCarter, identifying each individual for him.

"Kim Yeo is known to us. It's been difficult proving anything against him. He has strong protection from the Chinese. We have been looking into his business dealings, and we know he works with the mainland Chinese. He supplies goods they want. Anything from cars to domestic refrigerators. He has contacts that reach all across Southeast Asia. If he is dealing with the North Koreans, he's moving into dangerous territory. Lucrative but risky. The Koreans are hard people to do business with, and they do not tolerate mistakes."

"The authorities in Beijing let this go on?"

"If it causes unrest in the region, especially where the Americans or any Western government is concerned, they turn a blind eye."

"Still up to their old games?"

"Which is why we have plenty to do."

McCarter tapped one of the images. "Sun Yang Ho?"

Lee nodded.

"Not a person I would be happy being around. He's one of North Korea's dealers. His job is to try to sell their weapons. A shrewd negotiator. Also very successful. Now that the sea lanes are being monitored for illegal cargoes, Ho sees this a challenge. He will find other ways to move his merchandise if he can."

"Sit down, Henry," McCarter said. "You want a drink?"

"Coffee would be nice."

McCarter crossed to a small table and he picked up a Thermos jug. "Had some sent up just before you got here." The Briton filled two cups, handing one to the Chinese. They sat facing each other.

"Tell me what is behind all this," Lee said.

"We believe Iraqi ex-fedayeen members from the old Hussein regime are looking to buy some serious weaponry. Not just AK-47s and a box of grenades. They'll need those for sure, but these blokes are in for the long haul so they want big stuff, as well. The Koreans are in that business. They'll sell providing the buyer has the big bucks. You've heard about the bombing in the U.S?"

Lee nodded. "A terrible thing to happen. So many people dead. Families. A whole community."

"Khariza has been purchasing small arms for some time. We confirmed this when we broke up his buy in South America. But he has bigger plans from what we've been able to work out. He needs larger ordnance. For that he needs to get his hands on the bulk of the money the Hussein regime banked in secret accounts."

"These stories about missing billions of dollars. They are true?"

McCarter nodded. "Hussein's cronies salted away so much money you wouldn't believe it. They had it in secret accounts spread all over. They had a problem when one of their blokes got pissed off and quit the regime. Before he did, he planted a virus that wiped all the account codes from their system. It meant they couldn't tap into the funds. The Koreans wouldn't hand over the shopping list until they actually had payment."

"And?"

McCarter smiled. "The guy who went over the wall made disk copies of the account codes and took them with him. The fedayeen found out and went after him. We tried to keep the disks from getting into their hands but we dropped the ball."

"So now these Iraqis will be able to get their money and buy their weapons?"

McCarter sighed. "Don't rub it in. I feel bad enough we let them snatch those bloody discs back. And take a hostage."

"Even so, there must still be time to do something. You said yourself these people are looking for heavy ordnance. Not the sort of equipment you can place in the back of a car and drive home with."

"Kim Yeo?"

"He operates a diverse company. He has restaurants in Kowloon and Hong Kong. Couple of hotels. Also a shipping company that trades all over the South China Sea farther up the coast in the New Territories. His ships are involved in all kinds of freighting. Including much for the mainland Chinese."

"He do anything for the Koreans?"

"Oh, yes. He does quite a trade with North Korea. We only found this out recently because the amount of traffic has increased."

"And the search ships can't be everywhere all the time."

"What are you thinking?"

"That it might be worthwhile taking a close look at the Chang Li company."

"Where is the rest of your team?"

"In another hotel," McCarter said. "We didn't want to show up in a group in case it attracted too much attention."

"Good idea. I'll arrange things for you and get back by late this afternoon. As I said the Chang Li warehouses and main offices are up the coast a way. We can go in by boat."

"Henry, we came in clean. Had no choice. Anna said you might be able to supply us with weapons."

"I'll bring them along before we go in."

After Lee left, McCarter used his cell phone to contact Encizo and Manning to bring them up to date.

"Let's hope we find something," the little Cuban said. "David, this could get close. The Chinese aren't going to like it if we make a noise, especially if this Yeo character is under their protection."

"We'll handle it, Rafe. Okay?"

"You're the boss."

"Don't bloody remind me."

THEY WERE BEYOND the glitzy tourist area of Kowloon, farther along the coast in the direction of the New Territories, in among the commercial trappings of the dock area. The bright lights were far behind them, a neon haze in the darkness. The busy period had passed and the dock area was less hectic than it was during the daylight hours. The slow-moving junk, the Chinese workhorse of the water, chugged across the harbor, staying in the shadows of the moored freighters and cargo ships that worked the South China Sea. They were one among many and no one paid them any attention. Two of Lee's men worked the boat as crew.

McCarter, Encizo and Manning stayed beneath the canvas-covered area at the stern of the junk. They wore plain, dark clothing. Their hurried move to Hong Kong, by commercial flights, had prevented them from bringing along any specialized gear, so they had been forced to rely on civilian clothing.

The same had applied to weapons. The Hong Kong Chinese authorities were known to be hot on security, so Phoenix Force had been forced to arrive clean, depending on Mei Anna's Pro-Democracy group to help. Henry Lee didn't disappoint them. Once they were on board the junk and away from the shore, he produced a leather bag that held a selection of handguns.

There were two 9 mm SIG-Sauer P-226 pistols, a pair of Glock 17s, also in 9 mm and a .357 Magnum Ruger GP-100 revolver.

"Some mix there," Manning said as he hefted a P-226.

"We have to get our weapons where we can," Lee explained.

"Hey, I'm not complaining. These are damn fine weapons."

"There are magazines in there, too," Lee said. "Plenty of spares."

While the others chose their weapons, McCarter and Lee went over the floor plan of the Kim Yeo building.

"The two lower floors are where the goods are stored and dispatched. Doors open onto the loading dock at the front. There are facilities at the rear for handling trucks. The top floor is where Yeo has his offices. His personal office suite is here on this corner section, overlooking the harbor."

"What about alarms? It's not going to help if the bells start to go off the minute we go in."

Lee smiled. "Already taken care of."

They cut across to the dock area near the Chang Li Ltd. building. The helmsman guided the junk through the darkness and into a narrow dock that had been cut into the main area. A vessel was moored there, in total darkness, and the junk eased up alongside it. The motor was cut, and all they could hear was the soft slap of water against the sides of the junk and the other vessel.

"This is a dredger," Lee explained. "Only used when there is a buildup of mud in the shallow sections of the harbor. When it is not in use it just sits here. No crew, so it's ideal for what we need. A place to hide."

Lee spoke to his crew. They produced mat-black A-K47s and took up defensive positions on the junk's deck.

"They've done this before," Encizo said.

"A few times."

Lee led the way up the crusted ladder fixed to the dock wall. He checked out the area before stepping on to the dock. Phoenix Force followed him as he crossed the dock and they all flattened against the front wall.

"Anyone on watch?" McCarter asked.

Lee shook his head. "Kim Yeo is under protection. The criminal fraternity knows that. No one would even consider trying to steal from Yeo. So he has no need of guards."

"Why does that make me feel uncomfortable?" Manning asked.

"Because the guy has the Chinese army on call," Encizo pointed out. "And all I got is a P-226."

"Stop complaining," Encizo said. "You've got three full magazines to go with it."

"Enough chatter, girls," McCarter snapped. "Let's get to it."

He tapped Lee on the shoulder. The Chinese moved along the wall until he reached a single door, a simple wooden slab with a standard lock. Lee produced a small leather case from his pocket. When he opened it he took out a number of steel lock picks. He bent over the lock, inserting the picks and manipulating them until he heard the tumblers click. He put the picks away, gently turned the handle and the door swung inward with barely a sound.

McCarter followed the Chinese inside, Manning and Encizo following close. Once they were in, Encizo, bringing up the rear, closed the door behind them. He was about to turn away when he spotted bolts on the inside. He slid them into place. It was a precaution against anyone coming in behind them.

The deep spread of the storage area was in shadow, with faint light filtering down from lamps set high overhead.

"Where do you want to start?" Lee asked.

McCarter had taken in the huge expanse of the warehouse facility.

"We could spend all night and the next bloody day going through this lot. I think checking out the offices might save time."

They made their way to a set of steel stairs that led

to the upper floor. Reaching the level, they turned to the next set of stairs.

A blaze of light burst in their faces, dazzling them. There was the rattle of weapons, the sound of rushing footsteps.

A harsh voice reached out from behind the blinding glare. "Put down the weapons and show your empty hands. Refuse and you will die now. A simple choice."

Figures stepped forward, assault rifles trained on Lee and Phoenix Force. The men behind the rifles were Chinese. McCarter counted four of them. To one side an unarmed man moved closer. He had his hands clasped together, resting against his rounded stomach. McCarter recognized him from the photographs Lee had shown him.

Kim Yeo.

"The guns?" he asked.

McCarter was the first to place his pistol on the floor. The others followed suit. Lee was the most reluctant.

"Do it, man," McCarter said. "Dead, you're no good to anyone."

"Your friend is right," Yeo said.

Lee dropped his weapon and stepped back. "Who betrayed us?" he asked.

Yeo smiled. "One of your loyal people saw a chance to redeem himself and make a little money in the process. When he learned about your proposed interference with my business he took the opportunity to make amends for his lapse of conscience and informed me of your imminent arrival."

Lee glanced across at McCarter. "I have let you down."

"*You* haven't."

Yeo turned to his armed men, raising a hand. He spoke in rapid, harsh tones. The armed men moved to group around McCarter and the others. One of them retrieved the weapons placed on the floor, dropping them in a leather satchel hanging from his shoulder.

"You wanted to see what we were doing here? Very well, I will show you. And then we will go and see someone who is anxious to meet you."

Yeo led them deep into the large warehouse. It stretched for a long way, the floor space filled with stacks of crates and drums, pieces of machinery that ranged from car engines to farm tractors and harvesters.

"What we supply for our special clients is all part of the business," Yeo explained as he led the way. "One tool is just like another. All that differs is the use of that tool. And the price, of course."

They stepped through a sliding door into a further extension of the warehouse building. Here the area was smaller, but still expansive by most standards. In neat bays, cases and boxes were neatly stacked.

"Here," Yeo said, stepping into one of the bays. He lifted a top from a long crate. "AK-74s. New. Ten to a crate. There are fifty crates in each bay here. Next to them are more 74s. These are used. All have been reconditioned and are in perfect working order. Again ten to a crate. Along here the smaller boxes hold filled magazines for the 74s. As many as the client wants. In the next bay we have two hundred SR-88As. 5.56 mm, made in Singapore. A fine weapon. The manufacturer has failed to find out where the missing batch went."

The catalog of ordnance went on as Yeo pointed out the large cache ready for shipment. McCarter recognized box markings for SIG-Sauer P-226 pistols, Russian fragmentation grenades, cartons that contained C-12. There were detonators, timers. There were a number of containers marked USA—LAW rocket launchers, M-249 SAWs.

"These I am particularly proud of. One hundred Russian SA-18 Igla surface-to-air missiles, an extremely efficient and powerful weapon."

"You've been shopping around," the Briton commented.

"I go where the market offers the best. Our current client is extremely demanding when it comes to quality merchandise."

"Can we stop playing games?" McCarter snapped. "We all know who your client is. Call him by his bloody name. Razan Khariza. Ex-fedayeen. One of Hussein's regime."

Yeo turned to stare at the Phoenix Force leader. His face bore a faintly amused expression.

"If nothing else, I admire your honesty. Before you were evicted from Hong Kong, you British always managed to maintain face. In some ways I miss the British administration. Beijing has not yet managed to grasp the complexities of being handed the most cosmopolitan of colonies in existence. Global enterprise, Hong Kong style, is something new to them. Their heavy hand sometimes leaves me wondering if we did wrong. Perhaps it would have been better to let the British stay for another ninety years. Raising the rent, though."

"Why? So *you* can go on supplying weapons to whoever wants them?"

"Coming from a British subject, I find that slightly hypocritical. Or am I wrong when I mention your country, and the United States, both having extremely lucrative arms dealings? Should I list all the countries they have done deals with?"

"We've paid for our mistakes. I'm not denying what happened."

"Now *you* are on the receiving end," Yeo said. "Somehow that strikes me as ironic."

He turned and spoke rapidly to his own men. The armed escort closed in around their captives, gesturing with their weapons.

"We will go now. As much as I would like to carry on, our discussion time does not allow me the privilege."

They were walked through the warehouse, emerging on the far side, where a number of trucks were parked.

McCarter and his team, along with Henry Lee, were made to climb into the rear of one of the trucks, the armed Chinese following them.

"The journey will not be long," Yeo said. "We will transfer to an aircraft for the main trip."

Negev Desert, Israel

DRY WIND BLEW IN across the sandy terrain. Grit peppered the sides of the IDF combat helicopter resting in the shallow depression. The pilot cut the power and the rotors began to slow.

Calvin James slid open the side hatch and swung his lanky frame from the cabin, one hand steadying the H&K MP-5 he carried. He was clad in desert camou fatigues, a long-peaked fatigue cap on his head. Protective goggles hung around his neck. He moved out from the chopper, scanning the surrounding terrain as T. J. Hawkins followed him. Ben Sharon brought up the rear.

As well as the SMGs, each man carried a holstered handgun and a sheathed combat knife.

The pilot, a young Israeli, called Davi, exited the chopper on the far side, his 9 mm Uzi carried in one hand. His task was to remain with the helicopter, maintaining contact with the combat team via their Tac-Com units. The equipment had been checked and tested during the flight in from Beersheba. They had landed a half mile away from the isolated oasis, where, according to data from Rasheed's organizer, a fedayeen unit could operate from. The information had been clarified and confirmed as likely to be genuine from one of Ben Sharon's informants. The man, working inside a pro-Iraqi group in the West Bank, had been gathering his data for a number of weeks and had only just made his findings solid enough to contact Sharon. James and Hawkins had already been on their way to Israel to meet up with Sharon. The Mossad agent had returned to his homeland when McCarter, Manning and Encizo had shipped out to Hong Kong. He had immediately contacted James and Hawkins, arranging for them to join him and pool their information.

Stony Man had satellite information on the *Petra*.

Zehlivic's boat had made a rendezvous with another ship on the approach to Cyprus, and though they hadn't witnessed any actual transfer, it was felt that the *Petra* had transferred a number of its passengers to this new vessel. Kurtzman's skilled manipulation of his satellite eye had managed to get some identification of this ship. It was a cargo steamer that plied its trade around the Mediterranean, calling in at a number of ports along the North African coastline. This particular voyage was finalized when it docked in Tripoli.

With the unrest already escalating in the Middle East, including more unexpected incidents between Israel and the Palestinians, attacks by Turkish military units against the Kurdish oilfields, and the sudden murders of a number of the new Iraqi governing body, the fragile peace in the region seemed to be teetering on the brink of collapse.

"We don't have definite proof that any of Khariza's group jumped ship," Barbara Price said as she gave James the information via sat phone. "But the way things are moving at the present we have to make some assumptions and go for them. Join up with Ben Sharon and see if his and our intel fits together. Something is happening out there. Find it, Cal, and deal with it."

In Israel the two-man Phoenix Force unit met Sharon in Tel Aviv. They passed along the data from Rasheed's organizer and Sharon gave them what he had.

"In all that information there's got to be something that gels," James said.

"Let's go for the common denominator," Sharon replied.

They had shipped out within the hour, flying to Beersheba, where the combat chopper was waiting for them. James and Hawkins were equipped courtesy of Mossad, and after a quick meal they boarded the helicopter and took off for the Negev, where they were now.

"Let's move out," James said.

He raised a hand to Davi. The pilot nodded and spoke into his Tac-Com unit.

"Good luck."

His voice came through their headsets.

The three moved out, staying within the depression that cut its way across the dun-colored desert terrain. They moved steadily forward, aware of their scant cover and accepting the possibility of arriving at the oasis to find it deserted. Even so, they had to check it out. Rasheed's entries had, so far, been fairly accurate, and Sharon's information had the ring of truth to it.

There was nothing else they could do in the face of what had happened at Bucklow. The intention of Razan Khariza's group couldn't have been made more clear following the attack on the Texan community, since the bomb burst there had been, and still were, attacks on targets in the U.S., the Middle East and Israel. On the flight in from Beersheba the combat team had received an update. Two suicide bombers had struck in London. There had been more strikes against Israel, supposedly by Palestinian militants. Equipment and clothing that had survived the explosions had been identified as the type used by the Palestinians. There had been strong denials from the Palestinians. The Israeli armed forces, already on alert, had started to close in on the West Bank and the Gaza Strip. As well as mobile units, Merkava battle tanks rumbled along the streets. Tensions were at their most explosive. It was a situation that could erupt into full-scale violence at any moment. There was a need to defuse the standoff.

Rasheed's scant entry, on one of the final pages Erika Dukas had translated, gave a map reference that had turned out to be an oasis in the Negev Desert, followed by a single word.

Dimona.

The location of the Israeli nuclear plant.

A possible and likely target for Khariza's terrorists, backed up by the information smuggled out by Sharon's undercover man.

James called a brief halt as they neared the oasis. He checked out the Tac-Com link.

"You still picking us up, Davi?"

"I hear you."

"We're close. We'll leave the link open so you can follow progress. If you hear anyone yell 'help,' come running."

"Understood."

Sharon had edged forward to scan the terrain ahead. James and Hawkins joined him. "There," he said, pointing.

They saw the collection of ancient buildings, stone-built and in a state of semicollapse. Just beyond the buildings was a patch of greenery, a few palm trees and the gleam of water.

"See any movement?" James asked.

Sharon shook his head.

"If there is anyone there they'll be keeping out of sight in case any overflying planes spot them."

"How far to the Dimona plant from here?" Hawkins asked.

"Around ten miles."

"They have to have some kind of transport available," James said. "If they're going for the plant, they'll need more than a couple of assault rifles."

"Maybe this is just a forward post," Sharon said, "gathering intel and passing it back."

"It's worth considering. Main force standing by, waiting for the go. Could be they'll fly in the attack group along with heavy weapons."

"Coming from where?" Hawkins asked. "Jordan? Egypt?"

"Khariza could have allies in either country. There are sympathizers for his cause all across the Middle East," Sharon reminded them. "Syria, even Saudi Arabia."

"Nice to know we could be attacked from more than one direction," Hawkins remarked.

"Hey, listen up," James said. "I see movement."

They turned their full attention on the oasis and saw a single figure moving out from one of the buildings. He wore desert camou clothing and had a Kalashnikov slung over his shoulder. The man made his way across to the pool of water and went down on his knees to fill a canteen.

"Makes me thirsty just watching," Hawkins said.

"I have heard tell the water here is very fresh and

sweet," Sharon said. "It comes from an underground source."

"Right now all I'm interested in is who is down there."

Sharon checked his MP-5, cocking the weapon. "Shall we go find out?"

They waited until the water carrier had trudged back into the building before they moved, staying low, and skirting the perimeter of the buildings. The undulating terrain aided their approach. They were able to crawl the final hundred yards flat to the ground, using the hollows and the wind eroded ridges to conceal their approach.

"Let's spread," James said softly into his microphone. "T.J., you take left. Ben, go right. I'll take the center."

They continued their advance, coming in against the facing walls of the clustered buildings.

James, his back pressed to the warm, crumbling stone, heard the affirmative calls from Hawkins and Sharon. Turning his head he was able to see, some twenty feet away, Hawkins crouching at the base of a wall. Sharon was just visible at the other extreme, partly concealed behind a pile of stone from a collapsed wall. The Israeli held up a hand, fingers pointing to his eyes. Then he moved his hand to show three fingers.

Three spotted.

Until they actually moved in, there was no way of knowing how many more there might be.

James risked a verbal command. "Okay, we go in on three. One..two..three…"

In unison they pushed to their feet and made their assault.

Las Vegas, Nevada

PHILO VANCE WORKED out of a truck dealership situated at the northern end of Vegas, in sight of the intersection of I-15 and U.S. 95.

Able Team had driven in from McCarron International, where a USAF jet had landed them, just after 8.30 p.m. They picked up the Lincoln Navigator waiting for them courtesy of Stony Man. Schwarz, his torso heavily bandaged beneath his civilian clothing and still showing severe bruising, took the wheel, adjusting the power driver's seat to his satisfaction. Blancanales took the rear seat, a large canvas bag containing their weapons and equipment. Carl Lyons slid in on the passenger side. He glance across at Schwarz.

"We're in your hands."

"Just how I like it."

He started the SUV, switched on the headlights and rolled it across the tarmac, heading for the side gate that would take them to the main highway. Schwarz picked up I-15, easing the Navigator into the slow lane that would let him ease into the off-ramp when they reached their intersection. The powerful SUV covered the short trip quickly, and Schwarz was able to make his exit without fighting traffic. The blaze of the Vegas lights lay behind them.

Blancanales had passed out weapons. Lyons holstered his big Colt Python and dropped a couple of speed loaders into a pocket. Blancanales and Schwarz had Beretta 92-Fs.

Schwarz pushed the SUV along the feeder road and pulled to a stop just short of the wide lot that fronted Vance's truck agency.

"Some place," Blancanales said, eyeing the rows of trucks lined up on the concrete strip.

There were lights on in the low building at the rear of the lot.

Lyons took out his cell phone and called Stony Man. When Barbara Price came on she answered his question before he asked it.

"Local law enforcement has been advised to stand off until they get the call from us to go in. They've been instructed this is a matter being dealt with on a federal level and you are to be treated accordingly. Feel better now, Carl?"

"Better than Vance is going to. Thanks for the assist."

"Good luck."

Schwarz drove across the lot, easing the SUV to a stop near the glass doors that led into the showroom. Lyons and Blancanales climbed out.

"You still want me to stay here?" Schwarz asked.

"Cover our backs," Lyons said.

Schwarz nodded. He understood Lyons's reluctance to let him go inside. His body was still stiff and sore from the beating he'd received, and Schwarz would have been the first to admit he wasn't one hundred percent able-bodied. If he went in with his partners, he would have been putting them under pressure because they would have worried about his ability to cope with any emergency situation. That concern could have got them killed. Schwarz stayed with the vehicle, his Beretta across his lap.

Lyons led the way inside. The glass doors were automatic and they slid open to let the Able Team duo inside. The showroom held a couple of tractors, all gleaming paintwork and shiny chrome fittings. At the rear of the showroom were glass-fronted offices, furnished in plain but expensive furniture, pale wood and stainless steel. Each of the desks they could see held a large screen computer and enough telephones to keep a small company in business.

The offices were deserted, but the reception desk was occupied. The man lounging there was hard-looking. He blocked Able Team's way.

"Closed," he explained.

"We're looking for your low-life boss, Vance," Lyons said.

The man took a long, slow look around the showroom.

"Looks like he isn't here. Now you have to leave."

"Maybe he's upstairs," Blancanales suggested.

"I was thinking that myself," Lyons said.

The security man pushed his jacket open to expose a heavy pistol tucked in his belt.

"Just move your fuckin' asses back outside."

"It's the high-class people you meet in Vegas that makes it so appealing," Blancanales said.

"The hell with high class," Lyons said, and delivered a solid kick to the guard's testicles. The man let out a shivering groan, knees starting to buckle. Lyons timed his next move perfectly, driving his right knee up into the guard's descending face. Bone snapped and blood squirted in long streams. The guard went over on his back, crashing hard onto the showroom floor. "Give me a hand."

Between them Lyons and Blancanales dragged the

limp form across the floor to one of the showroom tractor units. Lyons pulled some plastic cuffs from his back pocket. He looped one around the guard's wrists, then used a couple more to secure the man to a towing loop under the tractor's front bumper bar. He took the guard's pistol, ejected the magazine and took the weapon apart, throwing the bits across the showroom.

"Upstairs?" he asked. Blancanales nodded.

Lyons headed for the open-plan chromed-metal stairs that led to the upper office. He went up fast and didn't stop when he reached the top. He raised a hard foot and kicked open the pale wood door. It swung in and thudded against the inner wall. As Lyons stepped inside he pulled the Colt Python, his gaze covering the large room.

A lean figure, blond-haired and tanned, was standing at a desk, pushing papers into a briefcase. He glanced up in alarm as the door was smashed open.

"Who the hell...?" he said.

"Still not learned any grown-up words, Philo?"

Vance leaned forward, peering hard at Lyons. Recognition dawned.

"Son of a bitch. I know you."

As he spoke, Vance pushed papers aside and grabbed for a stubby pistol in his briefcase.

Lyons crossed the office in long strides. His right hand came down, slamming the barrel of the heavy pistol across Vance's hand. Bone cracked. Vance howled in pain. He was still moaning when the Able Team leader caught the front of his shirt and swung him around. He swept the Python across the side of Vance's head, blood spurting as the blow turned the man in a half circle.

Lyons raised his foot and planted the sole of his shoe against Vance's buttocks, shoving hard. The force threw the man across the top of the desk, scattering everything aside. Vance crashed to the floor on the other side of the desk. He was still trying to gather himself when Lyons stood over him, grabbed his jacket and hurled him against the wall. Vance crumpled to the floor, blood streaming down his face, dazed and moaning in pain.

Lyons bent over the trembling figure, bunched a fist into the man's shirt and held him rigid. The muzzle of Lyons's Python ground into Vance's cheek, hard against the bone.

"Look at me, Philo," Lyons ordered. "Look at me and listen. I was there. At Bucklow. I saw it happen. All those people. Women, kids, whole families burned to ashes, Philo, and you're responsible."

Lyons drew the hammer back, screwing the cold, hard muzzle deeper into Vance's cheek.

"No. You can't hang that on me."

"The jury is already out, and I see a guilty man. And there's no appeal on this one, Philo. You've walked away for the last time. Hell you're out of your league. You should have stuck to selling Saturday Night Specials, Philo."

Vance's frightened gaze looked beyond Lyons to the figure of Blancanales as he moved up behind his partner.

"Tell him he can't do this. Jesus, this isn't the way. This is America, not some jackshit country."

"You sold out, Philo," Blancanales said evenly, "so the rules don't apply now. I'm here to see he doesn't miss, is all. If he only blows out half your brain, I'll have to finish it. I'll tell you, though, I'm not such a good shot. Might take me some time."

Vance looked between his two tormentors, fear showing in his eyes. There was no way he was going to talk his way out of this—except by giving them what they wanted.

"All I did was set up the deal. Paid off the guys at the airbase. They delivered the bombs to my crew and fixed it so they could drive out of the base. We switched vehicles and lost the military truck. We delivered the consignment to…"

Vance stopped. He refused to meet Lyons's angry stare.

"Who to?" Blancanales asked.

"His name was Kerim. He had his own drivers. I passed over the truck. He paid me and I took off."

"How much did you get?"

A faint gleam of hope showed in Vance's eyes. "More than enough. Hell, there's plenty to go round. I could cut it three ways and we'd all still be able to buy a small country each. You know what I mean?"

Lyons eased off the pressure.

"Christ, you guys play rough," Vance said, some of his confidence returning.

"Yeah," Lyons agreed. "It's a shitty game we're in."

"So?"

"You think we're going to let you walk away without proof? We get screwed and you sail into the sunset with your stash intact."

"Hey, would I fuck around with you guys? You think I'm stupid? I can take you to the money right now. Give me an hour and you can be driving back home with more cash money you ever thought existed."

"And what happens if we end up burned extra crispy when the next bomb goes off?" Blancanales said.

"That's crazy."

"Think about it, Philo. The odds might be long but it could happen. For all we know it might be set to go off down the road in Vegas. Those Iraqi mothers want to make big noises. They're going to choose somewhere high profile for the next one."

"Money's no good if we get wiped out, Philo," Lyons said. "You're a gambler. Would you take those odds?"

Blancanales leaned forward, shaking his head. "No way I'm risking it. Finish it. Shoot the bastard and let's get the hell out of here."

"Works for me," Lyons said. "Back off. This close it'll get messy."

"Hey, why make it easy for him?"

"What do you mean?"

"Dead men get away easy. Put a couple of shots through his spine. Paralyze him so he can't ever move again. Remember Gilman? Took a slug in the back three years ago. He's still alive. Can't move anything below his neck. If you call that living."

Lyons reached out to turn Vance over. The man began to scream and yell, struggling to stay upright.

"Don't fight it, Philo," Lyons said. "With all that money you'll be able to buy the best medical attention around. Nurses round-the-clock to hold your drinks and wipe your ass."

Blancanales reached down to help. It took their combined strength to turn the hysterical Vance onto his front. Blancanales put a foot against the back of his neck, holding him secure.

"This a softwood floor?" Lyons asked.

"Hard to tell. Why?"

"Don't want any slugs bouncing back and blowing his balls off too."

"Won't make much difference. He isn't going to be needing them."

"Damn, you're right."

Lyons pushed the Python against Vance's lower spine, grinding the barrel into the flesh.

"About there?"

"Just do it. I want to get the hell out of here."

"Shame, Philo, we could have cut a deal. Say good-bye to your ass."

"Oh. Jesus Christ, don't fuckin' do it, man. I'll tell you. Just…please…don't…"

He began to sob, his whole body shaking in sheer terror.

"I want to hear, Philo, and don't give me any crap. Think about it. If you give me wrong information I'll come back and I *will* shoot out your backbone. Don't believe otherwise."

Five minutes later they had the information. Philo Vance told them everything he knew about the mainland operation. Even down to where he had hidden his payment for the services he had provided to Khariza's fedayeen.

"Only reason I know is 'cause I saw his laptop. He had it open on my desk. His guy, Ramsey, called him out to deal with something. I was curious so I sneaked a look. He had data on two sites. One was Bucklow. Something about April 9. Didn't mean much to me at the time."

"The other site?" Lyons asked.

"Some place along Interstate 20. An airstrip outside Dallas. Coyote Field. It had a date next to it, as well. April 12. That's all I know."

Blancanales walked out of the office, taking out his cell phone.

"Hey, what's he doing?"

Lyons managed a cold smile. "Canceling our reservations at the Dallas Holiday Inn."

Vance chewed that one over. Something clicked in his mind and he stared at Lyons.

"You lying mother. That...all that crap with the gun was a fuckin' con. Just to get me to talk. Well, the hell with you, buddy, 'cause I was doin' *you*. Yeah. Dallas ain't the place. I told you something you wanted to hear. So find out for yourself."

"You told us the truth, Philo. You were too scared to make anything up."

"So you say."

"Okay, Philo. You screwed *us*. So I'll take you on a trip. To Dallas. Make sure you have a ringside seat so you can sit through the blast that isn't going to happen. Then you can have a big laugh on us when you don't get crisped."

Vance's desert tan paled visibly as he stared at Lyons's impassive face. The Ironman's expression was fixed.

"No way. I ain't going anywhere with you maniacs."

"Philo, you don't have a choice. If you lied, there's nothing to lose. All it means is you get to stay out of jail a little longer."

Blancanales reappeared. He nodded to Lyons. He had called Stony Man and asked them to check out Coyote Field.

"We're taking Philo on a road trip. He's decided Dallas isn't the site after all, so I told him he can confirm it by sitting it out until after the deadline."

"Pretty smart way of proving his point."

"Oh, sure. Philo's really smart. Right, Philo?"

Vance realized he was on the spot. He had talked himself into a corner and there was no comfortable way out.

"No need for the trip. Dallas *is* the real site."

"Maybe we should still take him," Blancanales suggested. "Be embarrassing if it turned out he was lying."

"The hell with you bastards," Vance screamed. "You some kind of sick mothers, or what?"

"That's open for debate," Blancanales said.

"Time we left," Lyons said.

He used more of his plastic cuffs to secure Vance's ankles and wrists.

"Hey, hey," Vance yelled, struggling. "I need to change my pants. I wet them you fuckers scared me so bad."

"At least it'll give the police shrink something to talk to you about," Blancanales said.

Vance's yelling and ranting accompanied them down the stairs and outside.

"Vegas P.D. should be here in the next few minutes," Blancanales said as they climbed back in the SUV.

"We get a result?" Schwarz asked as he rolled the Navigator back toward the highway.

"Yeah," Lyons said. "Back to the airport. We're going to Dallas."

CHAPTER TEN

Chechnya

Conditions at the camp were far removed from those on board the *Petra*. As far as Razan Khariza was concerned, it was a mere passing thought. His time on the *Petra* had been an enjoyable but transitional period between then and now. Khariza had no problems with his current surroundings. They served their purpose and that purpose, had little to do with personal indulgences.

Khariza looked around the stone shelter. He had, in his time, lived in worse. He reminded himself he was an Iraqi warrior, a fedayeen who could mount a horse with ease and ride across the desert to face his enemy. That wasn't such a bad life to contemplate. Let the Americans, with their modern weapons, face a force of mounted and armed Iraqis. Then they would see how a war should be fought.

Khariza uttered a self-deprecating sound, snapping out of his reverie and back to the present.

To immediacy.

He pushed the wooden chair he was using away from the battered desk and crossed the chilled room to gaze out of the grimy window at the bleak Chechen landscape. There was no sun here, no sweep of dusty desert with a lone hawk circling the blue emptiness. Only gray rock and barren slopes, smoke rising from the other stone buildings of what had been a living village full of people. Now it was a mute reminder of its former self, windswept and wet from the cold rain that seemed to be a permanent feature at this time of year.

Khariza saw a battered, ex-Soviet military truck lurch into sight around the bend that signaled the beginning of the village. He watched it bump and bounce over the rutted ground, sending heavy spurts of water from beneath its wheels. Khariza watched it jerk to a stop. It lurched as the driver forgot to put it into neutral before he took his foot off the clutch. That meant the driver would be Dushinov. The Chechen Muslim, though an eager driver, hadn't yet mastered some of the techniques, so that driving with him was a new experience each time.

The driver's door crashed open, almost coming off its hinges, and a large, bearded figure, clad in bulky clothing, climbed out.

Zoltan Dushinov stood six foot four inches tall. He was broad, as well, making him a dominating presence. His resistance to the Russians was legendary in the area. Depending on which side you were on, Dushinov was either a hero or a murderous brigand. If he had been forced to choose, Dushinov would have favored the brigand title.

Not wanting to appear inhospitable, Khariza crossed the room and opened the door, moving to stand in the passage so that he was the first person Dushinov saw when he entered the building.

"Welcome back, my brother," Khariza said.

"Razan."

The two embraced, then stepped back. Khariza's eyes searched the other's face for a trace of the news he was expecting. Dushinov remained silent for a moment, then smiled, briefly, and nodded.

"We have the weapons on the truck. As we suspected, the airdrop was affected by the storm. It blew the consignment away from the drop zone. But we found it. Intact."

"That *is* good news."

Dushinov spread his arms. "Tomorrow you can start to train those recruits of yours. By God, they need training. Most of them can't tell one end of a gun from the other."

"I cannot fault them for that," Khariza said. "Those faithful have come great distances to help our fight. It would have been foolish of me to expect all of them to be seasoned fighters. But we will show them. Between us we will make them into fedayeen, into the fighters who will help to reshape Iraq."

"What about your Korean friends?"

"Much more receptive now I able to access those accounts. Already we have started to transfer money into a new facility where I will be able to withdraw without so much difficulty. The Swiss may be good at storing money and keeping it safe, but when it comes to paying it out they suddenly become like snails. There is so much protocol to go through. So many regulations. They are such a dismal people."

"You should let me put it in my bank," Dushinov said.

"You mean, the one under your mattress?"

Dushinov laughed. It was a loud, booming sound that rattled the windows.

"Maybe. But I can get to it when I want. Day or night, my bank never closes."

"Zoltan, do not forget I will be bringing you some of the money when I finish dealing with the Koreans. A small way of thanking you for what you have done."

"I won't refuse it," Dushinov said. "It will be very useful. You know I would have helped you, anyway. The money is secondary to how I feel about you and what has happened to Iraq."

"With your help I will train my soldiers and we will do what is needed to drive out the Americans and their allies."

"I'll get some help and have that truck unloaded for you."

Dushinov turned to go, then paused and turned back to Khariza.

"Is something wrong?" the Iraqi asked.

"These people who have been interfering with your plans."

"What about them? Are they here?"

"My people tell me they have heard of men offering money for your whereabouts."

"Who? It doesn't sound like the ones who captured Rasheed. Or who killed Rasifi and Kerim. They were professionals. Not the kind to offer money. If they come, it will be unexpectedly and they will have guns not checkbooks."

"So who are these men?"

Khariza shrugged. "If they show up again perhaps we will find out."

Dushinov turned and left the building. After a few moments Khariza made his way to the rear of the building, where Abdul Wafiq and Saeed Hassan were packing thick stacks of hundred-dollar bills into backpacks. The money was to be used to purchase a number of vehicles for use when Khariza went back into Iraq. There were faithful fedayeen in Iraq who could use the cash to buy vehicles and arrange hiding places for Khariza and his group. Within the country hard cash would be a necessity. Khariza needed secure places to hide prior to some of the hard action he had promised his faithful.

Khariza sat at the table and idly toyed with the thick wads of dollars.

"The Americans gave us the money in the first place," he said. "Now we use their money to destroy *their* hold on Iraq. Quite fitting."

"We were listening to some of the radio reports about the bombing in Bucklow. Do we accept it as a success, Razan?"

Khariza glanced across the table at Wafiq.

"Of course. The death toll will make the Americans reconsider just how safe their country is now. I could tell them that. It is not safe. Not any longer. We have proved we can enter America, purchase weapons and use them in our struggle. America's size and the diversity of their culture makes it easy for us. The country is too large to keep fully secure. And their communities are spread out so widely the authorities are unable to be in all places at once. So we strike here, there, many different locations. No pattern so they will not be able to trace us. Given time they might form some kind of trail after us. But by then our people will have completed their tasks and moved on."

"What about the cells the Americans have raided?" Hassan asked. "The locations lost and the people arrested?"

"Regrettable," Khariza said. "I have to admit something puzzles me. How the Americans suddenly seemed to become aware of those locations. How they walked in on Kerim during his visit to negotiate with that Mexican gunrunner. Coincidence? No. Too much happening at once. There has to be a sound explanation."

"Has someone betrayed us?" Hassan asked.

"It is to be considered," Khariza admitted. "As much as I hate to accept it."

"Sharii betrayed us," Wafiq reminded him. "Others could do the same."

"Then we will have to be vigilant."

"Trust no one," Wafiq went on.

"Does that extend to us?" Hassan asked.

Wafiq simply raised his shoulders.

"If we fall out among ourselves, all it does is benefit our enemies. Abdul is suggesting that we take care.
My brothers, we have too much to achieve. Dissent
within our own ranks is not an option." Khariza held out
his arms, smiling. "Come, let us go and inspect these
new weapons Zolton has brought. Then we should sit
down and discuss our upcoming strategy."

They left the building and commenced the walk to
the large storage building where the new consignment
of weapons was being offloaded.

"This is a miserable country," Wafiq said. "I fail to
see why Dushinov wants to fight over it. Does the sun
ever shine here?"

Khariza laughed, "Abdul, no one could ever accuse
you of being an optimist."

The truck was being unloaded into one of the stone
buildings. Khariza led the way inside and they located
the crates Dushinov had brought. The Iraqi released the
catches holding down a top and raised the hinged lid.
Inside the crate, resting on polystyrene-molded shells,
were SA-18 ground-to-air missiles.

"Kim Yeo has more of these at his warehouse, ready
to be shipped," Khariza said. He looked at the other
boxes in the consignment. There were more assault rifles, handguns, ammunition.

"I will feel better once we have completed our deal
with the North Koreans," Wafiq said. "All the rifles in
the world won't deter the Americans."

"Now we have the main accounts back in our hands,

that will happen soon. Kim Yeo will be talking to Sun Yang Ho anytime now. Once he does, the Koreans will start to move our consignment."

"Including the nuclear devices?"

"Especially the nuclear devices," Khariza said. "If we have to use them, the effect in Iraq will far outweigh what we are doing in America."

Stony Man Farm, Virginia

"LISTEN UP," Kurtzman said. "Something interesting came through from the FBI. While they were going through Vance's books they found a couple of semi-trailer units missing from the list. According to the stock records, they were still on site, but when they checked them out they were gone. So the Feds had a hard word with Mr. Vance, and it came out he let the rigs go to the wood-chip mill at Bucklow."

"Son of a bitch," Lyons said over the link to *Dragon Slayer*.

"We also have a preliminary report from the CSI investigation team at Bucklow. They've established the detonation point. Turns out the MOAB was mounted on a semi-trailer. The vehicle was burned down to the steel chassis, which was buckled to all hell, but the manufacturer's production number on a plate was still readable under lab analysis. The CSI team checked out that number and it was one of the missing units from Vance's lot."

"So the vehicle we're looking for can be identified from a similar chassis number if we need to?"

"Exactly."

Blancanales voice came over the link. "Question. The MOAB is supposed to be launched from an aircraft. Dropped by parachute over the target, then guided in by laser control. How the hell did they do it from the back of a trailer?"

"I spoke to some people at the facility where the MOABs are built. The bomb is fitted with a device that detonates it six feet from the ground. No hardship to mount the bomb that height on the trailer. It was probably concealed under a canvas sheet and driven to the picnic ground with all the other local vehicles. From what we learned there was a parade of trade vehicles as part of the celebration. The wood-chip mill was part of the local community. Who was going to question it being there? The driver only needed to position the vehicle and wait for the chosen time. My contact at the MOAB builders said it would be possible for a manual detonator to be fitted. All the driver had to do was set the detonator and wait to push the button."

"He went up with the truck?"

"It would be a surer way of setting the device off than relaying on a distance detonator. Too much interference from electronic equipment around the site. It could have blanked the signal. So they chose the easy option."

"Easy? Not for the guy who pushed the button."

"A suicide bomber, Pol. It's nothing new in the terrorist world."

"What the hell has it come to?"

"How close are you to Coyote Field?"

"I'd say we should be over the place in thirty," Grimaldi said.

"I'm trying to get some access to a satellite eye. See if I can spot the field and anything on it."

Akira Tokaido broke in. "I'm sending through details on the semi-trailer and the chassis number for ID."

He tapped in the transmit code and sent the data through to *Dragon Slayer*'s onboard computer.

"DO I HAVE TO GO through this again?" Brognola asked. "Just tell me which part you didn't understand, Captain Douglas."

The voice on the other end of the line rose again. The hard twang of the speaker's Texas accent grated on the big Fed's nerves, and he was fast losing patience with the stubborn attitude of the Ranger captain, who seemed to have taken everything Brognola had explained on a personal level. It was as if the man felt Brognola was treating him like a child. The fact he was acting like one hadn't escaped Brognola's attention.

"Now listen, Douglas," the big Fed snapped, dropping the rank, "I've had enough of your crap. I tried polite. I tried diplomatic. Obviously neither of those things are within your mental reach. So we'll do it your way. You stay away from the designated area. You make certain those roadblocks stay in place and you keep civilians away. I don't have time to argue. This isn't a request. It's an order that comes from as high as it gets. Try playing hero and we might end up with a second Bucklow. I take it you heard what happened there?"

"We heard. You think we don't have communications down here? Mister, this is Texas we're talking about, not the ass end of Hicksville."

"Then understand me, Douglas. Do what you've been told. I don't care if it upsets you, or makes you look useless. I'm trying to prevent a catastrophe and personal feelings do not bother me in the slightest."

"Mister, you are starting to piss me off."

"Douglas, is this number where you can be reached anytime?"

"Damn right it is."

"Stay by the phone. In about five minutes you could very well be getting a call from someone who will convince you and your people to stay put."

"The hell you say. The only man who could make me do that is the President of the United States."

"Douglas, I take some of my comments back."

"Huh?"

"Just don't make him mad, because he's not having too good a day."

Brognola broke the connection and punched in his White House direct number. He was smiling when he heard the President's voice on the other end of the line.

IN THE COMPUTER ROOM there was an air of expectancy as Kurtzman's SARS satellite came online. As soon as Kurtzman had control, he set the tracking coordinates and directed the satellite's electronic eye to scan the area of Texas where Coyote Field was located.

He had done some preliminary work and the field was used infrequently now, mainly by a few locals. The facilities had never been kept up to date and Coyote

Field had lagged behind other, more sophisticated establishments. There was a rundown control tower and a couple of dilapidated hangars.

Kurtzman saw these now as the SARS focused in on the derelict field. He brought the image up close and scanned the perimeter of the dusty, overgrown area, setting his computer to make a record of everything he was picking up.

The first item of significance was the main hangar, its doors open wide. Shadow prevented Kurtzman from making a detailed identification, but he did make out the rear end of a semi-trailer.

Coyote Field, it appeared, wasn't as deserted as might have been expected.

Kurtzman made contact with *Dragon Slayer* to pass on the news.

Aboard: Dragon Slayer

"HOW DO YOU WANT to do this?" Grimaldi asked.

He had the combat chopper on hold, some distance from Coyote Field, the engines on silent mode to reduce the chance of detection.

Lyons glanced up from viewing the monitor screen. Stony Man had patched through the SARS images for Able Team to absorb, giving them time to make their decision.

"I say we go in fast. You drop us, then ease off and use your weapons to back us if we need them."

Grimaldi nodded. "You got it."

"You okay for this?" Blancanales asked Schwarz.

Schwarz raised his eyebrows. They were about the only part of his face that didn't ache.

"I take that as a yes? Or are you impersonating Roger Moore again?"

They were in blacksuits, armed and ready to go. Able Team and Grimaldi were all aware of the importance of getting control of the second MOAB. The Bucklow atrocity was still on their minds. The images they had seen would be with them for some time to come and the taped message broadcast from Khariza still lingered in their thoughts.

Khariza and his fedayeen were intent on causing as much damage and suffering as they could within mainland U.S. Because of the information that had come from Rasheed's organizer, the local and federal agencies had been able to take out a number of the strike teams situated around the country. There were others still to be handled, and everyone involved was aware that Khariza might still have other cells, not listed by Rasheed, who would now be staying out of sight. Those cells, possibly now denied supplies of weapons, wouldn't go quietly. Their intentions would still be as they had been. To make strikes against vulnerable American targets. To create as much unrest as they could.

They might not find their way as free and clear as they had anticipated. Now that Khariza's plans had been identified, the American agencies and the American people would be ready to fight back. And fight back they would. Putting the U.S.A.'s back to the wall would make a difference.

A big difference.

"COMING ABOUT," Grimaldi said.

Lyons tapped him on the shoulder. "Put the pedal to the metal, Jack. Time to rock and roll."

Dragon Slayer dropped from the sky like a huge, sleek, black bird. Under Grimaldi's sure touch, the chopper streaked in across Coyote Field's weedstrewed strip, then swept broadside on as she hugged the ground, coming to a controlled hover a few feet above the concrete apron. The side hatch hissed open and Able Team went EVA, hitting the ground running, fanning out with their weapons online.

The second the last man exited the chopper Grimaldi hit the power and took the black aircraft into a rapid climb, bringing her nose around to cover the hangars and control tower.

"ON YOUR LEFT," Lyons snapped into his mike.

"Got him," Blancanales replied.

An armed figure had emerged from the control tower door. Lean, dark and wielding a 9 mm Uzi, the man opened fire as he spotted the black-clad Blancanales. His rapid burst was well short, chipping the concrete.

Blancanales, equipped with an M-16, pulled it to his shoulder, aimed and triggered a quick burst at his target. They punched him in the center chest, knocking the guy off his feet. He hit the wall behind him and fell facedown, his Uzi clattering across the concrete.

Somebody began to shout in Arabic and there was a flurry of movement from the second hangar. Armed men opened fire on Able Team. The Stony Man trio had already spaced themselves well apart. They returned fire from three positions. Schwarz had an M-203 grenade launcher attached to his M-16. He had loaded it with a smoke canister which he fired in through the hangar door. It landed with a soft thump, coils of thick smoke starting to issue from the canister when it detonated.

Lyons had cut off to one side, coming in at the hangar from a sharp angle, firing his SPAS shotgun as he neared the hangar opening. He caught one armed figure as the guy leaned out, coughing from smoke inhalation. The powerful charge took him in the left side of his torso, close to his shoulder, tearing out bloody flesh. The man went down on his knees, screaming wildly, clutching at his left arm as it hung by bloody tatters of flesh.

Gunfire erupted from both hangars, clipping the concrete around Able Team as they moved in with relentless determination, laying down steady and accurate return fire. Their shots pushed the hangar defenders back from the openings, deeper inside the structures where their ability to respond was reduced.

One man tried to clear the main door of the hangar holding the semi-trailer, exposing himself so he could take aim. He was targeting Lyons, briefly ignoring the other Able commandos. It was a fatal, final mistake. Schwarz, his M-16 snug against his shoulder, tracked the guy and fired. The M-16 jacked out two close shots. They hit the would-be shooter over the heart. He took a faltering step back, then sank into a sitting position on the hangar floor, remaining upright for a few seconds before folding over at the waist.

Blancanales hit the outside wall of the hangar, flattening against the metal. He edged along the wall until he reached the open doorway. From his position he could see the semi-trailer's rear. He could also hear movement from the shadowed interior—the scrape of footsteps. He held his position for a few seconds.

"Going in," he said into his throat mike.

Without further delay Blancanales ducked low and went inside, moving instantly to his left, eyes searching the comparative gloom of the hangar. He could still hear movement deeper inside the structure. Blancanales dropped to a crouch and closed in on the semi-trailer's rear. He lowered his head and flattened out, sliding in beneath the vehicle, checking out the back section of the hangar.

He saw legs and feet. Counted three people.

Blancanales took the farthest target first. He brought his M-16 into target acquisition and triggered fast shots that ripped through the hardman's lower limbs, dropping the guy to the floor. As the screaming gunner's weapon clattered to the floor, Blancanales hit him with a single shot to the head, laying the guy out flat. Swiveling, Blancanales tracked a second guy as the man began to move. He caught his target on the run, putting 5.56 mm slugs in through his ankles, splintering bones and removing the man's ability to remain upright. As the man collapsed on his knees, the Able Team commando put three shots into his lower torso, one of the slugs blowing out the far side of the man's body. He fell sideways, his skull cracking against the concrete as he sprawled on the floor.

The third man took off for the rear of the hangar, his footsteps hard against the concrete. Blancanales rolled out from beneath the semi-trailer and pushed to his feet, scanning the interior, and spotted the guy heading for the far end of the building and a possible exit.

The rear section of the hangar held a lot of equipment that had been pushed there to keep it out of the way. Blancanales's quarry missed his way and found himself blocked off from the building's far wall. He paused, looking for a way through, then realized he was losing ground. He turned, brought up the SMG he carried and laid a burst in the direction of the man following him.

Blancanales heard the slugs hit the concrete, lifting thin flakes from the surface.

"Give it up," Blancanales yelled.

"No." The man raised his weapon.

Blancanales hit him with a short burst from the M-16, knocking him back into the metal barrier. The guy bounced off and fell facedown, his blood spattering the oily floor.

There was a rattle of sound behind Blancanales. He spun and spotted a moving figure in the cab of the semi-trailer. The man was pulling an assault rifle into position, freeing the driver's door at the same time. The Able Team commando raised the M-16 and jacked off another burst that blew out the windshield and went on to punch into the gunner's chest and throat. The man jerked in agony, falling back against the seat, the rifle slipping from his dead fingers.

Blancanales scanned the hangar. There was no more sound or movement. He headed back toward the semi-trailer. Reaching the rear, he yanked the locking lever and released the doors, swinging them wide open. As light flooded the interior, Blancanales saw the orange-yellow, thirty-foot outline of the MOAB, resting on a metal trestle.

"Bomb located," he said into his mike.

SCHWARZ HEARD Blancanales's words as he returned gunfire coming from the hangar into which he had lobbed the smoke grenade. The thick smoke was still rolling out the door. No one else had come out of the hangar, which concerned Schwarz to a degree. He was sure there were more of the opposition in there but their no-show had him puzzled.

"Hey, Pol, is there a back door in these hangars?"

"Yeah."

"Great," Schwarz said.

"You want backup?"

"I'll handle it. You keep your eye on that bomb."

"Watch yourself."

"And you."

Schwarz moved to the wide doorway and peered inside. The thick, curling smoke obscured his vision. He saw that the density was less on the far side of the hangar, so he slipped inside and angled across.

The building contained two panel trucks and a dusty Ford 4x4.

As Schwarz emerged from the smoke, he saw two armed figures making for the parked vehicles. One man wrenched open the driver's door of the Ford while the other turned, attracted by Schwarz's footsteps.

Schwarz raised his M-16. "It's not going to happen," he said. "Put the guns down and get on the floor. Do it now so I don't have to shoot you."

"Why should I listen to you?" the closer man asked.

"We have the bomb now. You don't get to use it."

The two men exchanged glances. "No. You are lying. As all you Americans lie."

"Just don't start with old propaganda speeches. I'm not in the mood. Put down the guns."

The man who had been opening the Ford's door became agitated. He began to yell at Schwarz in Arabic, punching the air with his fist. He stepped away from the 4x4, still shouting.

"I told you…" The guy suddenly brought his SMG up from where it hung by his side.

"Damn you," Schwarz breathed and fired, laying a pair of slugs into the man's chest. The impact kicked the guy backward, bouncing him off the side of the 4x4. He slithered to his knees, then toppled back, ending up halfsitting against the front wheel.

The moment he pulled the trigger Schwarz moved the muzzle of the M-16 to cover the second guy. He had turned to look at his fallen partner, then swiveled at the hips, his own weapon angling up in Schwarz's direction. The trigger went back and the SMG stuttered loudly, shell casings jumping from the eject port to bounce as they hit the concrete floor.

Schwarz felt something burn across his left hip, the force of the impact pulling him off balance. Even so, he held the M-16 on target and returned fire, and saw his shots punch the other guy in the high shoulder. Dark flecks blew out from the guy's shirt. Schwarz hauled himself upright and gripped the rifle, taking a second to hold his aim before he fired again, jacking two, three shots at the target. This time his aim was on line and the 5.56 mm slugs thumped home with deadly effect. One shot shredded the side of the man's throat, blood starting to pump out almost instantly. The guy fell against the Ford, hands splayed out across the front fender. Blood jetted across his hands, streaking the paintwork of the 4x4 as the guy lost his balance and hit the concrete.

Schwarz clamped a hand over his aching hip. He could feel blood leaking out of the rip in his blacksuit, wetting his fingers.

"Damned if this isn't my week," he muttered to himself. "Hey, Jack, you picking me up?"

"I'm here."

"Could do with a bandage."

"You got it, pal."

CARL LYONS KICKED IN the door to the control tower. He went up the worn wooden stairs two at a time, the SPAS shotgun tracking ahead of him. As he neared the top he picked up excited voices and the scrape of footsteps on the floor above him.

His blood was up.

Lyons was as angry as he could be. Over the past few days the intrigue and the twisted plans of Razan Khariza had pushed the Ironman to the edge. He had seen enough death and destruction caused by the fedayeen crew to last him a lifetime. Bad enough what they were doing in their own region of the world, but they had brought it to America, to *his* country, importing their fanatic hatred, their stolen money to buy off whoever they wanted, and the sheer baseness of their brutality.

Bucklow, Texas. A small community where the population most likely carried little, or no, hostility toward Iraq. Where families only wanted the same as any family the world over. To live safe. To get on with their daily lives. And to watch their babies and children grow and play and laugh in the Texas sun. That right. That simple, God-given right, at the heart of every family in America, had been wrenched from their grasp in those terrible moments when the bomb had detonated at the Bucklow picnic ground. The hungry, grasping, life-devouring fire had denied them their birthright.

Carl Lyons's eyes mirrored those dying moments as he reached the head of the stairs and turned to face the trio of fedayeen loyalists, the barrel of the shotgun already on line. His face was hardened by his thoughts, lips peeled back from his teeth in a snarl of utter contempt for the men who were willing and ready to bring down the same fate on yet another American community.

The sound of a single pistol shot was drowned by the hard boom of the 12-gauge. Flame and smoke gushed from the muzzle as Lyons tripped the trigger and used the remaining shots in the magazine.

He fired and traversed and fired again, his bursts blurring almost into a single rip of sound. His targets, their own attempts at defending themselves snatched from their hands by the relentless onslaught, were blown across the control room in a welter of blood, pulped flesh, splintered bone and shredded clothing. Blood spattered the control tower windows, splashed the control board.

When the SPAS locked on an empty chamber, Lyons stood stock-still, silently observing his kill zone. He heard one of the hit men groaning, moving slightly where he had slumped across the control board. He was bloody and in shock, one hand flapping ineffectually.

Lyons moved closer, easing his Python from its holster. He put a single shot through the wounded man's head, then he turned and did the same with the other two downed terrorists.

The radio crackled into life and a voice began to speak in Arabic. Lyons crossed to the control desk and leaned over it. He picked up the hand mike and pressed the transmit button.

"Who the hell is this?" There was a pause, then a voice spoke in accented English.

"Am I speaking to Coyote Field?"

"Damn right, you prick, and I'm guessing you were expecting your fedayeen brothers. Am I right?"

"Who are you?"

"I'm the American son of a bitch who just blew your buddies all to hell."

Lyons picked up the approach of a heavy aircraft. He peered out the control tower window as the sound grew louder.

"Permission to land denied. You won't be picking

up your bomb load, sucker. Not today. Not ever. You came to my country and tried your shit. Well, not this time. You want pain? You want suffering? You can have it."

Lyons cut the connection and spoke into his throat mike.

"You get that, Jack?"

"Affirmative."

"Can you get a lock on that bastard?"

"Already have. He's starting to turn away. Looks like you scared him off."

"Take him out, Jack. That fucker doesn't go home."

Dragon Slayer slid into view, then accelerated as Grimaldi boosted the power. The combat chopper climbed rapidly, tailing the dark bulk of the aircraft that had been making its approach to Coyote Field.

The radio crackled again and the accented voice came through the speaker.

"American? American, are you there?"

"Want to beg now?"

"I want to negotiate. We are unarmed."

"Negotiate? Like you let all those people in Bucklow negotiate?"

"That was an act of war. And as this is war, we must be treated as prisoners. You will accept our surrender. We will land and you must take us prisoner and recognize our rights."

"Jack, you get that?"

"I heard."

"What do you say, Jack?"

"I say I got these suckers in my sights."

"Finger on the button?"

"Just so."

"Hit it."

The heat-seeker missile shot from the weapon pod under *Dragon Slayer*'s stub wing and it lanced across the sky, curving slightly as it picked up the source from its target.

The explosion was hard, flame and smoke blossoming as the aircraft's disintegration was aided by its own fuel tanks blowing. Debris was scattered in a wide arc, dropping to the empty ground below, followed by the broken, blazing carcass of the plane itself. A secondary explosion followed the impact. Dark smoke billowed into the sky, the rumble of the detonation rising, then rapidly fading back to silence.

"Welcome to America," Lyons said. "Fuck with us we fuck you."

CHAPTER ELEVEN

Negev Desert, Israel

Calvin James cleared the low, crumbling stone wall and dropped to a crouch, eyes scanning the immediate area. The first thing he saw was the large camouflage net extending out from the roofs of the low buildings, across the area where they had been secured on posts driven into the ground. The sandy enclosure concealed by the net held the accoutrements of a small group, kept neat and stored so that the camp could be quickly evacuated.

He didn't have time for much more thorough scan. On the far side of the enclosure an armed guard turned, alerted even though James had made barely a sound. His hands swung the AK from his shoulder, eyes seeking the intruder.

The Stony Man commando was already ahead, his H&K on line the moment he had touched down from his jump over the wall.

James eased back on the trigger, firing a short burst that hit the guy in the chest, tumbling him back and off his feet. The guy landed hard, starting to gag as blood bubbled up his throat from a punctured lung.

There was movement from inside the building, more from around the far side where Hawkins had made his entrance, and the camouflaged enclosure erupted with the sounds of autofire.

FOR BEN SHARON the next few minutes became the most important of his life as he battled to stay alive while defeating the invaders of his country.

He had, like the others, breached the enclosure and found himself confronted by a startled man carrying an ammunition box. As they held each other's gaze for a heartbeat, it was Sharon who broke the frozen moment. He was almost touching the other, so he swung his MP-5, slamming it hard across the terrorist's head. The brutal blow spilt the guy's skin, blood welling up instantly and streaking his face. As the hardman stumbled back, dropping the ammo box and grabbing for the pistol on his hip, Sharon stepped in close. He drove one knee up into his adversary's testicles, drawing a shrill cry, then delivered another kick with the hard sole of his boot into the guy's left knee. Sharon didn't hold back and he heard the crunch of shattered bone as the leg gave and guy fell, his leg unable to support his weight. Briefly in the clear, Sharon stepped back, brought his H&K around and fired a burst that punched into his opponent's heart.

Moving on, Sharon caught a glimpse of someone ahead of him, emerging from an opening door. The Israeli caught the gleam of a rifle barrel as it swung in his direction. He dropped to the ground, hearing the crackle of autofire and the vicious snap of the slugs hitting the wall behind him. Gritty dust showered his back. Sharon rolled, twisting, and pulled his H&K from under his body. He saw the shooter turning to find him, then he was triggering the H&K, angling the muzzle up in the direction of the moving figure. The spray of shots climbed from the target's waist up to his chest. From his almost-prone position Sharon fired again, his second burst coring in under the guy's jaw, through his head, lodging just beneath his skull.

Sharon was on his feet before the man hit the ground, heading directly for the door the guy had exited by. He ducked below the low top of the door and was confronted by a guy pushing up off a canvas seat in front of a communication system. The man was reaching for the assault rifle leaning against the com set table. Bringing the H&K on track, Sharon hit the guy with a burst that pushed him across the room and slammed him against the wall. The stricken man slid down the wall and lay curled up at its base.

THE SOUND OF AUTOFIRE was heavy in the air as T. J. Hawkins came face-to-face with his first adversary. The guy was big, stripped to the waist, his torso muscled and toned. He lunged at Hawkins as the Phoenix Force warrior stepped around the edge of a crumbled wall. Hawkins swung his H&K into play, but the terrorist was too close. The guy's big hands snatched at the SMG, using it to swing Hawkins off balance. He let go with one hand and used it to back-fist the American across the side of the head. The blow dazed him and sent him reeling. The other guy moved in fast, his free hand swinging and clouting Hawkins across the face.

Hawkins tasted blood as he dropped to the ground, still holding his SMG. The other guy clung to the other end of the weapon, refusing to give Hawkins any advantage. It meant he had to bend over to maintain his grip, and Hawkins launched a full leg kick, connecting with the guy's face. The terrorist grunted from the solid kick, his grip on Hawkins's H&K slackening, giving the American the slight advantage he needed. Hawkins yanked the H&K from the big man's grasp, rolled until he was clear, then came up on one knee. The muzzle of the MP-5 targeted on the other guy, then spit out 9 mm slugs that cored in through the target's chest and destroyed his heart and lungs. The guy went down without a sound.

Hawkins pushed upright, moving forward. As he rounded the corner of a wall, he saw James ahead of him, there was a body on the ground close by the black Phoenix commando.

Movement caught Hawkins's eye and he spotted two armed figures emerging from a doorway behind James.

"Cal, behind you," Hawkins yelled, and ran forward, his H&K tracking the pair.

James dropped to a crouch, twisting to face the newcomers.

Hawkins targeted the hardman closer to his team-mate, firing instantly, his shots punching in through the guy's side. Bloody slugs burst from the guy's body as he collapsed to the ground.

James and the second terrorist fired together, their shots merging.

Hawkins saw James jerk to one side, pain etched across his face. The guy the black commando had fired on stumbled, then went facedown in the sand, body jerking in response to the sudden pain.

Hawkins ran across to where James had sunk to his knees, hand pressed to his hip.

"Cal? You hit?"

James shook his head. "Thought I was."

He moved his hand and Hawkins saw the shattered handle of the sheathed knife on James's belt. A bullet had struck it a glancing blow, driving the knife against James's hip.

"You are one lucky dude."

"Yeah. And only a bruise to show for it."

Hawkins turned, checking their surroundings. It had been the sudden silence that had unnerved him. He remained alert until Ben Sharon stepped into view.

"I think we're clear," he said, glancing at James. "You okay?"

"A bruise is all," James said. He unsheathed his knife and held it up. "Close, but no cigar."

"Come and look at what they had in here," Sharon said. He led them into the airless room and the communication system.

"Small generator on the outside wall for juicing up the battery pack, and a radio for vocal communications. The laptop here is connected to a satellite uplink."

Sharon led them around the edge of the wall and indicated the dish antenna mounted on an extendable aluminum pole that could be raised up through the open roof and through the camouflage net.

"Gives them plenty of range and access to satellite scanning," James said. "They can talk to anyone they want from here and use digital scanning to pinpoint ground images."

Back in the communication room James bent over the laptop. There was an image on the screen that looked like a satellite terrain scan. He used the keyboard to access data input and was confronted by text in Arabic.

"Anybody?" he asked.

Neither Sharon nor Hawkins could help.

James perched himself on the canvas seat and began to access the computer system. He worked silently for a few minutes until he found the e-mail facility and established contact with Stony Man.

"Can he do that?" Sharon asked.

Hawkins nodded.

Once he had the e-mail link established, James was able to send a message to Stony Man. He worked quickly, explaining what they had found and advising that he was going to transmit the data. He informed Stony Man that the documents would need to be translated, and that the team might have to move on. Any intel would have to be sent to Sharon's Mossad contact in Tel Aviv.

James sent the message. He waited until he received confirmation it had been received, then deleted all the current information.

"Ben, why don't you call Davi in with the chopper?"

Sharon nodded and moved outside to use his Tac-Com unit.

James and Hawkins searched the communication room. Apart from the radio and laptop, there was nothing else of value. The occupants had committed nothing to paper. Everything they had was on the laptop. James noted that it was a high-end Japanese machine. The radio equipment had been manufactured in the same country.

"Somebody is probably making big bucks selling this equipment," he said.

"Always a market for this kind of stuff, Cal. Same as the arms dealing. If you have the money, you've got all you need."

Sharon reappeared. He had a bundle in his arms and threw it on the ground.

"Our dead guys are a mix. Iraqi, possibly Algerian. No Palestinians. But look at this. All Palestinian-made clothing. The bastards even left the labels inside."

"Little crude, isn't it?" Hawkins said. "Doesn't exactly scream genuine, does it?"

"The climate in the region is fragile at best," Sharon said. "If these were waved in front of TV cameras, people wouldn't ask why were they left behind. It would be enough to set off a few hotheads. Maybe a few hundred hotheads. By the time they reached the streets and spread the news, there would have been bodies found wearing those same clothes."

"Brushfire tactics," James said. "Start a small fire and before you know it you have an inferno. And by then it's too late to put out."

"Maybe we can use this stuff to turn things around," James said. "Get your TV people to show what we found here. Show the communication setup, identify the bodies, convince the Israeli and Palestinian public this is a ploy by someone trying to mix things between you both."

"We don't have anything to lose," Sharon said. "Davi should be here in a few minutes. I got him to contact the military. They're going to send in an armed unit to take over this place and deal with anyone who might turn up."

"What about the thought that maybe these guys were here to guide someone in? Namely something in the air," Hawkins said.

"There will be air cover over this region within the hour. Radar scanning, as well. Anyone who flies into this area will be tracked and challenged."

"They might still try," Hawkins said.

The sound of Davi's chopper reached their ears.

"I hope they do," Sharon said.

They waited until the helicopter had touched down. They would have to wait at the oasis until the military squad showed up.

"Come on, and I'll let you taste that water," Sharon said.

"I'm bringing along this laptop," James said, uncoupling the computer. He tucked it under his arm. "We might be able to pull more data from it."

Hawkins turned to follow Sharon. James trailed after them, his bruised hip starting to ache now. He took his time, but not just because of his hip. He had things on his mind, such as the fact that Khariza was willing to launch an attack on a nuclear plant, despite the possible aftereffects across the region. If radioactivity was released, it could drift across the border into Egypt, across into Jordan or Saudi Arabia.

James began to wonder if Razan Khariza was more than just irresponsible. He was thinking along the lines of maybe a little crazy.

There was another, heavier worry he was carrying—how was the other half of Phoenix Force faring in Hong Kong?

CHAPTER TWELVE

Over Korea Bay, Yellow Sea

McCarter leaned toward the window, peering out as the plane began to bank. They were over the Yellow Sea and gray light was starting to show in the early-morning sky. As the plane started to descend, he was able to see the ragged coastline of North Korea. Out in the bay were scattered islands, and McCarter realized they weren't aiming for the main landmass. Instead the plane had leveled out, coming down faster now. They were going to land on one of the islands.

Slumping back in the rigid seat, McCarter caught Encizo's eye. The Cuban leaned forward.

"This could be interesting," he said.

"That's one way of putting it."

Manning, sitting beside Encizo, opened his eyes. For the past hour he had been sleeping, or at least feigning sleep.

"You wanted to find out where they were getting their weapons. Looks like your wish will come true, Dorothy."

One of the armed Chinese stood and approached the Phoenix Force trio. He thrust his assault rifle in their direction, snapping harshly at them.

McCarter's slim knowledge of Cantonese got him the gist of the words. He didn't let on he understood. Playing dumb where the language was concerned could help at some stage, though not right now. McCarter simply shrugged, holding up his cuffed hands.

"What's got up your nose? What the hell am I going to do? Take over the plane?"

"They do not trust you. Even though you are secured."

McCarter glanced up and saw Kim Yeo standing to one side.

"You lot aren't as dumb as you look," the Briton said.

"You continue to bait me," Yeo said. "Be careful. I may rise to your taunts and decide to kill you now."

McCarter refused to back down, staring directly at Yeo until the Chinese looked away. He spoke to the guard who returned to his seat.

"Enjoy the rest of the flight. We will be landing in a few minutes."

"Hell, David, are you trying to get yourself shot?" Encizo asked.

"He hasn't brought us all this way to kill us now."

"You're one-hundred-percent sure of that?"

"No."

"I didn't think so."

They felt the bump as the plane touched down, then sped along an uneven runway. The brakes were applied and the aircraft began to slow. Glancing out his side window again, McCarter saw they were running parallel with the sea. The wing of the plane extended out over the edge of the island. Even though McCarter was able to see the choppy water of the bay, he could barely make out the North Korean coastline. The plane slowed, rocking slightly as wind buffeted it, then came to a full stop. The engines were cut and as the noise faded, the sound of the wind could be heard.

"No sunblock needed here," Manning said.

"You will come now," Yeo ordered. "Remember you are now on North Korean soil. They really do not like Westerners. I suggest you contain yourselves. Unlike we Chinese, these Koreans have little sense of humor."

"Would you if you lived here?" Manning asked.

Yeo only smiled briefly.

STANDING BESIDE THE PLANE Phoenix Force and Henry Lee looked around. The outlook was bleak. The island, larger than they had realized, had little to recommend it. Rocky and flat, with barely any form of vegetation, it was open to the extremes of weather. The wind they had felt rocking the plane was stronger in the open. It buffeted them, tugging at their clothing and chafing their exposed skin. There were frequent sprays of sea water, picked up by the wind as it swept across the island. The spray was chilled.

Yeo called out orders to his men and they ushered their captives across the open landing area. Some three hundred yards away were rows of long, low buildings. As they got closer, they were able to see that the buildings were large, with wide, roll-up doors. A number of open trucks were parked outside one of the buildings and a lesser number of Jeep-type vehicles.

McCarter glanced across at Manning and Encizo, who nodded slightly. The Briton turned to look in Lee's direction. The Chinese gave him a similar response.

Yeo directed them toward one of the buildings. One of the Chinese ran ahead and pushed open a small door set to one side of the main one. They all trooped inside and the door was closed behind them.

The interior of the building was lit from banks of fluorescent lights suspended from the roof beams. They threw cold illumination onto the floor of the building.

Down the left side of the structure a line of rooms, built from wood panels and glass partitions, ran half the length of the building.

The main floor area was given over to storage. Here were lines of wooden packing cases of various shapes and sizes. A number of men in plain coveralls were busy with open packing cases, filling them from pallets being moved around on forklift.

"It's all very impressive, don't you think?" Yeo asked. "The first time I saw it I realized how efficient these North Koreans are."

"Not so efficient at feeding their own people, are they?" Manning said. "Too busy building missiles and statues to the Great Leader."

"You could put that to our host," Yeo suggested. "His reaction would be interesting to see."

He turned, indicating a slim figure dressed in a simple black tunic and pants. There was something in his manner, his thin face with its high, prominent cheekbones, that warned them he was a man of distinctly hostile moods. He moved quickly, hands at his sides, the hard-soled shoes he wore making sharp rapping sounds on the hard floor.

A silent pair of black-clad men followed him closely. The carried auto pistols in holsters on their belts.

Kim Yeo turned to face the man, inclining his head as a form of greeting. The other made no response. Instead he stopped to inspect the four captives.

Sun Yang Ho, the North Korean weapons negotiator, the man who was offering Razan Khariza his deal.

"Why have you brought these people here?" Ho asked in English, it being the common language between himself and Yeo, because neither could speak the other's native tongue.

"I am on my way to a rendezvous with Khariza after we complete our business. He will want to see them. And I thought it would interest them to see how efficiently your operation is run. After all, they have been interfering in Khariza's operation for some time. Now they can see how futile their efforts have been."

"Keep them out of my way, Yeo. They are American garbage. We have matters to discuss. There is no time to be wasted on these animals." He was about to turn away when he saw Lee. "Why is he with them?"

"Their contact man. He belongs to one of those irritating freedom groups working against the government."

"Then you should have killed him immediately. Not wasted valuable time bringing him along. Yeo, have you not learned anything? Alive, your enemies are dangerous. Dead they can do no harm."

Yeo considered the Korean's words. As he fell in beside Ho, he spoke quickly to one of his men.

The Chinese turned around and raised his assault rifle.

Encizo, watching the Chinese, realized what was going to happen. The Cuban pushed by Manning, already forming a shouted warning, but he was too late.

The assault rifle punched out a harsh volley of shots that hit Henry Lee in the torso, knocking him back. Lee stumbled and fell to his knees, his face showing an expression of stunned horror. He started to fall over, pushing out his bound hands to stop himself. The Chinese triggered more shots and they burst through Lee's upraised hands, taking off fingers, before they struck him in the face. Lee hit the floor, his body shuddering.

"You piece of…" Encizo yelled.

He would have gone for Yeo if one of the Chinese guards hadn't stepped in front of him. He raised his rifle and slammed the butt across the side of Encizo's head. The solid blow dropped the Cuban to his knees, head down.

"You see how they react," Ho said. "Too much emotion. They act before they understand the situation. And ultimately they suffer for it."

HO LED YEO ACROSS the building, pushing open the door to one of the rooms. He indicated for Yeo to sit across from him at the table dominating the room. There were computer terminals and telephones on the table. Ho used one of the keyboards and brought data on to the screen of the monitor in front of him.

"Khariza's deposits have been transferred to our account," the Korean said. "Shipments are already under way. Further shipments will now follow."

Ho tapped more keys, and on a side table on the other side of the room a printer began to push out a continuous sheet. The Korean pushed to his feet and collected the printout, folded it and handed it to Yeo.

"Please deliver this to the colonel when you see him. It is a list of the ordnance in the first shipment."

Yeo took the printout. He placed it on the table, gently tapping it with the fingers of his right hand.

"Am I detecting some impatience, Kim Yeo?"

"Much of Khariza's strategy revolves around the availability of the nuclear devices. He will be asking about them when I meet him."

The Korean nodded. He leaned forward and worked at his keyboard. Finally he raised his head.

"Purchase of the warheads from our Russian contact took time. Following the actual delivery, my technicians had to convert them from the original configuration to something capable of being carried easily. And there was the matter of the trigger devices." Ho stood and crossed the room. A coffeemaker stood on a wheeled trolley. Ho poured two cups and returned to the table, placing one in front of Yeo.

"Understand this, Yeo. I am not offering excuses. It is not in my nature. I am merely explaining the longevity of this operation. It is not as simple as making this coffee."

"I was not suggesting any deliberate lateness. It is more a need to placate Razan Khariza. Now that he has his operation under way, he is becoming increasingly anxious to carry it through."

"Which I understand. Military strategy requires forward momentum. Too many delays and the advantage can be lost. You can inform the colonel that his nuclear devices are now complete and are being loaded as we speak. They will leave within the next half hour. Delivering nuclear devices is not the same as sending out crates of rifles. Assure the colonel that we are taking every precaution possible. He will get his bombs. He needs to remain patient a little longer."

Yeo nodded. "I will pass along your message. And thank you, Ho, for being so direct. I understand the reasons for your caution."

Ho sipped his coffee. He placed his cup carefully on the table, nudging it with the tips of his fingers.

"Tell me something, Kim Yeo, and this conversation will not go further than this room. What are your feelings about Colonel Khariza? Do you truly believe he is capable of carrying out his plans for Iraq?"

Yeo smiled. "I have had the same thoughts myself. When Khariza first contacted me, it took me a little time before I accepted he could do it. I believe he can. He has people placed within the U.S. Weapons and funds are available to them. Many of his people have been in America for a number of years. After the first Gulf War, Hussein ordered Khariza to infiltrate America with loyalists prepared to sit by and wait for the day the call came. They were told it could be years but nothing had to be done until then because it was to be an all-out campaign. Since the Iraq war, those infiltrators have been put on alert. Many others have been smuggled into America from many places. Islamic believers have volunteered, willing to sacrifice themselves. And Khariza's people have recruited Americans themselves, people willing to work for the vast amounts of money being offered."

"Greed can close the eyes to anything," Ho said. "We have had a number of our own people selling out for money and a new life. Some have succeeded, others we have caught and dealt with."

"It was a cell of Khariza's people who organized the theft of the two MOAB bombs from the American airbase in Florida," Yeo informed him. "They worked on that for almost six months. They used computers to access personnel files, seeking out likely individuals they might recruit. In the end they found two people with Muslim backgrounds and went to work on them."

"Blackmail?"

"Extremely direct. They kidnapped a member from each family and made them vanish. Then they contacted each man and sent them tapes showing them their family members being tortured. The threat was simple and explicit. If the men did not cooperate, further members of their families would be taken and subjected to the same situation. Both men and their families were to carry on as normal. They were being watched and to prove it they were sent photographs of themselves going about their everyday existence. There was no discussion. No negotiation. To make the two men realize they were not making empty threats, they were each sent a package. The packages contained a severed hand from the kidnap victims. Not very sophisticated. Or even original, but it emphasized the severity of the threat. And of course if there were any approaches to the authorities in any way, the packages would start to arrive regularly."

"And they got their bombs," Ho confirmed.

"Indeed. One was detonated as Khariza had planned. On April 9."

Ho managed a smile. "A clever touch. A date significant to both Iraq and the town of Bucklow. What about the second bomb?"

"I believe it should have already been detonated. I sensed a little reluctance on Khariza's part to discuss it when I last spoke to him. He was disappointed that a number of his weapon caches within the U.S. had been discovered by the local and federal authorities. Not all, by any means, and there have been a significant number of attacks on the American mainland."

"He seems to be having better results from his decoy attacks around the Middle East region. And within Iraq itself."

"An easier option," Yeo said. "The Middle East is an area already restless. States are eyeing their neighbors with suspicion, fearful who will be next. And Khariza's loyalists are there to keep the fires stoked. An attack here, another there. Implicate the neighbor over the border and let the fires burn. If Khariza can keep things going, he could have the whole region in uproar."

"His plan to use the nuclear devices? Has he given you any details on this?"

Yeo shook his head. "That one he is keeping silent about. No matter how many times I have asked him Khariza is not talking."

"No matter. As long as he was willing to pay for those three bombs, I am happy to sit back and wait."

"My commission for arranging the deal will satisfy my curiosity."

Ho finished his coffee. "Let us have another cup, then we will go and look at what Khariza's money has bought him."

War Room, Stony Man Farm, Virginia

"I STILL KEEP SEEING the look on Aaron's face when you stood up to him," Barbara Price said. "It was worth the wait."

Erika Dukas, seated across the table from Price, shuffled her papers. They were the first to arrive in the War Room following Brognola's call.

"To be honest, I was ready to run at first. Then I figured, why not go for it? What could happen? He wasn't really going to eat me." She caught Price's eye. "Was he?"

Price grinned. "No. And you proved your point. There's something I wanted say before but never really got a proper chance. That was brilliant work you did on the translation, Erika. It gave us some important pointers."

"Thanks. But like I said, it's what you got me here for. So I was just doing my job."

"Some job," Price said.

They heard the secure door open, and several people entered the room.

Kurtzman led the way. Akira Tokaido was close behind, a pleased grin on his face when he spotted Erika at the table. Able Team was here in force. Hermann Schwarz took his time as he crossed to the table. His face was badly bruised, the swelling increasing the effect. Dukas had heard about the beating he had received at the hands of Khariza's people during his captivity. This was the first time she had seen him since Able Team had returned from the field, and she was a little shocked at his appearance. If anything, it brought home to her the reality of the work these men did. The risks they undertook to keep the peace as it were.

Seeing Schwarz returned Dukas's thoughts to what had happened in Texas. The entire Farm had been shown the TV footage of what had happened at Bucklow. It had been the simplest way of demonstrating how far Khariza and his group were prepared to go to maintain their threats. The sights and the distress of the survivors had been sobering viewing. Nothing had prepared Erika Dukas for the utter callousness of the attack. As the newest recruit to the Stony Man roster, Dukas had become a part of what was a group who worked out of the limelight and who faced on-the-spot crisis with a calmness and a dedication that surprised her. It also made her realize she had been granted a chance to be part of this team. For that she would always be grateful to Barbara Price for thinking of her.

Hal Brognola was the last to take his place at the table. He placed a file in front of him and opened it, then paused for a few seconds.

"Still no contact with Phoenix," he finally said. "Two of Henry Lee's team found dead isn't a good sign, but it doesn't mean we write Phoenix off. No way that's going to happen."

"What's the answer, Hal?" Blancanales asked. He looked around the table. "Do we go in and look for them? Cal and T.J. are still on assignment in Israel. No way we can pull them out."

"We're working on something right now."

"What about Mei Anna?" Lyons asked. "She knows the territory out there. Why not ask for her help?"

"Barb spoke to her some hours ago. Anna is on a USAF plane heading right for us as we speak. They flew her out of Lakenheath. She'll land at Andrews. I'm going out to meet her once we wrap this up."

"So let's move on for now," Price said. "We need to cover other things. Aaron?"

Kurtzman passed out thin files containing copies of data he had extracted from his computer searches.

"Everything we've been able get from the stuff you people brought back. Cell phones. Credit cards. Anything we could check on. Telephone accounts. Numbers called."

Tokaido held up one sheet. "We hacked into anything with a name attached to it. Like this guy, Radic Zehlivic. On the surface he's a clever guy who made his fortune buying and selling. Very smart. So smart he started to get lazy. It could be he figured no one would connect him to what he was doing on behalf of Khariza—providing a lot of supposedly covert assistance soon after the Iraq war started. All in the background. Telephone calls are the quickest way to make contact. Trouble is, they leave traces, and Zehlivic seems to have believed using the Cadot's Nest account would hide everything from prying eyes. Once we made the connection between the business and Zehlivic, it gave us a base to start from."

"We have enough to connect Khariza to all the players in the game," Kurtzman said. "The gunrunners in Santa Lorca. In Mexico. We cross-checked calls back and forth. Luiz Santos. Jafir Rasifi. Philo Vance. Read the lists. It all starts to come together. In brief, Khariza has one hell of a network running his operation. We've hit him where it hurts and done a great deal of damage to his plans—cut off his South American arms supply, terminated a good number of those weapons caches throughout the country, stopped the second MOAB from being used."

"Not the first," Schwarz reminded them all.

"We can't always be in the right place at the right time," Brognola said. "We don't win every round. David is still kicking himself because Khariza's people snatched those disks right from under his nose. Come on, people, we haven't come out of this too bad."

"There's a way to go yet," Price reminded him.

Brognola leaned back in his seat. "Let's hear what Erika has for us."

Dukas passed out her printed sheets. "The data Phoenix sent us from Israel translated as a timetable for Khariza's forces in the Middle East. It's written in a way that encourages his followers to forgo any kind of survival expectation. Their mission is all-important—to destabilize the region and cause much confusion among the various countries. He calls on all loyal Islamics, regardless of where they are from, to rally to the cause. Khariza has three main objectives. Major disruption within Israel. An ongoing guerrilla campaign within the U.S. and the U.K. He holds the U.K. as responsible as the U.S. for what happened in Iraq. His third objective is the restoration of Ba'athist-fedayeen control of Iraq. There is to be continued resistance within the country. All outside agencies, whether military or civilian, are to be targeted. In his words 'the Infidels who have defiled Iraq must be made to pay in blood.'"

"How does he expect to achieve that?" Blancanales asked. "No way is he going to walk in and take over. And how does he expect to defeat the U.S. coalition force? If Hussein's entire military machine couldn't, how does Khariza figure to do it?"

"He simply says if his followers keep their faith, God will show the way," Dukas said.

"And will they believe that?" Tokaido asked. "I mean, are they so easily persuaded to accept Khariza's word as given?"

"They have an abiding faith in what they believe," Dukas said. "Much stronger than Western ideologies. Their faith, their way of life, is so different from ours. What we call democracy, freedom? They see the opposite. Our open society is as alien to them as theirs is to us. In the end it's a diversity of what's right as seen by both sides. Each is convinced it has the correct path. If we don't compromise, step back and consider what we're doing, this division is going to go on forever."

"Nicely put, Erika," Schwarz said.

"So how do we stop it?" Tokaido asked.

"Isn't it the old political two-step?" Lyons said. "Same dance, different tune. We have to stop all this jigging about on the edge. Get everyone in the circle and hammer at it."

"I'm not disagreeing, Carl," Brognola said. "Haven't we all been coming up against this time after time? Stop one bunch and another jumps into the empty space. This goes deeper than a handful of extremists with guns and bombs. Look hard at it. We're up against people who have been taught from birth that we are the enemy, that we're the most corrupt and evil people ever to walk on two legs. We can't be trusted. We're unholy, cruel, greedy. We have no values. And we use the excuse of democracy as a cloak to hide our misdeeds. Did I miss anything? It's what we're up against. They see what we do. What we say. And they don't forget the wrongdoings against them. A generation on, they don't forget.

They live in their back streets and sit watching pictures of the West on television. They see our excesses and our vices, and we do ourselves no favors by the way we squander our riches. That must hurt them. So they listen to their leaders and advisers and they believe because—and don't doubt this—they take their religion far more seriously than we do. Just as Erika said. They see it as their mission to make us atone for what we do and what we have done."

"You don't think we have that kind of faith?" Blancanales asked.

"Pol, I'm no theologian. There are days when I'm not even sure I have any religious beliefs left. I just know that what we're facing is a hell of a lot stronger than anything the West has to offer in its place."

"You make it sound as if we don't have a chance of beating them in the long term," Schwarz said.

"Hell, if I believed that, I wouldn't be here. I'm just trying to say we need to view the threat by trying to understand it."

"Hard to do when you're staring down the barrel of a gun," Lyons pointed out.

"I didn't mean try to convert them. More to understand what drives them. Know your enemy and you have an advantage."

"FDR?" Dukas said.

Brognola smiled. "We know Khariza is determined to get back into Iraq and some sort of control. We also have confirmation he's negotiating a deal with the North Koreans through Kim Yeo. And he's intent on causing as much confusion as he can both here in the U.S. and the Middle East."

"My people will continue to monitor every angle," Kurtzman said. "We're still sifting information, checking out all our sources in the Middle East. There's so much going on over there at the moment we could choke ourselves on data. The main problem is sorting it into some kind of order. The minute we hook on to something useful you'll have it."

TEN MINUTES LATER Brognola, and Price and Kurtzman were alone in the War Room. At the conclusion of the meeting Kurtzman had indicated he'd needed to talk with the pair of them.

"I need to show you something. I set a search on something I spotted, that had to do with the calls between Khariza and Zolton Dushinov. They were intercepted on a computer belonging to the CIA. The odd thing is they were picked up and isolated before they could be logged on the main CIA system."

"Someone blocking input into the CIA?" Price asked. "Someone running a covert program?"

"It's happened before."

"Aaron, can we get a fix on who it was?"

"Already ahead of you. The computer had password protection and enough firewalls to hold back the Mississippi. It took a little time, but my program doesn't give up, and it eventually came up with a name."

Kurtzman hit the keyboard set in the surface of the

conference table and one of the wall-mounted monitors activated.

"Remember that name Erika came up with? It didn't mean anything at the time. That's where I started. Rod McAdam. CIA. When my search broke the password on that computer, it identified it as McAdam's."

The screen showed the image of a middle-aged man. Sandy hair and intense blue eyes. He was staring directly into the camera lens, almost defying it to show him as he really was.

"My search brought up some interesting links. McAdam knows General Chase Gardener, U.S. Army. Gardener is a dedicated hawk. So much so, I'm surprised he doesn't have feathers. He doesn't go much for the government's stance and thinks we're letting the country down. If he had his way, Gardener would most probably nuke the Middle East and North Korea based on gut instinct."

Gardener's image showed him as a lean, tanned man in his late forties, a professional soldier through and through. His graying hair was short, his mouth held in a taut line.

"Sleeps at attention," Price said softly. "Arms at his sides."

"Do I detect a trace of hostility?" Brognola asked.

"Just an observation."

Kurtzman brought up a third image. An immaculately dressed and turned-out man whose silver hair was worn slightly long.

"Senator Ralph Justin. He's one of Gardener's staunchest allies. When they're together they demolish any argument like an advancing army. He's well-known in Washington. Like Gardener, Justin is independently wealthy. Treats the world as if he owns it. Probably does have a large percentage. Word is, Justin is an arrogant bully. And our CIA man, McAdam, knows Justin, too."

"What detail do you have on McAdam?" Brognola asked.

"He's a busy man. His CIA file has him running his own section, which the honchos at Langley use when they need something special done. He's worked a lot of covert ops for the Agency over the years. He must have dirt on a lot of people in the service. His file has him as extremely ambitious, and likely to take risks. He's considered to be crowding the edge. Could be why he hasn't advanced as quickly as he might."

"So what's his connection to Gardener and Justin? And why show up in Rasheed's notes?"

Brognola turned to Price.

"Gadgets and Grimaldi can go take a look at what those three are up to. Confirm or eliminate them from our current involvement. Set it up. I'm heading out to see Mei Anna. I want Carl and Pol on standby to go with her to Hong Kong."

Andrews Air Force Base

"Is there anything I can get you?" Hal Brognola asked.

Mei Anna shook her head. She glanced around the interior of the Air Force Gulfstream C-20F.

"They looked after me very well during the flight."

Brognola sank gratefully into one of the seats. It was comfortable. Almost too comfortable.

"You look tired, Mr. Brognola."

"It's been a busy time."

"As I have been hearing."

"Miss—"

She held up a hand. "Anna. Please."

"Then call me Hal. Look, Anna, I wish I didn't have to ask for your help again so soon."

"I owe you and your organization more than I can ever repay. Never feel you are asking too much."

"When you spoke on the phone you said there was something important you needed to discuss."

Mei brushed black hair back from her cheek. Her eyes were fixed on Brognola's face. "I found out why David and his team were caught by Kim Yeo. They were betrayed by one of my own group. Someone who has abandoned us and informed Kim Yeo. That is why Henry Lee and your team was captured."

"Do you know who this informant was?"

Mei nodded. "Yes. The traitor has been identified, though he does not realize he has been discovered. We decided to leave him feeling safe until he can be compromised. Then we can question him and try to find out where David and the others have been taken."

"Let's hope it works."

"When I show up in Hong Kong, our betrayer will see a chance to hand me over to the authorities. They would like very much to get their hands on me."

"Anna, that's a hell of a risk."

"Life is a risk. Every day is a risk. I have stayed away for too long. London has become an easy option. It's time I returned and picked up the pieces."

Brognola studied her for a moment, seeing the determination in her bright eyes. The set of her firm jaw. "Now I can understand what David sees in you."

"Flattery from a handsome man," Mei said. "Worth the trip just for that."

"Two of Able Team will go in with you. One way or the other, we have to locate David and his team."

"My only worry is that Yeo might have involved Sun Yang Ho. That man has a bad reputation. If David and the others are near Ho, they could really be in harm's way. Ho is totally indoctrinated into the North Korean ideology. He has no regard at all for Westerners. He considers them to be below him. Less than nothing. Ho is a perfect creation of the revolution."

"Then the sooner we get you back on home ground, the better." Brognola took a long look at her. "Are you sure you're up to this?"

Mei Anna reached out to touch his cheek.

"I am much better. Almost back to normal. All that rest and care you arranged has paid off. I know David still believes I am too weak to do anything but look nice and let him pamper me. I'd be lying if I said I hadn't enjoyed it. But it is time I moved back into the real world. For the past weeks I've been working out each day. Hal, I'm stronger than I look."

"I can believe that, Anna. Now tell me what you need."

CHAPTER THIRTEEN

Hong Kong

Hard rain swept in across the harbour, the junks and smaller boats rising and falling on the heavy swells.

Mei Anna turned away from the hotel window and paced across the room, impatience showing on her face.

"Anna, sit down," Blancanales said. "I'm wearing out just watching you."

She glared at him, the tension between them almost visible. In the next breath she relaxed and went back to sit in the chair she had been using earlier.

"Sorry. I shouldn't take my feelings out on you. It's just—"

"You just want to get on with the job. Nothing wrong there."

"That and the fact I'm still getting back into the business."

"You don't get out of this business," Lyons said.

"You can take a break, but it's still going to pull you back."

The telephone rang. Mei picked it up and spoke rapidly. She replaced the receiver.

"The car will be outside the hotel in five minutes. We should go."

THE CAR WAS a large BMW. The rear door swung open as Mei Anna and Able Team stepped out of the hotel. They climbed in, Blancanales pulling the door shut as the car began to move. It swept around to the street and eased into the traffic, headlights on against the mist of torrential rain. The windshield wipers were working hard to keep the glass clear.

The man seated beside the driver turned to face Mei. He stared at her, then smiled and reached out to grab her hand. He began to speak in Cantonese until the woman shook her head.

"We have company, Tony," she said in English.

"Of course." He acknowledged Lyons and Blancanales. "Forgive me. I forgot myself."

"No problem," Lyons said.

The Chinese reached out to shake their hands. "I'm Tony Chan. We have much to thank your people for. Anna is important to us. Very."

"Tony, you are embarrassing me."

"Mei Anna embarrassed? Never."

"Tell us what you know."

"Okay. As far as we can work out, Kim Yeo was waiting for Henry and the others when they reached his warehouse. We couldn't understand how it happened until one of our people saw Tsui Kwan with two of Yeo's men. They were acting extremely friendly and money was passed to Kwan."

"Tsui Kwan?" Mei leaned forward and grasped Chan's arm. "There is no mistake?"

"No mistake. It was only after this discovery that things became clearer. Kwan had been acting a little strange recently. Disappearing often. No one thought too much of it until Kwan was seen with Yeo's people. We have been keeping watch on him ever since. He is behaving oddly."

"Having second thoughts?" Blancanales suggested.

"Or maybe nervous because he has been asked to stay with the group and offer them more information," Chan said. "He reacted when he heard you were coming back."

"Remember what we talked about on the flight?" Lyons said. "That this guy might be waiting so he can turn you in? Maybe that's why he's nervous."

"He won't get the chance," Mei said.

"We have to be careful," Chan pointed out. "If we expose Kwan too soon, he might not talk. He may be our only lead to where Yeo has gone."

"Maybe not," Lyons said. "These people who work for Yeo. You know them? Where they hang out?"

"Of course," Chan said. "Why?"

"If they work for Yeo, they'll know where he is. Kwan might not have been given that kind of information."

"Anna, I think I like your friends."

"Then let's do it."

"THE VIDEO STORE is one of Kim Yeo's enterprises here in Hong Kong," Chan explained. "Just one of his sidelines."

"He doesn't make enough money from selling guns?" Blancanales asked.

Chan laughed. "The store is nothing but a cover. Yeo has a video pirating operation going on. He distributes his products across Asia, and it brings in a lot of money. Kam Leong and San Tung work out of here. They front for Yeo in Hong Kong."

They were parked across the narrow street from the video store which had just closed for the night, along with the other businesses. The staff had already left. The continuing downpour had cleared the street.

"Tung has rooms behind the store. Most nights he and Leong work late after the store has closed. That is Leong's car parked in the alley."

Chan pointed to a sleek black Porsche.

"Business must be good," Lyons said.

"Do they have any backup?" Blancanales asked.

"Why would they need backup? They work for Yeo, and he has official protection. Local criminals know better than to move against someone like Yeo."

"Being out-of-towners, we wouldn't know about that," Lyons said.

He opened the rear door and stepped out, turning up the collar of his jacket. Blancanales followed. They were both armed with pistols Chan had provided. Chan's driver stayed in the car.

"Lead the way, Tony," Lyons said.

The Able Team commandos followed Chan and Mei

across the street and down the side alley. They skirted the Porsche, and Chan indicated a side gate. He pushed it open and they moved into the dark rear yard.

The back of the store had been extended. A concrete-and-brick structure that added another twenty feet onto the original building. The one window in the wall that faced them was shuttered, but some light showed through the overlapping slats.

"The door is this way," Chan said, and led the way. The door was plain wood with a metal handle. He tried it. Locked.

"Looks like we have to do it the hard way," Lyons said. "When we get inside, let me handle it. Just translate anything I say and don't cut them any slack."

"I don't understand any way but hard," Chan said.

"Your kind of guy," Blancanales said, smiling when Lyons scowled at him.

Lyons checked the feel of the door. He put his weight against it, pushing to see where the secure areas were, then stepped back. He drew the SIG-Sauer P-226 that Chan had given him, then launched himself at the door, hitting it hard with his left shoulder. The door gave, wood splintering as it burst open.

Lyons went in, Chan and Blancanales close behind. Mei followed, quickly closing the door and staying close by it, her own pistol in her hands.

The room was filled with banks of both VCRs and DVD copiers. Shelves were stacked with blank tapes and disks, with others holding already-copied material. At one end was a desk and a couple of chairs. Ducted ceiling fans spun, pulling out the heat generated by the running machines.

Just as Chan had predicted, there were only two men. As Lyons crashed into the room they jerked up from what they were doing, surprise etched across their faces. They recovered quickly, one of them turning for the desk, reaching for the handgun he kept there.

Lyons kept moving. He took long strides across the room and reached the man going for the gun. The Able Team leader caught a handful of the man's thick hair, yanking back and pulling the man to a dead stop. Still clutching the hair, he spun the man, swinging him across the room and into a bank of DVD machines. The impact knocked a number of the recorders off the shelf. They crashed to the floor, taking the Chinese with them.

The other man, seeing the weapons trained on him, held his hands up in front of him, offering no resistance. Blancanales used his own pistol to indicate he wanted the man to move aside.

"Who?" Lyons asked as he bent over the Chinese on his knees.

"That's Tung," Chan said.

Lyons moved so he was standing to one side of Tung. As the man started to get up, Lyons launched a kick that drove into his ribs. Tung gasped, lurching across the floor, the big American following him and delivering another hard kick. The force drove Tung up against the desk. He was still attempting to steady himself when Lyons reached him. He caught hold of Tung's expensive silk shirt and hauled the man upright. The thin material split. As Tung's head came up, flushed with rage, the Able Team leader backhanded him with the barrel of the SIG, drawing blood and knocking him to the floor. Lyons picked up Tung's pistol off the desk and threw it to Chan. Bending over the moaning figure, he dragged Tung upright, slamming him against the wall, then pushed the muzzle of the P-226 into the man's throat.

"Tell him I want the answer to a simple question. Where has Yeo taken our people? If he doesn't tell me what I want to hear, I'll shoot him in the knee."

Chan delivered Lyons's message. Tung's eyes flicked to his tormentor's face. The look in the American's eyes told him he had no easy way out. He replied to Chan's words in rapid Cantonese.

"He says how does he know you won't shoot him, anyway."

"He doesn't. And I will."

Lyons moved his gunhand until the SIG was aimed at Tung's left knee. The Chinese gave a frightened cry and began to speak.

"Yeo took our people with him on a flight to see Sun Yang Ho. He had dealings with the North Koreans on Khariza's behalf. All Tung knows is they flew to an island off the North Korean west coast. He doesn't know the location."

"You believe him?"

"The man does not want his kneecap shattered."

"Ask him why Yeo took our people all the way to this island."

"It seems that when his business is done, he flies on to deliver your team to Khariza himself."

Stony Man Farm, Virginia

"WE NEED TO LOCATE that camp in Chechnya," Kurtzman said. "If we want a chance at Khariza, it's possible that's where he is."

"Can we get satellite time?" Wethers asked. "Give us that and we might have a chance."

Kurtzman looked at the time on his monitor.

"Give me an hour and I can get some SARS time. It's our best shot right now."

Hong Kong

CHAN CALLED IN A CAR that had been waiting a couple of streets away. Kam Leong and San Tung were bundled into it and driven off.

"We'll follow," Mei said. "We have a safe house. Kwan will be there."

It was a thirty-minute drive to the house. It was out of the city, in the hills, isolated.

"I have told the others to wait a few minutes before they bring the prisoners inside," Chan said.

They went inside the safe house. The moment Mei appeared she was greeted by the four Chinese in residence. Only one held back for a moment before he greeted her.

"That is Kwan," Chan explained to Lyons and Blancanales.

"I don't think he expected to see her so suddenly," Blancanales stated.

"He'll have a heart attack when he sees his buddies," Lyons said.

"Yes," Chan said, "I believe he just might."

When San Tung and Kam Leong were brought into the room, Lyons saw the shock that crossed Kwan's face. He looked like a man caught in a trap of his own making.

"Nowhere to go, Kwan," Mei said. "Now we have you all. Tell me, was it worth it? Did the money these two give you take away your guilt?"

Tsui Kwan looked around the room, seeing only hostility in the eyes of his former friends. He saw nothing when he looked at his confederates.

"They can't help you," Chan said. "They have their own problems."

Lyons edged away and joined Anna. "I know you have your own way to deal with these guys," he said, "but we're on a tight schedule."

"If Yeo still has weapons in his warehouse, we can't ignore them," Blancanales said. "Wherever they end up, the U.S. is going to be on the wrong end. They could go to the mainland to be used against the American public, or they might end up in Iraq killing more U.S. military personnel. Either way, those weapons need to be neutralized."

"You are right," Mei said. "The matter we have to deal with here is ours. It shouldn't interfere with your mission."

She went to speak with Chan. He nodded and followed her back to Lyons and Blancanales.

"I will arrange things. We can show Yeo he doesn't have everything his own way."

New Territories Docks

THE RAIN, STILL SWEEPING in across the bay, had covered their approach. There was no junk used on this trip. A fast powerboat brought them in close to shore, Chan at the wheel. He knew the waters and the pattern used by infrequent patrol boats. There was a risk, and they all knew and accepted it. The possible price that might have to be paid if Yeo's stored weapons were destined for anti-U.S. targets was more than either Lyons or Blancanales were prepared to gamble with.

Mei Anna, clad in black like the rest of them, kept watch as Chan negotiated his way between moored boats, working them closer to the dock where Henry Lee had taken Phoenix Force. He brought them to the same mooring, alongside the dredger, cutting the powerful motors. The powerboat drifted in alongside the dark bulk of the dredge.

"The warehouse is the one directly in front of us," Chan said.

"We make this a simple in-and-out," Lyons said. "Get inside, plant the charges, then leave. If we meet any opposition, we take them out with the minimum of fuss. Understand?"

Chan and Mei nodded.

"Let's do it."

Mei's group had provided them with weapons and

explosive charges from one of their caches. Lyons and Blancanales had backpacks to carry their equipment. In addition to the handguns, they also had matte black Kalashnikovs.

Chan led the way across the rain-lashed dock. By the time they reached the warehouse frontage everyone was soaked.

"This place alarmed?" Lyons asked.

"Probably," Chan said.

"What's the likely response time?"

"On a night like this I'd say at least half an hour. That's if everything is working. If not, there might not even be a response."

"You guys like living on the edge," Blancanales said.

"They're crazier than you," he added for Lyons's benefit."

"Door here," Lyons said.

Chan used a set of steel lock picks, and it took him only a short time to free the lock. He eased the door open a little, then used his hand to explore the interior, his fingers seeking any alarm trips. Satisfied, he opened the door far enough so they could all slip inside. Chan closed the door behind them and they crouched in the semidarkness. While the others adjusted to the shadowed interior Chan checked over the door as a precaution. He eventually found a broken contact.

"Looks like we did trip some kind of alarm," he said.

"Then we'd better move," Lyons said. "We'll do this faster if we split into pairs to locate what we came for and set charges. We can detonate with the remote. Check your watches. We get out of here in…ten minutes from now."

Mei and Chan took one backpack and moved off to one side of the warehouse. Lyons and Blancanales went the other way.

IT WAS A LONG ten minutes.

Both teams had to locate and identify their targets, then set charges before moving on. The deeper they moved into the cavernous warehouse, the more the chance of discovery increased.

If the alarm had been picked up, any interception seemed to be taking time to show up. That was Lyons's greatest concern. He didn't let it deter him from completing the exercise. If the hammer came down, they would handle it at the time. Until then he and Blancanales carried on laying their charges.

They were nearing the end of the ten-minute period when they came across the bays of weapons Kim Yeo had shown McCarter. The consignment had still to be sent out. They identified the weapons—rifles and rocket launchers, SA-18s and cartons of C-12.

They placed their final charges.

"We got any spare detonators?" Lyons asked.

"Always bring a few spares."

They opened a number of the C-12 packages and added the detonators.

"Time to go," Lyons said.

They backtracked, reaching the door they had entered seconds before Mei and Chan returned.

"Everything set?" Blancanales asked.

Mei nodded.

"All our charges set. Little red lights flashing."

"We clear the dock before we detonate," Lyons said. "If all the charges go, we should expect one hell of a bang."

Chan eased open the door. The hiss of the rain deadened any sound coming from outside. He slipped his assault rifle from his shoulder before he moved outside. Mei went next, with Blancanales close behind. Lyons was the last to leave.

"Damn," he heard Blancanales mutter. "We've got company coming in, and I don't think it's to say welcome."

"Yeo's protection squad," Chan said.

Lyons caught the bouncing beams of powerful flashlights cutting through the sheeting rain, heard the sudden sharp commands. Dark figures raced toward them across the dock.

The shouts were punctuated by the crackle of assault rifles. Slugs whined off the concrete.

Lyons brought up his AK-47, aiming at, then slightly above, the flashlight beams. He touched the trigger, feeling the rifle jerk against his side. One of the light beams jerked skyward as the man holding it went down, punched off his feet by the 7.62 mm bullets.

The others turned their weapons on the advancing crew, cutting a swathe through the front rank. The Chinese were firing on the move, reducing their accuracy. Figures stumbled, hit the wet ground, light beams shooting in all directions.

"Head for the boat," Lyons yelled. "Get the damn thing fired up before we have the Red Chinese Army down here."

Chan, with Blancanales on his heels, ducked and ran. Blancanales laid down cover fire once they reached the edge of the dock, leaving Chan clear to go down the ladder and drop into the powerboat.

"Get to the dock," Lyons told Mei as she snapped in a fresh magazine.

The Chinese had scattered, their return fire sporadic as they sought to relocate themselves.

Lyons maintained his bursts, pausing only when he had to reload. He used short, selective bursts, his aim accurate, taking down a number of the dark, hunched figures. Out the corner of his eye he saw Mei scuttle across the dock, then drop flat on the edge alongside Blancanales. The pair set up covering fire for Lyons as he ran to join them.

Below the dock, the powerboat's engines burst into life.

"Let's go," Chan yelled above the noise.

"Move out," Lyons said.

Blancanales and Mei went down the ladder.

A number of the Chinese started across the dock, heading directly for Lyons's position.

He pulled the remote from inside his jacket, extended the short antenna and flicked the power switch. The indicator light flashed red. He pressed the button.

Rain hissed across the dock, autofire crackled from the darkness.

Nothing happened immediately, and Lyons found he was holding his breath.

Seconds slid by. Lyons looked at the remote in his hand. The red light held steady. Then he saw it flicker for a microsecond.

The warehouse blew apart. The detonation deafened them. Heat washed out from the center of the blast, singeing Lyons's clothing, stinging one side of his face. The concussion came, pushing Lyons over the edge of the dock. He let go of the remote and grabbed hold of the metal ladder as his body went over the edge.

The Chinese, upright and exposed, took the full brunt of the blast. They were enveloped by the heat, clothing igniting, flesh charring. The force of the blast picked them up and hurled them across the dock into the water below. Other lacerated and scorched bodies were scattered across the dock, clothing and flesh alight. The front wall of the warehouse vanished in the initial blast.

Lyons, feeling the heated air, slid down the ladder as scattered debris began to rain down on him. He felt something strike his left shoulder.

The warehouse was rocked by a second, even larger explosion as the extra C-12 Lyons had activated detonated with all the other material. The roof of the building was torn open, a massive fireball rising into the dark sky. Lyons felt the dock wall tremble as the blast reached its peak.

He dropped the last couple of feet, grabbing the side rail as Chan gunned the engines to maximum and took the powerboat out across the water, away from the inferno that had been Kim Yeo's warehouse.

Flames were rising into the sky, smoke coiling in

thick clouds. Shattered debris was splashing back down into the water.

"Son of a bitch," Blancanales said softly. "It was worth being here just to see that."

"And worth coming back for," Mei said. "I just wish David had been here to see it."

Ho's Island

"RAFE?"

Encizo, his head still down on his chest and a hand pressed over the bloody gash, remained leaning against a wooden crate.

"I'm okay."

McCarter bent over him. "What are you up to?"

"When I go down, see if you can get one of those Chinese over here."

"Gary?"

"I heard. It's worth a try."

Encizo groaned and let himself slump to the floor. Manning knelt beside him, while McCarter held out his bound hands and gestured at one of the Chinese.

"Hey, give us a hand. Can't you see he's hurt?"

The Chinese glanced at his companions, saying something in Cantonese.

McCarter caught the words "What shall we do?"

"Go and look."

"You hit him too hard, Kee."

"You're no help."

Kee, ignoring the laughter from his companions,

turned toward the three captives, his rifle pointed at them as he approached.

Encizo groaned again.

"Help him," Manning pleaded.

Kee used the muzzle of his rifle to push the Canadian to one side. He peered down at Encizo's prone figure. All he could see was the blood streaking the side of the Cuban's face. Encizo continued to moan, holding Kee's attention.

"He will not—" the Chinese began.

McCarter leaned in closer and clamped his right hand over the butt of the pistol in the holster strapped to Kee's waist. He yanked the weapon free. It was a SIG-Sauer P-226, a benefit of working for someone like Kim Yeo, rather than having to use one of the Chinese home-manufactured weapons. McCarter flicked up the safety and jammed the muzzle into Kee's side. He pulled the trigger, drilling a 9 mm slug into the man's side.

As the stricken Chinese fell, Manning made a grab for the Kalashnikov, yanking it from Kee's fingers. He clamped his fingers around the hand grip, jammed the stock against his side and braced his arm against it. He turned the muzzle in the direction of the other Chinese and touched the trigger. The Kalashnikov began to jack out shots, the 7.62 mm slugs spraying the area, scattering the Chinese before they could return fire.

McCarter had turned away from Kee the moment he had triggered his first shot. Now the Briton faced around, the P-226 rising to track in on one of the moving guards. McCarter was in a better position to use his handgun, and his next shot caught its target on the move, the 9 mm slug punching through the side of the man's neck, opening a wound that began to pulse with blood. The Chinese stumbled, then skidded facedown across the floor.

Encizo pushed aside the body sprawled across him. He got to his feet, checking out the area around them. The proliferation of packing cases would give them good cover in the first instance, at least allowing them sanctuary even if it was only for a short time.

"Move back," he yelled.

Still firing the Kalashnikov, Manning moved to follow the Cuban. McCarter wasn't far behind, dropping and rolling behind the cover as Yeo's guards began to return fire from their own protective areas.

"Keep moving," McCarter said, measuring his shots from the 15-round magazine.

They edged back through the rows of crates, toward the entrance. They were ignorant of how many, if any, armed personnel Ho had on call. The only people they had seen were Ho's two bodyguards and the workers packing the crates. The packers had scattered the moment the gunfire started, leaving open boxes and tools strewed across the floor. It was Encizo who spotted a pair of cutters one of the workers had dropped. He snatched them up, turning to McCarter.

"Hey."

McCarter turned and saw what the Cuban was holding. He stuck out his bound wrists and Encizo cut the plastic loop. Moving to Manning, Encizo freed his hands, then passed the cutters to the Canadian so he could be freed himself.

"Now that feels better," the Briton said.

Manning, now able to manage the Kalashnikov correctly, began to lay down his shots with precision, keeping Yeo's two men from advancing.

McCarter kept watch while Encizo checked out some of the crates close by them. Peering into one after the other, he came across one containing fragmentation grenades and, without hesitation, picked a couple from the box. Pulling a pin, he hurled the grenade across the building. It landed just ahead of where Yeo's men were crouched. The grenade's sharp blast tore the wooden crates apart and threw splintered wood at the pair of Chinese. Bleeding, they stumbled away from the smoking remains of the crate and walked into Manning's controlled burst. The hail of slugs cut them down, their bleeding corpses tumbling heavily to the floor.

Encizo launched a number of grenades, in different directions, insuring that the explosions were close enough to the stacked crates to inflict damage on whatever they contained. One blast touched off something flammable, flame erupting in a boiling cascade. Sizzling trails of fire arced across the building.

When his P-226 locked back on an empty breech, McCarter tucked it behind his belt, turned and equipped himself with a couple of grenades. He launched his first one in the direction of the office block where Yeo and the North Korean had gone. It fell a couple of feet short, though the blast was still powerful enough to shatter glass and splinter door panels. McCarter ducked and moved closer, so that when he launched a second grenade it arced in through one of the shattered window frames and exploded inside the office block.

Armed with more grenades the Phoenix Force trio moved across the building, laying down a trail of destruction that turned the interior into smoking chaos.

"Look at that," Encizo said, indicating a cluster of weapons on a large, flat metal pallet, roped down and ready to be moved.

The recognition came quickly, from Stony Man briefings on ordnance: it was a North Korean heavy machine gun, designated M-1983, quad in 14.5 mm. Normally mounted on a battle tank, this weapon had been fitted to a base capable of being fixed to a truck chassis. The four-barrel machine gun operated on a recoil basis and was belt fed. A hefty weapon designed for use in rough terrain, it had a rate of fire that punched out around 600 rounds per minute from each barrel.

"You think these are for Khariza?" Manning asked.

"Could be," McCarter said.

He indicated the crates and boxes spread around the building.

"Grenades, rocket launchers, assault rifles, machine guns. All stuff he's going to need to make good his promise to make life difficult in Iraq. Let's face it, that bloke is serious. We know that already."

"Talking of rifles," Encizo said. "Take these."

The Cuban thrust Kalashnikovs into their hands. The weapons were already loaded. Encizo leaned into the crate he had discovered and pulled out one for himself. He handed McCarter and Manning extra magazines, which they tucked behind their belts.

There was a dull explosion some distance from where they stood. Something their grenades had detonated. Metal debris clanged to the floor. Smoke rose and gathered in the apex of the roof.

"I want Yeo," McCarter snapped.

"We should be making for that plane," Manning said. "Time we got the hell out of here."

"Yeo first. And if you see that bloody Korean, sort him out, as well."

Manning glanced across at Encizo, who merely shrugged.

They ran in the direction of the office block. Smoke was still swirling around the wreckage of the outer wall. Doors hung loosely from their hinges and glass crunched under their feet as they closed in.

A hunched and bloody shape lay against the inner wall, the left arm torn from the shoulder. One of Ho's bodyguards. The other bodyguard was nowhere to be seen.

"David, on your right," Encizo yelled as he spotted a dark figure emerging from the smoke.

It was Ho.

The Korean, his black clothing torn and streaked with dust, face bloody from glass cuts, swung around a door frame, holding himself upright with one hand, while a pistol filled his other. His mouth was open in what McCarter thought was the beginning of a yell. A closer look revealed that the left side of Ho's mouth had been blown away, exposing lacerated gums where teeth had been torn out.

McCarter half turned as he registered the Korean. He saw the rising gun in Ho's hand.

The Kalashnikov in the Briton's hands erupted on full-auto. The lethal burst of fire slammed into Ho at waist level, shredding the wooden door frame he was clinging to. There was a burst of splintered wood and bloody chunks of flesh as the 7.62 mm slugs impacted. Ho's slender form was almost shredded. He flew back, arms wide, and crashed to the floor in a grotesque slide, leaving a bloody trail in his wake.

A figure burst out from the shattered office block, firing a handgun wildly. It was Kim Yeo. The Chinese arms trafficker turned in an attempt to cover himself behind a stack of crates.

Manning opened fire, his stream of slugs chewing through the wood and blowing out the other side. The slugs, impacting against the wood, had distorted and ripped ragged holes in Yeo as he ran directly into their path. The man crashed to the ground. By the time Phoenix reached him Yeo was leaking copious amounts of blood from the half dozen pulped wounds.

While the others stood watch, McCarter knelt beside the dying Chinese.

"It is painful," Yeo said.

"I hope so," McCarter said coldly.

"Because I had Lee killed?"

"Bloody right."

"We all make choices."

"I choose to let you die right here, you bastard."

Yeo turned his head for a moment as the sound of jet-powered aircraft took off and flew over the building.

"Too late for you," he said. "I have at least fulfilled my contract with Khariza."

"Meaning what?"

"The most important of the weapons I negotiated on his behalf have just left, and you failed to stop them."

"The hell with you. Play your bloody games, Yeo. We handled Khariza's other weapons. We'll do the same with whatever just left."

Yeo struggled to stay coherent long enough to speak.

"You have no idea where that plane is going. Or the type of aircraft to look for. Time is not on your side. Khariza will have the cargo in his hands before you locate him…too late to stop those—" Yeo's eyes began to glaze over "—three nuclear devices…"

"Did I hear that right?" Encizo asked.

McCarter pushed to his feet. "Yes. You heard it right. It sounds as if our friend Khariza has just gone nuclear."

* * * * *

The heart-stopping action concludes in
FULL BLAST,
available in June.

Readers won't want to miss
this exciting new title
of the SuperBolan series!

Don Pendleton's **Mack Bolan**
Lethal Tribute

Wiped out a century ago in India, the ancient
Cult of Kali has been reborn. Organized, well
funded and with clandestine contacts in high
places, these Hindu death worshipers have an
agenda of serious destruction, backed by three
stolen nuclear warheads from Pakistan.

Mack Bolan heads a covert U.S. probe to the
subcontinent and uncovers a situation that borders
on the supernatural: an army of invisible soldiers
who kill swiftly and silently, at once unstoppable
and unseen. But Bolan deals in facts, not fiction—
and the high-tech secrets behind the mysterious
cult of killers lead to a hardcore shakedown in the
heart of Calcutta, where true evil awaits....

Available May 2005 at your favorite retailer.

Or order your copy now by sending your name, address, zip or postal code, along with a check or
money order (please do not send cash) for $6.50 for each book ordered ($7.99 in Canada), plus
75¢ postage and handling ($1.00 in Canada), payable to Gold Eagle Books, to:

In the U.S.

Gold Eagle Books
3010 Walden Avenue
P.O. Box 9077
Buffalo, NY 14269-9077

In Canada

Gold Eagle Books
P.O. Box 636
Fort Erie, Ontario
L2A 5X3

GOLD EAGLE ®

Please specify book title with your order.
Canadian residents add applicable federal and provincial taxes.

GSB102

THE DESTROYER

DARK AGES

LONDON CALLING...

Knights rule—in England anyway, and ages ago they were really good in a crisis. Never mind that today's English knights are inbred earls, rock stars, American mayors and French Grand Prix winners. Under English law, they still totally *rock*. Which is why Sir James Wylings and his Knights Temporary are invading—in the name of Her Majesty.

Naturally, Remo is annoyed. He is from New Jersey. So when Parliament is finally forced to declare the Knight maneuvers illegal, he happily begins smashing kippers...knickers...whatever. Unfortunately, Sir James Wylings responds by unleashing his weapons of mass destruction—and only time will tell if the Destroyer will make history...or be history, by the time he's through.

Or order your copy now by sending your name, address, zip or postal code, along with a check or money order (please do not send cash) for $6.50 for each book ordered ($7.99 in Canada), plus 75¢ postage and handling ($1.00 in Canada), payable to Gold Eagle Books, to:

In the U.S.	In Canada
Gold Eagle Books	Gold Eagle Books
3010 Walden Avenue	P.O. Box 636
P.O. Box 9077	Fort Erie, Ontario
Buffalo, NY 14269-9077	L2A 5X3

Please specify book title with your order.
Canadian residents add applicable federal and provincial taxes.

GOLD EAGLE ®

GDEST140

TAKE 'EM FREE

2 action-packed novels plus a mystery bonus

NO RISK

NO OBLIGATION TO BUY

SPECIAL LIMITED-TIME OFFER

Mail to: Gold Eagle Reader Service™

IN U.S.A.:
3010 Walden Ave.
P.O. Box 1867
Buffalo, NY 14240-1867

IN CANADA:
P.O. Box 609
Fort Erie, Ontario
L2A 5X3

YEAH! Rush me 2 FREE Gold Eagle® novels and my FREE mystery bonus. If I don't cancel, I will receive 6 hot-off-the-press novels every other month. Bill me at the low price of just $29.94* for each shipment. That's a savings of over 10% off the combined cover prices and there is NO extra charge for shipping and handling! There is no minimum number of books I must buy. I can always cancel at any time simply by returning a shipment at your cost or by returning any shipping statement marked "cancel." Even if I never buy another book from Gold Eagle, the 2 free books and mystery bonus are mine to keep forever.

166 ADN DZ76
366 ADN DZ77

Name _____ (PLEASE PRINT) _____

Address _____ Apt. No. _____

City _____ State/Prov. _____ Zip/Postal Code _____

Signature (if under 18, parent or guardian must sign)

Not valid to present Gold Eagle® subscribers.
Want to try two free books from another series? Call 1-800-873-8635.

* Terms and prices subject to change without notice. Sales tax applicable in N.Y. Canadian residents will be charged applicable provincial taxes and GST. This offer is limited to one order per household. All orders subject to approval.

® are trademarks owned and used by the trademark owner and or its licensee.

© 2004 Harlequin Enterprises Ltd.

GE-04R

DEATHLANDS · EXECUTIONER · SUPER BOLAN · OUTLANDERS · DESTROYER · STONY MAN

FREE

SCREENSAVERS
CELLPHONE RINGS
E-POSTCARDS
GAMES
and much much more...

Available at
www.cuttingaudio.com

STONY MAN · DEATHLANDS · EXECUTIONER · SUPER BOLAN · OUTLANDERS · DESTROYER

GECCGEN05MM